Peter Corris was born in Staw his family left the country fc Melbourne High School and ..cibourne. After taking a Master's degree at Monash University and a PhD at the Australian National University (both in History), he became an academic, teaching and researching in various universities and a College of Advanced Education. He published extensively on the history of the Pacific Islands.

In 1975 he gave up academia for journalism. He was literary editor of *The National Times* from 1980 to '81. He has travelled and lived for short periods in the Pacific, Britain, Europe and the USA. He has been a full-time writer since 1982 and has written over seventy books (see www.petercorris.net). His interests are reading and writing, weight training, golf and films. He is married to writer Jean Bedford and they have three daughters. He lives on the Illawarra coast of NSW.

The Journal of
FLETCHER
CHRISTIAN

Together with the history
of Henry Corkill

PETER CORRIS

V
VINTAGE

Random House Australia Pty Ltd
20 Alfred Street, Milsons Point, NSW 2061
http://www.randomhouse.com.au

Sydney New York Toronto
London Auckland Johannesburg

First published by Random House Australia 2005

National Library of Australia
Cataloguing-in-Publication Entry

Corris, Peter, 1942–.
The journal of Fletcher Christian.

ISBN 1 74051 351 7.

1. Christian Fletcher, 1764–1793 – Fiction.   2. Sailors – Great Britain
Fiction.   3. Bounty Mutiny, 1789 – Fiction.

A823.3

Cover artwork: Mutiny scene taken from 'Fletcher's Mutiny Cyclorama',
Norfolk Island; a large 360° panoramic painting of the *Bounty* voyage and mutiny
and the settlement of Pitcairn and Norfolk Islands. © Artists: Sue Draper and
Tracey Yager, 2002
Cover design: Nada Backovic
Maps and other illustrations designed by Anna Warren
Typeset in ACaslon 12/17pt by Midland Typesetters, Maryborough, Victoria
Printed and bound by Griffin Press, Netley, South Australia

10 9 8 7 6 5 4 3 2 1

For Sofya, Robert and Vincent

CONTENTS

Introduction

One day in 1970, I received a letter that would help to trigger the writing of this book, more than thirty years later. This letter was originally addressed to my father who had died three years previously, but had found its way to me. It was from a firm of solicitors in Workington, Cumberland, and concerned a relative of my grandfather, Robert Henry Corris. My grandfather had been born on the Isle of Man and moved to Cumberland* before migrating to Australia early in the twentieth century. This relative had died intestate and his small legacy was to be divided among Robert Henry Corris's descendants. These included my father's two sisters, both still alive, and his two brothers, only one of whom was still living. Consequently, a small amount of money came to several of my cousins on my father's side and to my brother, sister and me.

Accompanying the letter was a list of other beneficiaries on the Isle of Man and in England. One of the names listed was Christian.

As a small boy, aged about nine or ten, I was mightily impressed by the 1935 film *Mutiny on the Bounty* which I'd seen at a Saturday matinee. In the early 1950s, primary school students were called upon to give the 'morning talk' to the class on Monday accounting for what they had done over the weekend or any other topic of interest. Many

---

* In 1972 the counties of Cumberland and Westmoreland were merged to form Cumbria.

of my classmates dreaded this event and stumbled through accounts of playing football or going to a party. Being a show-off, I always looked forward to it being my turn. As an addicted reader my head was full of books and I was likely to talk about the book that had most recently captivated me. I was considered a bit odd. But going to the pictures was an experience common to us all and on this occasion I launched into an address on the subject of the film about the mutiny. I was full of admiration for Christian but gave Bligh his due. 'Captain Bligh,' I said, 'sailed his launch all the way from the Pacific, where the mutineers had left him, to England.'

'To Timor, Peter,' said the teacher, who was evidently well informed on the subject or had also seen the film. My embarrassment fixed this incident in my memory, but details of the mutiny and Charles Laughton's roared 'Mr Christian!' stuck with me and I read popular accounts and the regular newspaper features on the story over the years. I saw the 1962 film with Marlon Brando and Trevor Howard in the key roles as soon as it came out and thought it inferior to the earlier version, although by then my reading had shown me that both were wildly inaccurate, historically.

In 1967 I began work on a PhD in the Department of Pacific History at the Australian National University. Harry Maude, a professorial fellow in the department, had written articles on the mutineers and Pitcairn Island and the matter came up in casual conversation between us occasionally. Over time, I bought a few second-hand books on the subject, popular accounts, such as Nordhoff and Hall's *The Mutiny on the Bounty*. Beachcombers and castaways, sojourners on the islands not only fascinated me, they were legitimate subjects for academic study. I accumulated a small library of first-hand accounts.

So the 1970 letter from the Cumberland solicitors came as a revelation. I knew my grandfather was a Manxman who had moved to

Introduction

Cumberland, but if I also knew that Fletcher Christian was of Manx
descent and had grown up in Cumberland the facts hadn't registered.
I realised that, however distantly, I was related to the famous
mutineer, immortalised on film by the greatest male stars of their day
– Clark Gable, Marlon Brando and, in 1984, Mel Gibson.

From then on I would occasionally boast of my connection to
Fletcher Christian, joking that it was better to be onside with
Christian, with Gable, Brando and Gibson in the role than alongside
Bligh, portrayed far less attractively by Laughton, Howard and
Hopkins.

This flippant attitude changed in 2003 when my daughter, a
librarian interested in genealogy, began investigating the Corris
family history via the Internet. I told her about the Christian connection (although I had long since lost the 1970 documents) and her
researches confirmed it, discovering several Christian–Corris
marriages on the Isle of Man in the eighteenth and nineteenth
centuries. As Fletcher Christian's family were landed and professional people and at least some of the Corrises, before their migra-
tion to Cumberland, were farmers and merchants, it seemed possible
that the connection might have been reasonably close. It intrigued
me. I began to mention it when I was interviewed by journalists and
asked to write brief biographical notes for conference appearances
and when giving talks to writing groups.

Over the course of the next year I received many communications
from people who also claimed a Christian connection, some from
England but some also from Australia and the United States. The
name Corkill cropped up in this correspondence and my daughter
confirmed that this, a common Manx name, was also linked with that
of Corris.

One day a parcel arrived. It had been sent to one of my publishers
and forwarded to my agent and then to me. It was accompanied by a

letter from a Mr Joseph Corkill of Mornington, Victoria. Mr Corkill – the bearer of a now interestingly familiar name – had heard my claim to be related to history's most famous mutineer and said that a story of a similar connection had been current in his family, handed down from generation to generation.

Mr Corkill, who was then eighty, had been born in Australia, but his parents and some older siblings were born on the Isle of Man. Very much as my small inheritance had come to me, Mr Corkill had received some money and a few effects from a distant relative named Samuel Corris, who had died intestate in the United States some twenty years before. A busy man at the time, managing a number of hobby farms for their Melbourne-based owners, Mr Corkill had banked the money, forgotten the name of the distant relative, and taken little interest in the package, which was wrapped in an American flag. When he attempted to unwrap the package, the material had come apart in his hands and he had put it aside until time permitted him to handle it more carefully.

Joseph Corkill had lost the documents accompanying the package and was now resident in a nursing home, without family, frail and in failing health with severely diminished eyesight. He had heard me speaking on the radio about my Manx origins and the *Bounty* story and, having enjoyed my detective novels, he was reminded of the name attached to the neglected package. He decided to send me the package from his American Corris relative as a way of saying thanks for the pleasure the books had given him. Knowing that I had previously been an historian, Mr Corkill kindly thought that the parcel would be of interest to me and that I might make some use of them.

Someone in the nursing home had evidently posted the package, now with several layers of newspaper around the faded and threadbare flag, in a large padded post bag. I removed the newspaper and the old, faded cloth flag – possibly the 1795 version with fifteen stars and fifteen stripes – virtually disintegrated in my hands. Beneath it lay a small notebook in a sealskin pouch and a very old, larger volume wrapped in cracked, dried-out oilcloth but in a good state of preservation.

I let the package sit on my desk before opening it and my mind went back to the old film and the 1970 letter. As a professional historian I knew how chancy the survival of documents was – how much was lost forever, how the means for the reconstruction of the past was affected by major events such as fire or legal proceedings or things as slight as the depredations of silverfish. My own doctoral thesis had benefited greatly by the chance preservation of a tin trunk of papers. I felt that I was being granted something similar – a link with a past that involved me. But in this case, far more personally.

I sniffed the package and ran my hands over it as I had those documents that luck had brought my way before. Back then I imagined they had smelled of the Pacific islands – that ripe, moist smell, not diminished by time or place. I hauled myself back to reality from wild imaginings. Most old stuff is just old stuff. I slid the notebook out of the pouch and inspected it. What might be called the title page, written in a crabbed hand, read 'The History of Henry Corkill, Sailor'. The larger volume, strongly bound in leather like a ship's log, appeared to be older than the notebook and its cover was faded and stained. Its 'title page', written in a rounded, fluent hand, but in a language unknown to me, was incomprehensible apart from the words, 'Fletcher Christian'.

My throat went dry. That name, those two words – both with so many resonances and echoes that had played in my imagination for so long. The first thing I did, before even turning the pages in the volumes, was to telephone the nursing home in Mornington. But the parcel had taken some weeks to reach me, and Mr Corkill had died in the interval.

I contacted my daughter, whose researches had included accessing a Manx dictionary. She had emailed me a few Manx phrases for fun as she had pursued the Corrises and Christians and it was reasonable to suspect that the language in the bound book was Manx. I asked her if she could translate the title pages of the thick notebook which I scanned in to the computer. She reported that it was inscribed thus: 'The Journal of Fletcher Christian, Gentleman.'

With Joseph Corkill dead and no documentation available, absolute authentication and provenance of the notebook and the bound volume has proved impossible. However, on being provided with small samples, Professor I.A.H. Hancock of the Manuscripts Collection of the British Museum reports that the paper, binding, the ink used, the pouch and the oilcloth date from the late eighteenth or early nineteenth century. The ship's flag, too faded and fragmentary to identify, appears to be slightly less old.

I am indebted to two scholars for their translations. Dr Robert Macconochie of Durham University has translated Fletcher Christian's text from Manx. Dr Macconochie advises that several difficulties arose in rendering Christian's text into readable English. There were many crossings-out, attempted erasures and misspellings, so that at times the words were barely legible. Christian's grasp of Manx was sound, but sometimes his writing of it was more phonetic than accurate. While in no sense making a 'free' translation, Dr Macconochie has opted for some more modern usages than Christian employed in the interest of intelligibility. He has provided headings at appropriate points which are lacking in the original and followed conventions, such as the italicising of the names of vessels, titles of books and words in foreign languages, not observed by Christian. Dr Macconochie is preparing a monograph on linguistic questions raised and solved by what he calls 'this unique document in the Manx language of the late eighteenth century'.

Associate Professor Epelli Latekefu of the University of the South Pacific has translated those portions of Christian's journal written in Tahitian.

As I read through Corkill's 'history' and the translations of Christian's writing, my excitement mounted. I felt privileged to be the only person, other than the translators, to lay eyes on these remarkable documents for probably almost 200 years. Since much of the material in both Corkill and Christian's accounts is frank on sex and other matters, it was lucky that some puritan among the Corkill clan did not consign his journal to the flames and the other with it. Such things have happened, the most famous example being the burning of the explorer Richard Burton's papers by his widow. Burton's published works are explicit about sex for their time; his unpublished writings were probably even more so. We will never know.

Mariners' journals and diaries abound in archives around the world, but many are dry as dust accounts of sailing details and weather. Some of course, James Cook's journals notably, are masterpieces of writing and observation and have provided the basis for much of the history since written about the period they cover. What a treasure trove these accounts now in my hands would have proved for historians, not only of the exploration and exploitation of the Pacific, but for their insights into early American social life and manners, maritime history, sealing and whaling in the Atlantic, Polynesian society and the clash of cultures in the Pacific. While the outline of the *Bounty* story is widely known, few people know much of the mutineers' attempts to establish communities blending the Polynesian and European takes on the world – one a failure, one a qualified success – on two different, widely separated, Pacific islands. A detailed, unexpurgated first-hand account of these experiments is presented here for the first time.

It is no exaggeration to say that I was obsessed by these unique documents coming my way. The personal connection I spoke of took hold of me in an odd way. For a time I felt it so strongly and proprietorially, that I considered not publishing them at all; merely hoarding them for my personal pleasure and playing my part in their long concealment. But this gave way to stronger impulses of the writer and historian in me. The *Bounty* is a part of the heritage of many different kinds of people in many countries and no part of it can or should belong to an individual. I remain fascinated by an odd Christian–Corkill–Corris triangulation. My daughter's further researches revealed that a Jane Corkill was my great-great-grandmother. She was no doubt related to Edward Corkill, the father of the Henry of the 'history', and to the 'old Claude' Corkill referred to by Christian in his journal as a kinsman.

Obsession changed to empowerment. So much has been written about Christian and Bligh, not only about their fateful collision, but as individuals. Bligh's life is better documented, but, as with Christian, there are sidelights and questions. Did he inadvertently provoke the attack that killed Cook at Kealakekua Bay? Did he hide under the bed in the Rum Rebellion?

In Christian's case, apart from his motive in leading the mutiny, there are other questions that have fascinated writers. Did he escape from Pitcairn? Did his former comrade, Peter Heywood, actually see him in Plymouth around 1808? Heywood claimed he glimpsed a sailor whom he took to be Christian, hailed him and the man ran away. Others, acquainted with Christian, saw a gentleman traveller in the Lake District who closely resembled him. With several of the mutineers hanged by this time, the mind boggles at the danger Christian would have faced had he returned. Yet sober people claim to have seen him and a number of writers have taken the claims seriously and searched for evidence to support them. How romantic such a notion is, how attractive and how unlikely. In my musing about Christian over the years I entertained these thoughts myself – Christian as Alexander Selkirk; Christian as the Count of Monte Cristo. Henry Corkill's 'history' provides the probable answer to these questions.

Needless to say, I am proud of my connection to Henry Corkill and Fletcher Christian, and it is one of the quirks of history that the hitherto obscure American sailor, now shown to be a keen observer and chronicler of his times, preserved the journal of Britain's most famous mutineer. It emerges that Corkill and Christian – both sceptics at a time when religion ruled – were kinsmen, however distant, and it is instructive to read the former's story to get some insight into the elements of the character of a couple of tough guys of Manx ancestry pursuing a dangerous and demanding career in the late eighteenth century.

To put to sea in a wooden sailing vessel at that time was to take on a high level of risk. Countless trading vessels went to the bottom, holed by rocks and reefs or with their planks shredded by sea worms. Innumerable men-of-war were sunk by enemy action or storms, and when Lord Nelson himself could lose an eye and an arm and his life, how much more danger could an ordinary seaman or junior officer expect to face?

With a love of the sea in their blood and a rebellious streak combined with ambition, Corkill and Christian faced all these hazards and more with fortitude. They were formidable – as friends who could win trust, and likewise as bitter enemies when wronged. Both could love, fight, and kill. Both took command of a vessel and the fates of other men when the chips were down. To know the American is to know the Britisher.

No portrait of Christian exists. He was obscure until the mutiny made him famous. There are few such figures in history who remain so significantly mysterious. Until now all that survives of a first-hand kind is a handful of letters of no particular consequence. Similarly, all accounts of Christian's behaviour come from observers, and most notably from his enemies. There has been nothing confessional, defiant or apologetic – nothing from the inside of the man, from his keen and active but troubled mind.

So many statements made at the time of the mutiny and subsequent actions have remained enigmatic. What did Christian mean by his repeated claim that he was 'in hell'? What was implied by Bligh's last cry, 'Never fear lads, I'll do you justice if ever I reach England'? What secret did Christian entrust to his comrade Peter Heywood when they parted for the last time at Tahiti? At last, Fletcher Christian's journal throws a burning light on the question that has intrigued scholars, and fascinated poets, novelists, musicians, playwrights and filmmakers for over two hundred years: the root causes of the mutiny on His Majesty's Armed Vessel *Bounty*, under the command of Lieutenant William Bligh.

Peter Corris

Illustrations

Registry of Deeds, Official Copy.

PARISH REGISTER OF PATRICK

1799

Hugh Christian of this Parish (Bachelor) and Ann Corris
of the said Parish (Spinster) were married
in this Church by licence this Sixteenth
Day of November One Thousand Seven
Hundred + Ninety-Nine.
By me Ev. Christian vicar

This marriage was solemnized between us

In the presence of us	Hugh Christian my **X** mark
John Radcliffe	and Ann Christian late
John Corris my **X** mark	Corris my **X** mark

A re-creation of the official Isle of Man parish register recording
the 1799 marriage of Hugh Christian and Ann Corris.

Reproduced with permission of the Civil Registry, Isle of Man.

Registry of Deeds, Official Copy.

PARISH REGISTER OF PATRICK

Thomas Christian + Elizabeth Corris were intermarried
in this church by lycence this ninth day of June one
thousand eight hundred and thirty two.
By me T. Stephen Vicar

This marriage was solemnized between us Thomas Christian **X**
Eliz. Christian late Corris in presence of Thomas Moore
James Newlove

A re-creation of the official Isle of Man parish register recording
the 1832 marriage of Thomas Christian and Elizabeth Corris.

Reproduced with permission of the Civil Registry, Isle of Man.

Registry of Deeds, Official Copy.

REGISTER OF BAPTISMS, PARISH OF GERMAN

(PAGE 152)

BAPTISMS Solemnized in the Parish of *German*
in the Isle of Man, in the year *1838*

When Baptised	Child's Christian Name	Parent's Name	
		Christian	Surname
May 13th No. 1214	*Philip* *Son of*	*Patrick* *Jane*	*Corris* *Corkill*

A re-creation of the official Isle of Man parish register recording the 1838 baptism of Philip Corris (Peter Corris's great-grandfather), the son of Patrick Corris and Jane Corkill (Peter Corris's great-great-grandfather and great-great-grandmother).

Reproduced with permission of the Civil Registry, Isle of Man.

1870 **Marriage Solemnized** *at the Parish Church* in the *Parish of Ballaugh* in the ~~Count~~ *of Isle of Man*

No.	When married	Name and Surname	Age	Condition	Rank or Profession	Residence at Time of Marriage	Father's Name and Surname	Rank or Profession of Father
66 ~~154~~	1870 *June 16th*	*Edward Corris* *Mary Anne Christian*	*full age* *full age*	*Bachelor* *Spinster*	*Mariner*	*German* *Ballaugh*	*Philip Corris* *John Christian*	*Mariner* *Labourer*

Married in the *Parish Church* according to the Rites and Ceremonies of the *Established Church* by *licence* by me,

HG White Curate

This Marriage was solemnized between us, { *Edward Corris* *Mary Ann Christian* } in the Presence of us, { *John Corris* *Ann Cannell* }

A re-creation of the official Isle of Man parish register recording the 1870 marriage of Edward Corris and Mary Anne Christian.

Reproduced with permission of the Civil Registry, Isle of Man.

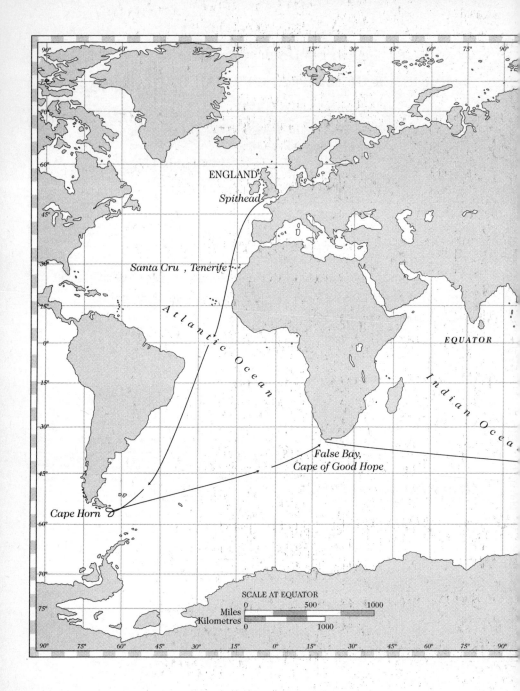

ENGLAND

Spithead

Santa Cruz, Tenerife

Atlantic Ocean

EQUATOR

Indian Ocean

False Bay,
Cape of Good Hope

Cape Horn

SCALE AT EQUATOR

Miles
Kilometres

0   500   1000

0   1000

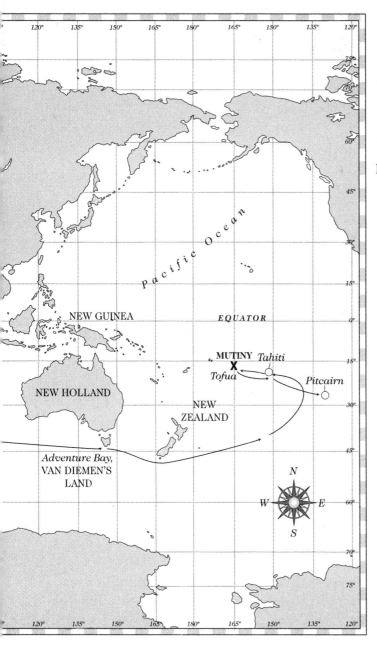

Voyage of
HMS *Bounty*

under

William Bligh and

Fletcher Christian.

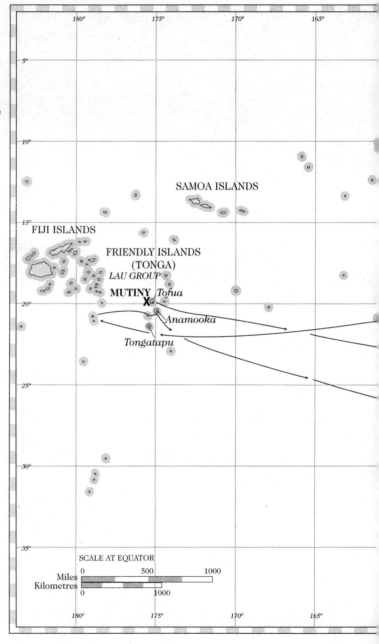

Detail of the

voyage of

HMS *Bounty*

under

the command of

Fletcher Christian.

180°   175°   170°   165°

5°

10°

SAMOA ISLANDS

15°

FIJI ISLANDS

FRIENDLY ISLANDS
(TONGA)
LAU GROUP

MUTINY *Tofua*
X

20°

Anamooka

Tongatapu

25°

30°

35°

SCALE AT EQUATOR

0   500   1000

Miles

Kilometres

0   1000

180°   175°   170°   165°

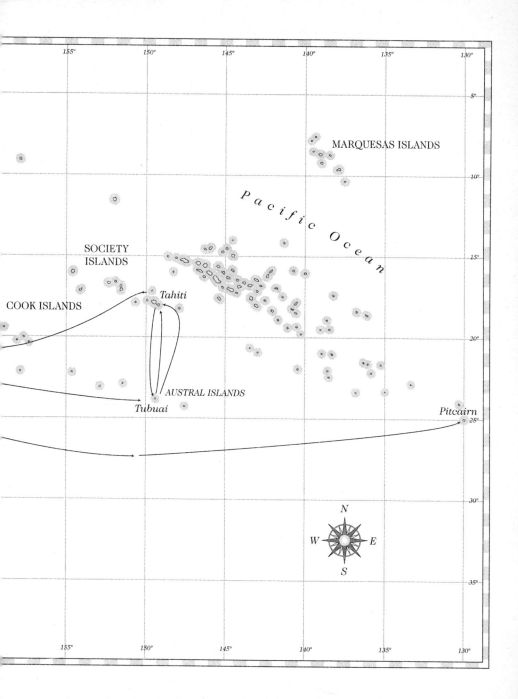

A hand-drawn map of **Matavai Bay, Tahiti**, sketched 'from recollection and anchor bearings' by William Bligh.

A chart of
**Pitcairn
Island,**
sketched by
Captain F.W.
Beechey in
1825.

Reproduced with
permission of the
British Library.
The original of this
image is found at
'Pitcairn Island', Maps
SEC. 15 (1113s).

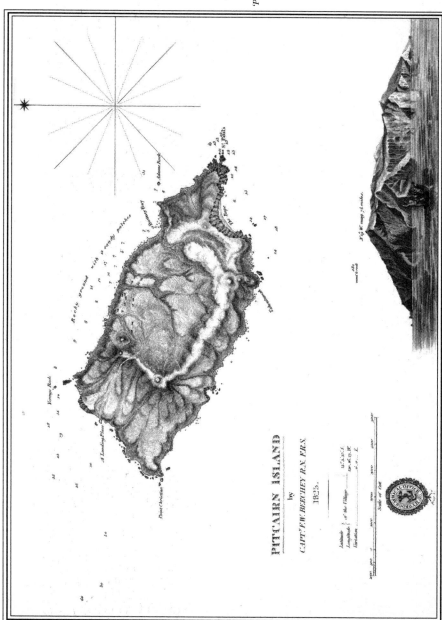

PITCAIRN ISLAND

by

CAPT.^N F.W. BEECHEY R.N. F.R.S.

1825.

Latitude } of the Village ....
Longitude }
Variations

The History of
HENRY CORKILL,
Sailor

ONE – In which I account for my family's condition, my interests and my appearance.

I WAS BORN IN BOSTON, Massachusetts, on 16 March 1775, the son of Edward Corkill and his wife Margaret, whose maiden name was Thomas. I had a brother, Robert, two years my senior, and two sisters, Sarah and Isabelle, my juniors by two and four years respectively. At the time of my birth, my father held a substantial interest in a sawmill. I say an interest because, although in part an owner, he also worked in the mill, doing most of the tasks, from handling the logs, to operating the steam-driven saws.

We lived in a fair way of comfort in a solid house a mile or so from the mill. From a young age, Robert and I were taken to the mill where my father showed us how the operation worked, in the expectation that we would follow him into this business. Robert did, I did not. The reason was that one day I witnessed an accident wherein a worker caught his arm in the machinery and had it torn from his body. I saw a strong, healthy man turned to a cripple before my very eyes. His blood soaked the sawdust to a depth of inches and his screams caused me to block my ears and I felt as though his pain was my own.

The mill workers were accustomed to such accidents and were quick with their remedies – swabbing and tarring the wound, keeping the poor man warm and dosing him with strong liquor to ease his pain and his passing if so it proved. The man survived and continued to work in the mill but in a reduced capacity. He took to drink and died miserably within five years of his mishap.

From that moment, although I said nothing of this within the family, I resolved never to work wood. Indeed my father had lost parts of several fingers and had a large scar on his shoulder where a plank had speared him, but he made light of these injuries. Robert had not seen the accident and when I asked him about his feelings towards the mill he always waxed enthusiastic.

'I love the smell of the cut wood,' he said, 'and the sound of the saws is music to my ears.'

For myself, I was drawn not towards the woods, or the farms or the city's industries, but to the sea. In time away from school, and increasingly avoiding the trips to the mill, I frequented the docks in the company of like-minded friends. When permitted, we boarded the ships, climbed the rigging, dodged the buckets of water flung at us by the sailors, and listened to their tales of faraway places, of painted savages and creatures from the deep.

Had I not fallen so under the spell of the ships and the mariners, I might have noticed their missing eyes, scarred hands and arms, rheumatic limbs and limps, but I saw none of this. I might have echoed my brother's words: 'I love the smell of tar, and sound of the wind in the rigging is music to my ears.'

Although I was not very studious, I attended school regularly under our mother's strict instruction and such learning as was imparted there was reinforced by her at home. She was ever setting us word and number puzzles of her own devising and contriving small treats for successful answers. By the age of thirteen I was competent at reading, writing and numbering, had memorised several poems, passages from the Bible, a good number of hymns and knew that reading books was no waste of time but at once a pleasure and a way of increasing knowledge of the world. To placate my father I read manuals on steam machinery; to please my mother I read devotional tracts; for my own enjoyment I read tales of the sea.

This interest had to be kept secret from my father because in his youth he had been pressed into the British navy. A native of the Isle of Man, born on a small farm into a big family, he had left for England to seek work. Like most Manxmen, he was competent in boats, and had found berths in the craft fishing for herring around England. While ashore in Liverpool and drinking in a tavern, he had fallen foul of a press gang and been put aboard an English man-o'-war. At night, by the fire, when in a good mood, he would tell us stories of his naval experiences. 'Depend upon it, children, there is no life worse than that of an English sailor aboard a fighting ship. The food is foul, the discipline harsh, the pay tiny and the chances of survival close to those of a snowflake in hell.'

My mother sniffed at the mention of hell, but he went on, always in the same vein. 'The English are the cruellest race on earth, especially to their own. They divide mankind up into ranks and those at the back and bottom are treated worse than animals while those at the top live like kings.'

He made no secret of deserting his ship when it stood in Boston harbour and hiding in the woods until it had left and for many a day thereafter. It was while in hiding and in fear of his life – for desertion was a hanging matter – that he met my mother whose family shielded and provided for him until it was judged he was safe. When in the woods he took note of trees and saw their number and quality and how, properly selected, they could serve many purposes from the building of houses to the manufacture of fine furniture and, benefiting from his sea-going, their usefulness as wharf and dock timber.

At a later date, questioning my sisters who had spent much time with our mother after our father's death at a not very great age, I learned that money lent by my mother's family, the Thomases, had established my father in the timber business. My sisters, by then both married and happy with families, made no bones about it.

'They bought him,' Sarah said, 'and it proved a good bargain on both sides.'

'Why the necessity?' I asked. 'She was a handsome woman with a dowry. Why come down to a runaway sailor?'

Isabelle winked at her sister. 'Brother,' she said, 'just to look at you impels me to tell you the great family secret, now that the children are abed and my Matthew is snoring aloft.'

I was in Sarah's house at the time, back from a voyage the details of which I will relate, with a pot of spiced rum in my hand and my pipe drawing well. 'Do tell, sister,' I said.

'Do you mark and remember our mother's appearance?' Isabelle said.

I drew on the sweet pipe. 'Handsome, as I said. A fine woman in every way who became somewhat heavy in later life.'

'God rest her soul,' Sarah murmured.

Never one to put any store in religion, I let this pass and indicated to Isabelle to continue.

'Regard yourself, Henry. Your dark skin and hair, those black eyes.'

I waved my pipe. 'Nothing to that. My father spoke to it more than once. Spaniards from the great Armada that attempted to invade England in the reign of Good Queen Bess were cast ashore on the Isle of Man where our father was born. A dark Spanish strain was thereby introduced to the blood stock of the island and I, and to a lesser degree, you, Sarah, are throwbacks.'

'Nonsense,' Isabelle said. 'Any Spaniards from the Armada setting foot on the Isle of Man would have been instantly killed with no chance to bed Manx women. Our mother Margaret Thomas's grandmother was an Indian. Her daughter, our grandmother, was dark. Our grandfather on that side, who died before you were born was a pale man, almost an albino. Our mother, unlike her brothers and sisters, bore the stain as do you. Our father, a great story-teller about the distant past as you'll recall, had a story to account for the colour, but it was just a story and nothing more.'

Of this I knew nothing as a youngster, being content with my father's story of the Spaniards, happy with it indeed, as it spoke of the sea which was my passion and was the only positive note of the sea he ever struck. In my fifteenth year I was a well set up youth having reached close to the full height I was to attain, namely five feet nine inches and tipping the scales at close to ten stones. Black haired and dark-eyed I was, with a brown skin in summer and winter. Yet this was no occasion of comment as there were many black Irish among us, along with French from the north and others no doubt carrying a measure of the native blood unacknowledged.

TWO – Where I describe myself in more detail and tell how I went to sea.

I COMPLETED MY SCHOOLING at the end of 1789. Robert was already at the mill and the expectation was that I would join him after the Christmas and New Year festivities were over. I was equipped with heavy gloves and boots, canvas trousers and jacket and a felt-lined coat, because at that time of year the mill and yard were cold. I was taller by an inch or two than my father and brother, well-muscled and limber. I was the fastest runner at my school, the best jumper at height and breadth, and could throw a weighty stone further than any of my schoolmates or even the older youths now at work at one trade or another. There was nothing to postpone my going to the mill – except my horror of so doing. I made my plans.

I remember Robert coming home, two days before I was due to join him, and collapsing exhausted into a chair.

'What's the matter, Rob?' I asked him.

He did not reply and I asked again in a louder voice. Still no reply. I realised then that, after only two years in the mill, he was already slightly deafened by the noise of the machines. My father was hard of hearing as well, a matter he had put down to being close to the blast of cannon when in the navy. I now thought otherwise. My heart went out to them, but my resolve was hardened.

That night I waited until the household was asleep, no hard task, for my father and Rob retired early as did my mother, and my sisters, still young and carefree, not yet back at school, slept easily after their frolicksome days. I had penned a note and left it prominently for my mother, always the first to rise, to find. I remember its wording well. It read:

Dearest Mother,

Having attained almost the stature of a man and believing I know my own mind with its strengths and failings, I have decided to leave home and make my own way in the world rather than follow Robert into the mill. I feel that the world is wider than the mill, our home and Boston itself, and I would fain travel it for a period of time.

I know father will be angered but I beg you to intercede with him on my behalf. He has Robert happily bent to his will and dutiful daughters in Sarah and Isabelle. He is blessed and should be able to endure one black sheep.

Do not fear for me, mother. Your example of book learning, polite behaviour and careful consideration of the needs and wishes of others will be ever with me and my major guide through life's storms. I will write as often as my circumstances permit so you will know I am always safe and always thinking of you and my dear family.

Your loving son,

Henry

I realised too late that in using words like 'wider world' and 'life's storms' I was almost spelling out that I had gone to sea. But I had concealed my attraction to ships and sailors so well that my family was slow to come to this realisation. Indeed, they were distracted by my apparent enjoyment of horse-riding which was more feigned than real. As I grew I became slightly bow-legged, a characteristic my father attributed to time spent on horseback. I was pleased for him to think so and to conclude (as indeed he did) that I would make my way inland, seeking new stands of trees. In fact, I truly believe that my gait was in imitation of the sailors I so much admired and longed to join.

Join them I did. The *Falcon* was a vessel engaged in the sealing trade. I had many times boarded her while she lay refitting and re-provisioning in Boston Harbour and had made myself useful running messages for her captain, one Silas Keaton, and mate, Luke Bruce, and yarning with members of the crew. They told me of their voyages south to bays and islands hunting the whales whose bodies yielded oil for lamps and seals for their oil and skins. In addition, they sought walruses for their tusks which, as ivory, was second in value only to that of the elephants of Africa and India.

Captain Keaton was a severe man and Luke Bruce scarcely less so; they were feared, but respected by the crew for their navigational and sailing skills which had carried the vessel through many dangerous storms and shoals.

'Careful Keaton, he's known as,' one of the sailors told me, 'on account of him taking few risks and only when justified by reward.' It was a dangerous business, working so much close to shore in places where charts were few and unreliable, currents and winds uncertain and the inhabitants of those faraway places often hostile. The sailors told of being becalmed, being stuck fast on sandbanks and of spear and arrow attacks. Some carried scars as testimony to their stories. Their living and working conditions were harsh but they had in prospect payment for the skins, oil and ivory they brought back for every man, from the highest to the lowest, rated a share.

From my visits I knew every inch of the ship from stem to stern. I resolved to stow away because the sailors told me that a stowaway not discovered until the ship was at sea became automatically a member of the ship's company. This may sound like a rash act, but

I was a calculator even then. I knew the captain cared for his vessel and his crew; I knew I'd have friends aboard once I emerged and also that the *Falcon* plied the waters south to the islands off the South American coast and that her voyages lasted months rather than years.

I made my way to the dock where the *Falcon* was drawn up preparatory to her dawn departure when the tide and wind would be right. I knew the night watch paraded the poop deck at intervals but stopped periodically to light and smoke his pipe, the action taking up to thirty minutes depending on what there was to look at and how his pipe drew. Wearing clothing intended to keep me warm in the mill with my other possessions in a haversack, I crouched in hiding on the dock until I saw the watchman's vesper flare. He was near the bow of the ship, out of sight of the gangplank. I crept aboard and made my way straight to where the ship's cutter was lashed down on the afterdeck.

As nimble as I was it was simple matter to conceal myself under the canvas cover of the cutter and to make myself comfortable inside a blanket. I'd taken care to piss and empty my bowels before leaving home and I had water, bread and cheese in case my stay in hiding proved to be longer than I thought. I knew that ships could sometimes be held up by such things as the late arrival of stores, hands needing to be scoured from the taverns and unfavourable winds. I pillowed my head on the haversack, drew the blanket around me and prepared to sleep.

For all my preparation and firm resolve, sleep was slow in coming. As I composed myself and listened with something like joy to the creaking of the *Falcon*'s timbers and whistling of the wind in her rigging, I experienced regret at leaving my family where I had received nothing but kindness, even from my father whose understanding did not reach to the kind of youth I was and the kind of man I wanted to be. I knew I would miss my mother and my sisters for their softness, my brother for his solid comradeship and the rowdy company of my friends.

I heard the footsteps of the watchman, once, twice, three times as he passed by the cutter and my heart leapt, for discovery now would bring all my plans undone. I never heard his next pass. I was young, with nothing yet in my life to grieve over, snug and well fed and tired after a day of planning and contrivance, and I eventually fell into a deep sleep, lulled by the motion of the ship as she strained at her moorings.

When I awoke I knew that I had broken free of the land and was at sea. The *Falcon* seemed to be skimming the surface of the water with scarcely a movement other than forward and the sails barely flapped as they caught and embraced the wind. I lifted the canvas and saw that it was broad daylight with the sun well aloft. The air was cold but the sky was clear and I took my first deep breaths of sea air and felt intoxicated like a man taking his first draught of strong drink.

Lifting the canvas an inch higher I peered around and saw the ship in all her glory – the deck newly stone-washed, the scuppers clear and the helmsman at his post handling the wheel with ease. I was stiff and sore from the unaccustomed sleeping position, but not cramped or cold. I took a long swig from my water bottle and ate some bread and cheese because the sailors had told me that stowaways were sometimes confined, even in irons, for a period of punishment before being entered on the muster. Thus fortified and after performing a few stretching exercises, I climbed from my hiding place and swung myself onto the deck.

Later, my shipmates told me it was like a miracle how I was able to walk easily with the motion of the ship, never having been at sea before. I stood upright and the first person to clap eyes on me was Luke Bruce, the mate.

'Who let this whelp aboard?' he roared. 'Whose watch? I'll flog him black and blue!'

He made reference to my age and not my size for I was much of a measure with him. 'T'weren't the watch's fault, Mr Bruce,' I said. 'I crept on board so quick and quiet no one could've seen me.'

He swung, intending to backhand me across to the railing but I stepped away to miss the blow and then stood my ground. That gave him pause. 'I know you, you're the saw miller's pup.'

'Yes, sir. Henry Corkill. I've done small services for you and the captain and our . . . the mill supplied you with decking timber.'

'And right good timber it is, Luke.' One of the seamen by the name of Cotter and a Manxman like my father, spoke up. 'The lad longs to go to sea as a good Manxman should.'

'I'm an American,' I said.

Bruce waved the few men who had gathered back to their tasks. 'You look like a bloody gypsy to me and I've a mind . . .'

Just then a stray wave hit the ship and she pitched and rolled. By long habit Luke and Cotter reached for ropes to steady themselves. I found it easy to do the same as if I had had a second's warning of the movement.

'He's a sailor,' Cotter said.

Bruce nodded. 'He is that. God help him.'

The *Falcon* was a three-masted schooner one hundred and thirty feet long with a breadth of thirty feet. Her crew comprised twenty-eight men and I became the twenty-ninth and was assigned the most menial duties shipboard life has to offer – assisting the cook, washing clothes, swabbing the decks and drawing up samples of the bilge water to allow an estimation of its quality. There was no talk of wages or mention of a share in the profits of the voyage, nor did I expect such. A hammock was slung for me in the foc'sle and I was assigned a tin locker for my few possessions.

Having observed something of a sailor's inventory I had equipped myself with a clasp knife, several large kerchiefs, a scrap of towelling and some soap, two shirts, a pair of cotton trousers for the southern clime and a light jersey. I was thus able to cut my bread and salt meat like the others, stay warm, clean myself and tie a kerchief over my head or around my neck in sailor fashion.

After some weeks when it became clear that I could work like a man, take the roughness that was part of a sailor's life and stand up for myself in disputes, I was accepted as part of the ship's company. I turned fifteen when we sailed east of Cuba and began our passage down the coast of South America. I told no-one about my birthday but it meant a good deal to me – I felt I had left childhood behind me, as indeed I had. That was brought home to me in strong fashion when we crossed the line.

THREE – In which I cross the line for the first time and am introduced to the sealing trade.

THERE WERE THREE OF us aboard the *Falcon* who had not crossed the line and some days before the vessel reached the equator we were made aware of what was in store for us.

'You'll be ducked deep several times each of you,' Cotter said, 'and it'll behove you to take it like men. Then you'll be dressed as mermaids or Neptune and paraded around the ship. Like as not there'll be a mock flogging for any that show a yellow streak and then you'll drink half a pint of rum. Some captains permit a tarring and shaving with a blunt razor but Captain Keaton fears it can cause injury and keep a man from his work too long.'

My companions in the ordeal were Peter Dent and Christopher Carter, both in their twenties and experienced seamen, but who had only plied the northern waters.

Dent was a well set up young man who looked likely to take the ceremonies in his stride, but Carter was a pale creature with a hacking cough who used laudanum to get him through his duties. He was English and rumoured to be well connected, although how that fitted with his status as an able seaman aboard a sealer, and an ailing one at that, no one could tell. After a life at sea and on land I can say that many are the people you encounter in humble circumstances who have fallen there from great heights. Carter was evidently such a one.

15

We crossed the line in the morning of 2 April 1790. I mark it well for, as the reader of this may have determined, I had a notebook and pencils in my haversack and seized such moments of privacy as the work permitted to scribble hasty notes on matters of interest. We three were paraded on deck and stripped naked – no great trial for, although the year was young, the heat of the day was great in that latitude and we did our work in a minimum of clothing. A rope and belaying pin were attached to a davit and in turn each of us was to be made to straddle the pin, grip the rope and be ducked deep beside the ship.

Dent and Carter had been given strong draughts of rum to steel them for the ordeal but I refused. Not because I was less afraid but because I had resolved to experience everything of a sailor's life as I had read about it for years, including this, and I wanted my wits about me. Dent was swung out first and ducked six times before he began to show signs of distress – a respectable performance. Carter lasted but two immersions. His coughing alarmed everyone and his normally pale complection took a blueish hue that indicated he had had enough.

'Now then young Henry,' Cotter the Manxman yelled as I settled myself across the pin, 'how many duckings do you fancy?'

I should add that the whole of the crew was fairly far gone in drink by this time, apart from the men in control of the davit.

'How many had you when you crossed the line?' I rejoined.

'Ten.'

'Then I'll try a dozen to start and see if I can double your score.'

A cheer went up and the ducking began. It may sound easy enough, a dunking in tropical waters, but it was far from that. The drop was deep and the light was shut out so that the thought entered my brain that if I came off the pin I wouldn't know which way was up and which down. I clung tight, held my breath and shut my eyes. As I have said, I was broad made and deep chested and could hold a deal of air in my lungs. Also, unlike many a sailor, I could swim, having learnt in the stream and pool beside the mill, so that immersion did not frighten me as much as it might others.

I roared out 'One!' as I came out of the water the first time and continued to shout the score as the ducking went on. I was thumped hard against the side of the ship and almost lost my grip at one ducking and saw a monster shark drift by me, its eye happily on other prey, but my nerve held and I heard the cheers each time I surfaced. Gasping for breath and my eyes half-blinded by the salt water, I saw Captain Keaton observing proceedings from the quarterdeck. My shoulders were racked with pain from gripping the rope and my legs felt numb but my brain was still working. I sucked in air before I went down for the twelfth time.

The water world seemed to hold me for minutes rather than seconds, and I had a sense of what it might be like to drown when that mighty world rushes in and eclipses the other. When I emerged I signalled to the men at the davit that I had had enough and they swung me in to cheers. I had wanted to show my mettle, but it was no part of my plan to humiliate Cotter, my supporter and fellow Manxman.

After that, there was further torture for Carter as he was dressed a mermaid and tormented by Bruce regaled as King Neptune and equipped with a trident. A number of the crew dressed as pirates, several as whores, some as naval men. I was given a cat o' nine tails and encouraged to whip any I chose. This I did in a bantering fashion doing no harm and only increasing the jollity when I brandished the cat in Captain Keaton's face, taking care not to touch him.

My fortitude in the line-crossing ceremony and my willingness to work won me the respect of the crew, or most of them, and before long I was doing the work of any sailor – hauling on rope, climbing rigging, reefing sails. Cotter gave me instruction in helmsmanship and, aloft in the crow's nest, I was taught how to spot a sail on the horizon and distinguish it from a cloud or a flock of seabirds.

The weather grew colder as we tracked south and I saw my first whale while in the rigging working on a twisted rope. I shouted 'Whale!' and was laughed at by those who had seen the huge beasts times without number. The whale rose in the water and then crashed down leaving a greasy slick where it had been. I confess I did not find the sight majestic or awesome and soon grew accustomed to seeing whales, old and young, in the southern waters. Some of the sailors had worked on whaling vessels and spoke of the dangers and rewards of that trade. Some admitted to preferring sealing as less dangerous.

'They whales can smash a ship to matchwood,' one sailor said, 'and sink a long boat with a flick of the tail. Evil creatures.'

I was inclined to agree with him, having seen a whale turn its eye on our vessel as it slid by. Baleful I thought it, as if it resented sharing its sea with any other large structure. Likewise dolphins, which I'd seen off the Massachusetts coast many a time. Some sailors claimed to have an affinity with them and to be able to interpret the sounds they made but I took this to be fanciful. I found them tiresome.

'You're a born sealer, Hank,' Cotter told me. 'Something of a cold heart, unless I miss my guess.'

'Not so,' I said. 'But I reserve my feelings for humankind and care little for fish other than to eat.'

'You'll be tested,' he said.

When we reached the forties the weather grew cold and blustery and I was glad of the padded coat and the rest of my mill-worker clothes. We began to work in towards the South American mainland, taking care not to be blown on shore, but testing the inlets and bays and offshore islands that abounded in the area.

'Worked out,' I heard Bruce say. 'We'll have to go further afield this voyage.'

'How far?' O'Brien, the bosun, asked.

Bruce shrugged. 'Careful Keaton may have to take a risk.'

'You mean the Cape?'

'Pray God not,' Bruce replied. 'Let's hope our luck is better in the Falklands and South Georgia.'

O'Brien, evidently a Catholic, crossed himself as he spoke. 'Pray God indeed, with all my heart.'

Bruce roared at me when he saw me eavesdropping and had me climb aloft in a bitter wind and adjust a sail lashing. The *Falcon* was rolling in heavy seas and the task did not have to be done at that moment, but a deck hand could not question the orders of the mate and I made the hazardous climb and freed the lashing. When I returned to the pitching deck, Bruce caught me by the collar of my coat.

'Not a word of what you heard to the other men.'

'Aye, aye, sir. But why?'

'Some have been round the Horn and would prefer not to do so again.'

'I'd like to.'

'You're a young fool who knows nothing, for all your book reading and scribbling and deep breaths. About your business.'

A man skilled at his job, Luke Bruce knew everything going on aboard his ship and no doubt had other eyes and ears working for him, so it was mere vanity making me believe I had any secrets. I kept silent about the conversation I'd overheard but I bore it in mind and fancied I could detect an increase in anxiety among the crew as we probed ever southwards. But it was as if the sea creatures had wind of our coming and so few were to be seen that it was not worth putting out the boats.

The day came when the captain gave orders to change to a eastward course and the mood of the men lifted, knowing they would not be risking the Horn. In truth the seas were so high at times and the winds so strong, I was not sorry myself to postpone this experience, although I made a resolve that I would voyage into the Pacific Ocean one day, if I was spared.

That provisional idea came to me when poor Carter died of his lung disease as we beat eastward. He had been ill for days with a raging fever and shivers that seemed to shake what little flesh there was from his bones. He could neither eat nor drink and coughed blood continually so that his passing was a mercy. Ever anxious for experience, I went below to look at the dead body, the first I'd seen.

'What think ye, Hank?' said the sailor preparing the canvas envelope for the body.

'He looks at peace at last.'

'Aye. Drowned in his own blood he did when his bellows collapsed.' He gave a harsh laugh as he lifted the grown man's body on to the canvas as if it were as light as that of a child. He wielded needle and thread with a practised hand and I helped him carry the body up to the deck, more to prevent it bumping against steps and sides than for its weight. Sailors lived with death constantly, and the ceremony for Carter was brief with the captain reading a Bible verse I have forgotten and the weighed package sliding into the sea, scarcely under the surface before hats were on and work resumed.

I scribbled some notes about the death that night by a flickering lantern light. As well to say here that I put no stock in religion even at that age. I had seen animals mate, defecate and die and had no reason to think they continued to exist in any sphere, and ourselves likewise. Of course, I hid these thoughts from my mother at home and bared my head like the rest at Carter's entombment, but it was all sham on my part.

And next I saw so much of death that my godlessness was multiplied a thousandfold. Possession of the islands off the coast of South America, I was told, was disputed among several European countries. The Spanish claimed them and called them the *Islas Malvinas*, the English name was the Falklands. As well as the two main islands there were two hundred or more smaller ones dotted about and it was among these that Captain Keaton hoped to find his cargo.

The islands were apparently well charted and it was possible to bring the ship in close to land where the reefs and shoals were known. A cry of 'Cargo' from on high brought us to the rail as we sailed close to a rocky island with the waves lashing a stony beach. Bruce ordered the boats lowered and I joined a party of ten in one boat with a few less in the other. Each man was armed with a stout club and a wickedly sharp knife. There were also a couple of muskets in each boat. We pulled for the shore with me on an oar keeping pace with older men. As we drew closer to the small bay I could see the animals sunning themselves on rocks and stony ledges all about us.

The order came to ship oars and we held the boat steady for a moment and then rode a breaking wave in to the beach. We dragged the boat up and secured it with a grapnel to a rock. The seals barked a harsh, unpleasant note and appeared to shuffle about before settling again.

'Don't they fear us?' I asked Bruce.

'Too stupid,' he said. 'Right lads, among them and watch for the bulls. You stay here, Corkill, and see how it's done.' The men walked briskly up to the seals, which lifted their heads as if to invite the blow. The clubs rose and fell, smashing the small heads to pulp, one blow often being sufficient. The animals watched the slaughter for some minutes, apparently unconcerned, until some kind of awareness dawned and they began to slither towards the water. But the sealers had so arranged themselves to cut off this escape and the killing continued, with more animals dying than escaping. The rocks and stones of the beach began to run with blood and the smell attracted hundreds of gulls that fluttered about uttering cries that drowned out the sound of the thudding clubs.

Indeed the animals appeared passive and stupid until one of the largest made a rush at a sailor who had turned his back to wipe blood and brain matter from his face. The huge seal knocked him flying and then mauled at him with its teeth as if it would have revenge for every seal killed that day. The sailor screamed and tried to fend the animal off but it persisted and his blood joined that of the seals on the rocks. Bruce seized a musket from the stand he'd made on the beach, advanced quickly, priming and loading the weapon. He put the musket to the enraged seal's head and fired. The seal flopped a dead weight on the sailor, and he screamed again as his ribs and spine cracked.

'God damn you!' Bruce roared. Watching from thirty feet away, I thought at first he was referring to the brave seal, but it became apparent that his curse was for the dead sailor, because the sound of the musket had sent the entire seal population of the bay slithering, flapping, barking, bound for the sea with such vigour than an army of men could not have stopped them.

FOUR – I reflect on death, am blooded and our voyage continues profitably.

I ANTICIPATE THAT IN time to come there will be those crying out against the cruelty of the sealing trade. Indeed, given the rate at which we sealers killed them such protest may be unnecessary for they may have vanished from the earth altogether. I understand such feelings but confess that I did not share them then or now. The seals were ugly beasts, half-formed it seemed to me, and impossibly stupid. They seemed to have no awareness of the danger a ship represented. In cove after cove we anchored, rowed ashore and killed them. In some places there were signs that others had been here before us – a rusty, broken knife blade, a stoven barrel – yet the seals learned nothing and died. Further, they were not incapable of a defence as the death of the seaman named Quinlan at our first landing showed, but such aggression was rare.

With first Carter and then Quinlan dying, with hundreds of seals dying also, I began to think that life was a small thing easily snuffed out. Like the others, I forgot the two men within a couple of days and the world went on as if they had never been. I concluded that we put too much store on life which is but a brief spark, a momentary glow in the immensity of things. The words 'life everlasting' when I heard them spoken made me smile – it was quite the opposite.

On our second killing I was given a club and a knife and, watched by Cotter, killed and skinned my first seal. I despatched the animal neatly enough with a powerful and well placed blow but made a hash of the skinning. Cotter looked at the hacked about pelt when I finally freed it from the carcass and laughed.

'A fine coat that would make, for a beggar or a leper or worse.'

Nevertheless, he dipped his fingers in the blood and printed two marks on my face. 'One for killing and one for skinning,' he said, 'and you'll do both till your arms and back ache and you'll hear the barking in your sleep.'

Cotter was right about the ache in my body but not about the trade disturbing my sleep. I was more perturbed by the smell that pervaded the ship from the moment the boiling down of the seal carcasses began. Only the fattest were chosen and the gaining of the oil was secondary to the skinning and preservation of the hides, but it went on constantly and the reek seeped into every corner of the ship, despite the washing with warm vinegar ordered by the captain from time to time. I assisted in all these operations and Bruce, O'Brien and Captain Keaton began to look more cheerful day by day as the weather held fair and the hunting was good. We were all exhausted by the end of the day and I confess I looked forward to the measure of rum we were allowed to raise our spirits and soothe our rest.

After almost four months on board ship the hard work and ample food had filled me out and caused me to grow so that I found my pants short in the leg and my shirts tight on my chest. I also had the beginnings of a dark down on my upper lip and cheeks. I was becoming a man and welcomed the development. After yet another day of killing, skinning and boiling, I was enjoying my rum when Bruce told me the Captain wanted to see me. I was alarmed and asked why but got no reply.

I smartened myself as much as I could, finished my rum to give myself courage and ventured to knock timidly on the door of the captain's cabin. Bidden to enter, I found him seated behind a table on which were spread charts and other papers. I stood respectfully. 'You wanted to see me, sir.'

He barely glanced at me. 'We have lost two men on this voyage. You, I have observed, have more than made up for their loss. I therefore propose to allot you a share in the profits of the voyage.'

'Sir, I said, 'would not their families . . .'

'Carter's family is rich and has no need of it. Quinlan had neither family nor friend aboard. You are entered for a share. That is all.'

I thanked him. He ignored me and I left the cabin, still worried. I confided the news to Cotter. 'Might not the other men resent it? Fewer shares mean more for each man.'

'Aye, you'll be challenged. Best to get in first if you have the nerve.'

As soon as the opportunity presented I issued my challenge. I said, 'In defence of my right to a share, I'll arm wrestle any one of you of about my size.'

Laughter greeted the challenge. 'And if you lose?' one growled.

'I forfeit my rum ration for a week.'

That gave them pause. None wanted to lose face by being beaten by a stripling, but the prize was too tempting for the rascally Peter Maynard as I had anticipated. He was too fond of drink and often bartered for others' rations. Maynard was at least ten years older than me and built solid, but I calculated I was longer in the arm, an advantage in such a contest as I had proposed, and that his passion for drink ashore and afloat had sapped his strength.

We took off our jackets and faced each other across a barrel top. We locked hands and, for all the hard work I'd lately done, my hand felt soft compared to the leathery surfaces of Maynard's palm and fingers. He grinned slightly as he felt the same thing, but the grin faded when he saw I had an inch or so of greater leverage. For all that he almost beat me, surprising me with a hard jerk and twist that I had to yield to or hear bones break. He had my arm halfway to the barrel and the sailors were cheering him and nodding wise heads. They were also betting and I sensed that the money was on Maynard by a wide margin.

But I held him there, bracing my arm against his and resisting the downward pressure with all my might. No chance of a twist now; to move in the grip would give me the advantage. Slowly I felt his strength ebbing and his breath began to come in gasps. A foul odour of rotten teeth and tobacco wafted towards me and I remembered that Maynard was one of those with a pipe seldom out of his mouth. It became not so much a trial of strength as a test of lungs and there he was no match for me. As his breath came in ever harsher pants the strength left his arm and I took it back to level and then began to press downward. Still, I remained wary for an old dog knows many tricks and a moment's slackness could turn the tables. He swore and spat but he was done and I pressed his hand down to the salt-stained boards.

To my surprise I discovered that Cotter, Bruce and a few others had bet on me and were pleased with their winnings.

'No hard feelings, mate,' I said to Maynard, but the man turned away and spat over the side before lighting his pipe.

'I hope a seal snaps off your balls,' he said.

FIVE – Sundry voyages over the years from 1797 to 1807, briefly described. Early stages of the voyage that changed my life.

I DO NOT PROPOSE to recount in detail my life as a sealer, whaler and merchant seaman over the next seven years. Suffice to say that I suffered no great injuries, profited well from each voyage and earned my first mate's ticket. Sadly, I was never reconciled with my father and was greatly grieved when he was killed in an accident in the mill in the year 1800 when I was at sea. My brother Robert and I remained on good terms and my mother was dear to me although she deplored what she called my 'heathen trade and way of life'. My sisters married worthy, if dull men, and the Corkill family was firmly established in its Boston respectability, with only myself as a volatile member.

Despite my mother's fears, I by no means led a riotous life. When ashore I drank in the taverns with my shipmates but never to excess and although I occasionally went to the brothels, especially after a long voyage, I took pains to visit only the reputable houses and to protect myself from disease. I saved my money with a view to buying an interest in a vessel and becoming a master and trader in my own right. In my own way, I had the same ambitions as the other members of my family, although exercised in a different sphere.

I sailed several times more with Careful Keaton and with Cotter the Manxman and learned something of the history of the Isle of

Man and picked up from him a smattering of the language which we used among ourselves occasionally when we wanted to annoy our shipmates or keep a conversation private. But our ways eventually parted when he took a berth on a northbound vessel for which I had no inclination. Another ambition had risen within me; I had tired of the cold and, having read accounts of the voyages of Captain James Cook, I longed to go round the Horn and sail the Pacific Ocean.

My chance came when a mate's berth fell vacant on the whaler *Emerald,* sailing out of New Bedford. Her captain, Eli Tarpone, had been in Boston and had been heard to lament the scarcity of whales in the northern waters and the Atlantic and to speculate about the prospects in the Pacific. When I heard of the vacant berth I was visiting with my family. I borrowed a horse from the mill and hastened to New Bedford to apply for the post. As it happened, Captain Tarpone was at the rail of his ship when I pulled my horse up close to the dock and requested permission to come aboard.

'Did you get the bow legs from riding nags?' he asked when I had presented my papers. We were standing aft with gulls wheeling around us, and sailors busy with ropes and canvas.

I was sensitive about my slightly bowed legs but tried not to show it. 'No, sir. A family trait I believe, but one which has given me good balance aboard many a pitching ship.'

He laughed. 'A good answer, and I see you have the years and the sea miles to your credit. Four voyages with Keaton – a good apprenticeship. What would you do with a man who thieved aboard ship, Corkill?'

I made a fist. 'For a first offence I would knock him down and have him make restitution. For a second, I'd knock him down twice and impose double restitution. There'd not be a third.'

He nodded his dark, shaggy head. He was a tall, spare figure, pock-marked and ugly and somewhat ill-kempt, but I'd noticed that his vessel was as clean as I'd ever seen any whaler which was no easy thing to achieve. He folded my papers and handed them back to me. His black eyes seemed to pierce me through.

'Ye could have taken a coach and been here in ample time. I sense an urgency in you, Corkill. It's not usual in a Manxman. Ye are a Manxman? I know the name.'

'An American. My father hailed from the Isle of Man.'

'Whence your colouring then?'

I trotted out the story of the Spanish ancestor from the Armada, not yet having heard my sister's sounder explanation.

'But your passion is not to slaughter whales, I fancy.'

'Not that alone, sir, I admit it. I yearn to round the Horn and enter the Pacific.'

'Do y'now? And what makes you think the *Emerald*'s bound that way?'

I told him that I had people placed in taverns along the coast alert for talk of a Pacific voyage, and that I'd undertaken to pay for the information. He laughed, took a snuff box from the pocket of his bedraggled jacket and sniffed and sneezed and spat overt the side. He then fell into a fit of coughing from which it took him some little time to recover. 'And have you paid?'

'The arrangement is, I pay when I get the post.'

He extended a hand wrinkled like a parrot's claw and spat again. 'Pay up then, man. The berth is yours.'

Eli Tarpone was an experienced and canny sailor and, what's more, one who knew how to pick and handle his men. Also, unlike other merchant sailors, he read the journals and memoirs of naval men and others who had sailed before him and learned by their experience. Consequently, he knew that the early months of the year were the best time for rounding the Horn. Later, the storms and tremendous seas made the route dangerous if not impossible. Taking care not to appear better informed than he, I let him know that I too had read Cook and others and had absorbed some of their wisdom.

Among the crew were several who had been to the Dutch East Indies as pressed men aboard British naval vessels, though none who had taken the direct route. Tarpone himself had sailed from English ports and into the southern oceans but only via the Cape of Good Hope. To use a woodsman's phrase, he considered himself to be blazing a trail for whalers. Not that others hadn't worked the Pacific, but none had published accounts of their voyages. I often had occasion to see him working long and late at his log, chewing his pen. Eli Tarpone yearned for the immortality of print.

His mastery of men extended further than picking experienced tars. As we made our way swiftly south to the Horn, as luck would have it we sighted whales in the southern waters. But Tarpone had convinced his crew that the pickings in the Pacific would exceed anything to be got in the accustomed grounds and that they would return to New Bedford with money enough to buy a tavern rather than just drink in it. Consequently, we sailed past the great, spouting monsters and the weather grew colder and wilder as we neared the Horn.

'Hard to believe that people live in these climes, Corkill,' the captain observed as we bore towards Tierra Del Fuego.

'Indeed, sir, although the same might be said of the northern frozen wastes – Greenland and such.'

'Ye've ventured there, then?'

'I have, captain, and for the last time I trust. I believe the Pacific will be more to my liking.'

He glanced sharply at me. 'Ye're not a sensualist, Corkill?'

'I'm unfamiliar with the word, sir.'

He coughed and spat and fought briefly for breath. He seemed to have lost some flesh and had little to spare. 'Do ye lust after the brown maidenly bodies described by Cartaret and Cook?'

'You have the better of me. I have not read Cartaret closely. And Cook's fate makes me think caution rather than boldness might be the mark among the natives of the Pacific, whatever allurements they may offer.'

'Aye. I doubt we'll venture north to those paradisiacal islands, anyway. Our prey lies further south, typically.'

There I had the greater knowledge, for I'd talked to some Pacific whalers and knew that the beasts went north to calve and feed before returning to the colder latitudes. Depending on the time of year, we could find ourselves chasing them as far north as New Zealand and Botany Bay. But Captain Tarpone had read me aright in part. The drawings of the natives, their dress, weapons, houses and so on, in the published accounts fascinated me and I longed to see them. And if some bare-breasted maidens should come into view and show themselves willing, so much the better.

As the Captain had anticipated, we rounded the Horn in conditions which, if not calm, were manageable for a good crew in a good ship. We had clear skies for most days and the wind held fair, not driving us towards the treacherous rocks around that forbidding shore. The *Emerald* was a sober, well mannered ship, by which I mean there was little sky-larking and no fighting. Every man aboard had crossed the line so there was the bare minimum of ceremony when we did so. It occurred to me that we should have had some ceremony to mark rounding the Horn and when I mentioned this to the captain he nodded and ordered an extra ration of meat and rum per man. That sufficed for the captain and crew of the *Emerald*.

And so I sailed into the vast Pacific which, as we bore north to pick up the forties, belied its name. We ran for days before howling winds that threatened to shred the sails under dark skies that prevented the taking of any readings. Good navigator though he was, and now somewhat skilled at the craft myself, the captain and I had no way of determining our precise location. The ship was sound and the crew in good health. By rights we should have been in no danger, but the spirits aboard sank day by day for two reasons. One, sailing blind as we were, there was always the chance of running into a reef or rock. Two, if there were whales in these wind-tossed seas, we were too busy manning the ship to spot them and no one would have wanted to enter a boat if we had. The swells were high and unpredictable and there was water enough across our decks without seeking more.

'Tis uncommon strong,' the captain said to me as we shared a dawn watch. 'In days gone by the sailors would have thought us likely to be blown off the edge of the world.'

'There's no talk of that, sir,' I said. 'Only of a wish to know where we are and to do our business.'

'I share both wishes, Corkill. At least there can be no talk of mutiny.'

'Captain?'

'It's been known to happen in these circumstances. A man like yourself might decide he could do better and recruit others to his cause. Ye'll have heard of that scoundrel Christian, the fool Bligh and the *Bounty*.'

I laughed. 'The British Navy. My father told me something of it. We're not subject to such tyranny. There's nought to do but run before this wind, and every man aboard has confidence in you.'

Almost as I spoke the wind seemed to drop. A light appeared in the east and the sun gradually rose into a clearing sky.

'Land, ho,' called the lookout in the crow's nest.

SIX – A Pacific Island paradise, for a time. A strange encounter. A dalliance. An initiation.

THE LAND TURNED OUT to be a barren rock, but under the clear sky Captain Tarpone was able to take readings and then, by consulting his charts, to determine where we were. He called a meeting of the senior members of the crew and announced that we had reached the Paumotu Archipelago, a collection of atolls and coral islets east of the Society Islands. This was good news because, according to the captain, there were no reports of hostile natives in these parts. The many European vessels as had passed by or sojourned – such as those commanded by Wallis, Cartaret, Byron and Cook – had met a friendly reception. On the other hand, the atolls and reefs were treacherous and had brought many ships to grief. The Spanish, the first Europeans to sight the Paumotus according to the captain, had named them the 'low islands' and stressed the dangers to navigation.

'How about whales, sir?' Carstairs, the bosun, asked.

Tarpone shrugged and I was about to say that the whales could well be heading our way from the warmer waters to the north, when Jacob Finlay, the ship's carpenter, knocked briefly before entering the cabin.

Tarpone looked up, annoyed.

'Beg to report, sir. The mainmast is strained in its housing and several planks in the hull have sprung. The copper sheathing has lifted and we're exposed to the worms unless we make repairs prompt.'

'God damn it!' Tarpone roared, turning his back on us. 'That long run before the wind has taken its toll.'

Finlay retreated to the door. Few had heard Tarpone swear, but Finlay had the courage of knowing whereof he spoke. 'We must make a landing, sir. And I'll need timber.'

Carstairs said, 'The bilges are sour, sir, and our water's low. Likewise the meat.'

Tarpone swung back on his heel. 'I thought you were break-a-neck to hunt whale, bosun?'

'Not in a wormy ship, sir, with a hungry, thirsty crew.'

Tarpone's smile was accommodating. 'So be it. Can we refit while afloat, Finlay?'

'I hope so, sir.'

'So do I. About your business and inform the crew we'll make landfall where we can avoid reefs and shoals and where there is timber and water to be had.'

The weather had become warm and calm after the blow of the forties and although it was reckoned to near enough to winter in this, the southern half of the world, to a northern it was like summer still. The crew cheered at the prospect of fresh water and food and the foc's'le hummed with stories of the island women and their winning ways.

'If the Spanish and French have been here the bitches'll be poxed,' said Henry Smith, an Englishman who all suspected was a deserter from the British Navy.

'And I suppose coupling with a Limey'd cure them,' replied Coltrane, an American.

I had to intervene to prevent a fight, indicating the shortness of the men's tempers after the hard voyage and their concern at the state of the vessel.

With our most expert taker of soundings, Renee Marat, dropping the lead, who had taken ships through dangerous waters in all parts of the world, the *Emerald* probed the reefs and sandbars of the Paumotus for a week before a safe passage through the coral and breakers was found to an anchorage in a bay of the large island of Rangiroa. Throughout this trying time, the sailors had manned the pumps constantly for the ship was taking on water. Captain Tarpone and myself had shared the task of steering according to Marat's soundings, by night and day and, like the sounder, we were both exhausted by the time the anchor was dropped. The crew gave hearty cheers, but whether it was for our efforts or at the sight of the canoes heading out from the beach towards the ship I could not say.

Ten canoes were paddled through the waves each containing a dozen or more people – men, women and children. In the time they'd seen us manoeuvring the ship into the bay they had loaded the canoes with bananas, coconuts and other fruits I could not then identify.

The captain summoned Finlay the carpenter to the rail. Finlay had been to the Sandwich Islands in the years after Cook and had learned a smattering of the language which apparently was spoken with small variation all over the Pacific.

'Tell them,' Tarpone instructed, 'that we come in peace and to repair our ship. If their chief is present we would welcome him aboard. Otherwise three men may board but no women. We will happily pay for the food they bring with trade goods.'

There was a moan of disappointment at this from some of the men but Carstairs nodded his sage agreement. 'They'd be over the ship like monkeys in minutes. The women would be handling your privates while the men would be stealing your pants.'

'Don't know as I'd mind,' one sailor grumbled.

'You'd mind when they stole rope and nails during your watch,' Carstairs said. 'You'd pay for every inch and every nail.'

The captain ordered men armed with muskets to stand by the rail while Finlay communicated with the natives. They had evidently seen such weapons before and showed them respect. When a few children attempted to swarm up a rope hanging from the rail they were ordered down by their elders.

Finlay was up to the task. After some exchanges that appeared friendly, he turned to the captain. 'They say they have not seen white men for some time and we are welcome. The chief is old and too fat to travel in a canoe. He will see us ashore.'

Tarpone ordered two sailors to lower a rope mesh over the side to facilitate climbing. 'Three men,' he said.

The natives conferred briefly and two canoes drew close with four men gripping the rope.

'I said three.'

'I'm sorry, captain. I must have used the wrong word and told them four.'

Tarpone roared with laughter, and his mirth was echoed by the islanders who swiftly climbed the ropes and leapt over the rail to the deck.

'They rub noses instead of shaking hands,' Finlay said quickly as he performed the salute with all four.

'Show them our way,' Tarpone said sternly, and the carpenter took the hand of the biggest of the natives and shook it vigorously while talking in the island tongue. Tarpone extended his hand and the natives shook it in turn, smiling and nodding amiably before looking down into the canoes and gesticulating for the foodstuffs to be attached to the ropes we'd lowered and sent up. These goods were stowed in baskets cunningly woven from some kind of hardy leaves and could bear a considerable weight.

The captain ordered a box of trade goods to be brought on deck and a judicious number of knives and hatchets were exchanged for the food. By this time most of the canoes had departed, but those that stood by each contained a couple of women who conformed to the sailors' expectations – tawny skinned beauties with lustrous dark hair and upthrust bare breasts with nipples the colour of blackberries. After so long at sea, I doubt there was a limp cock among the men gazing down at them. Certainly mine was in a more than ready state.

Under the captain's orders, Finlay continued conversing with the natives, whose eyes were wandering over the ship and the crew, although they appeared well satisfied with the trade goods. Finlay conveyed the message that we were in need of water, meat and timber and would need to stay for some time to make repairs to the ship. At this the natives fell into a conference, speaking so quickly that Finlay declared himself unable to follow the discussion.

At length one of the men spoke simply and plainly to Finlay who nodded his understanding.

'This man is able to speak for the chief, captain. He declares that we will be welcome at his village and along this stretch of coast but they have enemies inland and around the point. If you would fire our guns several times, their enemies would take it as a sign not to oppose us or them.'

'When should this be done?'

'Immediately, sir. The whole island is alerted to our arrival.'

Tarpone gave order for our four small twenty pounders, the only guns we carried, to be run out and fired, two shots from each gun. This was done with dispatch and the natives declared themselves satisfied. By now it was late in the day and Finlay was told to inform the natives that we would come ashore in the morning to greet the chief and that there would be further gifts. The natives shook hands again. We expected them to go over the side and down into their canoes and head for the beach, but their leader arrested their movement to the rail and approached me.

Like most of the men I was stripped to the waist on account of the heat and had been so for the last few days. My naturally dark skin had darkened still further so that I was of a colour with the natives, at least those parts of me that had been exposed to the sun. The islander, a strapping fellow with an inch or two on me and a greater girth, seized me by the shoulders and brought his face close to mine. I was alarmed but allowed him to rub my nose against his. He then shook my hand and spoke to me in his own language.

I looked to Finlay. 'He thinks you are a native like him, Mr Corkill, being so dark skinned and all.'

I smiled. 'Little use to tell him of my Spanish ancestry. Tell him he is mistaken but that I am honoured.'

Finlay did so and the native accepted the information with a good grace. All four then descended to the canoes. Again, we leaned over the side to look at the women, some of whom raised their arms in a gesture of farewell that lifted their breasts and sent our hearts racing.

'I fancy you will find favour ashore, Mr Corkill,' Finlay said, 'but the least favoured of us might do well enough with a knife or a few nails.'

'I'm grateful for your efforts, Finlay,' the captain said. 'And you will have nails aplenty, but for repairing the ship, not for wetting your pizzle.'

'Aye, aye, captain,' Finlay said.

Eli Tarpone was a master controller of men. In the days that followed he permitted all members of the crew to go ashore but only for brief periods. Exceptions to this were the carpenter, who supervised the cutting of timber, the bosun, who exercised discipline over the shore parties, the Captain himself and me. As it happened, I had a facility for languages and in addition to the snatches of Manx I'd picked up from Cotter, I'd learned some French, Italian and Spanish in the course of my sea-going career. For the first few days I pestered Finlay to teach me what he knew of the islander language and I acquired it quickly. I then set about communicating with the natives, enquiring the names for people, places and things and soon acquired a working vocabulary. My grasp of the language's grammar remained rudimentary, but with what I had, and gesture, I was able to converse on a practical level and soon outran Finlay's expertise.

The carpenter, happy to be relieved of the duty, communicated this information to Tarpone who congratulated me and put me in charge of negotiations regarding provisioning the ship and our standing with the village chief. This individual, named Binoka, was immensely corpulent, to the degree that he could scarcely walk and it required six strong men to carry him in a litter. Such was his lineage and prestige and, I gathered, his fame as a warrior in his youth, that his authority was unquestioned. He appeared to me to be shrewd and acquisitive, bargaining hard for every pig and coconut.

It became clear that what Binoka really sought was a supply of muskets, powder and shot. The few guns the islanders had were falling apart and they had no powder or balls. I had no doubt his plan was to increase his power on the island.

'I'm against that,' the captain said when I told him of my suspicions. 'Arming these savages would make them over-bearing when ships arrive needing succour. But play him along, Corkill, and we'll see who holds the best cards at the end of the game.'

The timber Finlay secured on the island enabled him to rebuild the stays to the mast and to replace some spars that had been damaged over time. As the *Emerald* held no cargo and was lightened by the distribution of trade goods and the floating of the cutter and longboat, she rode high in the water and Finlay was able to repair the copper sheathing and attend to the parted planks without needing to beach the ship.

The weather continued fair and the work went on apace. I spent much time ashore acquainting myself with the natives' language and customs. Having no interest in religion, I did not enquire into such matters but could not help learning that they propitiated a number of gods, mostly associated with the natural world, some with ancestors and a few requiring periodic sacrifices. Of more interest to me were their family and political relationships but these proved so intricate they were difficult to unravel. One fact was clear; they enjoyed sexual congress and had no shame about it. Older men initiated girls at a young age and sexual jealousy was unknown among them. Within strict kinship rules, fathers and brothers made their daughters and sisters available to other men and the women themselves had a great deal of choice in the matter. It was through this latter fact that I made the acquaintance of Tahuata.

She was the widowed daughter of a chief, inferior in rank to Binoka, but of some standing. Her husband had been drowned when his canoe had been swept out to sea in a freak storm. She had a son of about ten years of age and, as a high born widow with a son, she enjoyed a degree of freedom denied to other women. As we would have said in Boston, she took a fancy to me and I to her. She was lively and intelligent and acquired English from me as fast as I acquired her language from her, or faster. We were thrown together often as a pair who could best resolve a dispute – over the value of a pig or an axe – or explain a custom – as when the ship's company celebrated Independence Day on July 4, or when a woman gashed her head fearfully with a sharp shell when her child fell ill and died.

It was inevitable that we would share a bed as we shared so much else. We coupled fiercely and often and the natives regarded our union as something to be expected and acceptable. To me, who had only bedded whores, albeit of the better sort, it was a wonder. I had never had a woman so proud of her body and so ready to allow me to enjoy it in whatever manner I chose. A man who believes a whore loves him is a fool, and I knew full well that the women I'd been with cared nothing for me, got little or no pleasure from the act, and forgot me instantly it was over. Not so with Tahuata. She took her own pleasure seriously and often compelled me to go about my business more slowly or in a particular way. We made love in a naked state in the woods and on the beach and I pitied those many of my countrymen at home who did it in the dark and never saw their wives unclothed.

So useful were our translations that the Captain made no comment about our association, although he tried, with limited success, to prevent the same from forming among the sailors. The women gave themselves so freely that most of the men gloried in the number of their conquests as they saw them, rather than in any single attachment.

I admit it gave him some concern when I consented to be tattooed according to the island custom. Tattooing was something of a badge of honour, evidence of having travelled to the Pacific, and a good number of our company embraced it, painful though it was. I had a blue star picked out on my breast – that pattern for no particular reason. But the next marking had a history.

There were frequent conflicts between Binoka's people and the clans inland and further around the coast. This not infrequently took the form of kidnapping and enslaving children, perhaps sacrificing them, although I was never clear on this point. One day I was out hunting for a wild pig that had been devastating the village gardens and had wounded a man by slashing him with a tusk. I was armed with a musket, powder and ball, and set out along a trail leading to a

41

dense thicket where the animal was thought to be hiding. This took me about two miles from the village.

Unknown to me, Tahuata's son, Pakolo, had followed after me, making a game of concealing himself. I was approaching the thicket when I heard a loud squeal behind me. Thinking it was the pig, I swung around and brought my musket to my shoulder. To my horror I saw a man attempting to abduct the boy. He was a stranger to me and the axe in his hand showed his ill will. Fortunately, Pakolo, a strong, wiry child, was struggling. He shouted a word which I knew was used by our people to describe their enemies to the south.

Pakolo kicked and thrashed and broke free. The man cocked his arm to throw the axe. I shot him, the charge taking him high in the chest and dropping him instantly. Whether the ball would have killed him or not I was never sure but it was of no moment. Pakolo seized the fallen man's axe and with three or four blows cracked his skull and spread blood, bone and brain over the ground. He then dropped the axe and ran to me, shouting in triumph that we were two great warriors whose feat would be sung and danced for generations.

I had never had a part in killing a man before and I slumped down against a tree, not far from the body, with my musket in my hand. Pakolo sped away on his young legs and returned within what seemed like minutes with his mother and some of her male kin. Chattering too quickly for me to follow in detail, he told the story of how we had slain the enemy. First Tahuata and then each of the men embraced me and sang my praises. I was escorted back to the village by the mother and son and her father's brother who alarmed me by smacking me hard on the buttocks.

I was conducted to a hut where I was given food and drink and ordered to remove my pants. There were no women present and for a moment I wondered if I was to be subjected to some unnatural sexual practice, such as the islanders were said to indulge in. I began to protest but Tahuata's uncle explained, using the name they had assigned me. 'You are now a warrior, Korka, and must bear the warrior's mark.'

Although the men of the island usually wore a strip of bark cloth around their loins and some had exchanged curios for sailors' pants, I had seen some men naked while swimming and noticed a black stripe tattooed across their behinds. When I had asked Tahuata about this she refused to speak and I gathered there was something of a *tapu*, or forbidden secret, surrounding it. Now, I was enlightened. It would have given great offence to refuse and I lay on a mat and prepared myself for the ordeal.

I ventured to say that Pakolo had dealt the decisive blows and should be similarly adorned. I thought I was making a poor joke, relieving my anxiety, but the men agreed that he would be tattooed in the same way when he reached puberty. I snatched up a piece of stick from the dirt floor of the hut, bit down on it and tried to let my thoughts wander as the tattooist began his task. I tried to think of Boston and my family. Then of the profits to be made from this voyage which would bring me closer to my dream of a schooner of my own. But the only image I could conjure up was Tahuata's ripe breasts swinging close to my face as she rode me, and this gave me a cockstand that made the whole operation more painful. Happily, the pain killed all such impulses after a time. I spent several hours spread out on the mat and many more recovering under the ministrations of my mistress, whose skill with coconut oil, applied both to my wound and my organ, passed all understanding.

EIGHT – A temptation resisted. Departure from Paradise. Hunting the whale. An unexpected island and its people.

'I TRUST YE'VE NOT formed too strong an attachment, Corkill,' Tarpone said when next he saw me. He touched the glass with which he'd been surveying the horizon to the mark on my chest, although I was aware he meant the other tattoo.

'No, sir,' I said.

'Resist it with all your might. I've heard of men falling in love with these islands and remaining behind. They either find ways to brew spirits and go mad, or fall foul of some *tapu* and end up with a spear through their guts.'

'I'll warrant that's true.'

'It is. And where, may I ask, is the musket you signed out?'

I clapped my hand to my head in dismay. 'Good God, I've never given it a thought since . . .'

Tarpone laughed. 'Set your mind at ease. You'll not be charged for it, and one weapon can do no harm. 'Tis nothing compared with the goodwill your gallant action has brought us. The terms for the timber and provisions are favourable in the extreme.'

'It was hardly gallant to shoot a man armed only with an axe.'

'It sufficed. I want you to help the bosun supervise the loading of our supplies and check with the carpenter that all repairs are complete.'

'We're leaving?'

'As soon as may be. I've discovered that your information is correct – the whales will be travelling south at this time of the year and I mean to intercept them.'

Tarpone had a pale complection and as he remained on board almost all the time he took on no colour from the sun. Still, he appeared unnaturally pale lately and I fancied his hands trembled, though he fought to conceal this.

I was torn, I admit. I had become deeply fond of Tahuata and Pakolo and would have given a great deal to have been able to stay longer with them. I racked my brains for a way out of the dilemma. There was no possibility of taking them with me, none. Staying on the island would put me at risk of falling foul of precisely the dangers Tarpone had warned me of. In the end I took the coward's way out of telling them that I had to leave but that I would return. Whether any of us believed it I know not. Our parting was prolonged and tearful.

Eventually all was in readiness, and the last boats left the shore accompanied by canoes. The last coconut was stowed and the last straggler hauled up. Binoka, of course, was not there so the captain presented his representative with a finely made cutlass in a handsome scabbard. The man looked crestfallen, expecting a musket, but the natural politeness of these people prevented any protest.

'They have your musket, powder and shot and a cutlass,' Tarpone said as we stood by the rail. 'Not enough to do any damage to their fellows or to offer resistance to the next ship along.'

'Just so,' I said, but I scarcely took in what he said. The order was given to set the sails and the anchor was brought up. The ship began to move and the islanders paddled hard to keep us in sight for as long as they may might. My last view of Tahuata wrenched my heart – she stood weeping in the canoe, and slashing at her head with a sharp shell.

The real business of the voyage now began and our luck was good. In favourable winds, on smooth seas, in a well-founded vessel we patrolled the south Pacific waters and encountered the whales heading south. The *Emerald*'s crew was all experienced at whaling and her harpoonists were the equal of any I'd seen. The work was tiring and dangerous from the moment a whale was spotted through the chase and kill to the cutting up and rendering of the flesh. Despite the best efforts with sea water and warm vinegar, the ship soon smelled horribly of blood and blubber, but the smells were sweet to the whalers, betokening profit.

There were accidents aplenty – slipped knives occasioning wounds, falls on the bloody deck causing broken bones and a near drowning when a sailor fell from a longboat. But in a business when it was not unknown for the whales to smash a pursuing boat to matchwood and even to cause damage to a large vessel, these mishaps were minor and the captain and crew remained in good spirits.

The water, meat and fruit we had taken on at Rangiroa kept us fit and healthy and our rum supply was adequate for the purpose of rewarding good work and the occasional celebration, as for the captain's birthday. All in all, the *Emerald* was a happy ship and, after some time back at sea following my profession, I admit thoughts of the island and Tahuata faded. Such is the way of sailors.

Our barrels were almost full and the Captain decided it was time to head for home. If we encountered whales on our way we could increase our haul, if not the voyage was still considerably profitable. Tarpone made this decision when we were in the mid-Pacific, east of the Marquesas. His plan was to turn south, hoping to chance upon winds that would enable us to round the Horn once more, not a simple matter at that time of year. Although more venturesome than some captains I had sailed with and less so than others, Eli Tarpone was not one to challenge the elements out of bravado. If the approach to the Horn proved too hazardous, he announced, we would alter course and pick up the favourable winds for the Cape of Good Hope and return home by the longer but safer and possibly, given how long a ship might battle the Horn in vain, quicker route.

All went well on the southern leg of our journey until we had reached the mid-twenties latitudes. The lookout cried 'Land ho', and the captain came on deck holding a chart in his hand. I had a spy glass and confirmed the lookout's call.

'Where away?' the captain asked.

I passed him the glass and gave him the bearing. He looked long and hard and then shook his head. 'According to the charts this should be open ocean with no land for many miles in any direction.'

'The charts are clearly wrong, then,' I said.

He glanced at me. 'A dangerous assertion.'

The helmsman called for instruction and Tarpone didn't hesitate. 'Make for the island.'

I knew his thinking. His health was not good. He coughed and spat continually and his steward said he ate little. He was anxious to be home, but he had in mind the discovery of a new island, the marking of it on the charts and nautical immortality. Nor was I averse to the action. After the hard work of the past months some diversion, and fresh food, would be welcome.

'Aye, aye, sir.' There was enthusiasm in the helmsman's response.

The captain rolled up his chart, returned my glass and stayed on deck to watch the island grow larger. It rose from the sea like an enormous rock and we could see no prospect of landing, such was the fury of the waves beating against the massive cliffs. Tarpone directed that we should circumnavigate the island.

'You see the vegetation and the pools of fresh water, Corkill,' he said.

'I do, sir.'

'And the smoke. This island is inhabited and so must have a landing place.'

We sailed around the island, keeping clear of the rocks that ran for most of the way around it. Eventually, on the eastern side we spied a break in the rocks, at least a space where the breakers were less fierce, and an indentation that could be called a bay with a shallow beach before the land rose upward, but not as sharply as on the other coasts. It was more out of curiosity and ambition than a need for food and water that the captain put in to the bay and dropped anchor perhaps half a mile off shore. The day was clear and bright, though cool, and we could clearly see a path leading up the cliff and people on it.

Tarpone continued to study his charts and then went below for a time. When he emerged disappointment was written all over his face.

'I think this bloody rock must be Cartaret's Pitcairn Island,' he told me, 'which that fool has mislocated. A Frog by origin, no doubt. Never trust Frog navigation.'

I thought for a moment he was going to order the anchor raised but a shout from the rail took his attention. A canoe was being paddled out through the fairly rough sea by a couple of stalwart young men with a fat woman also paddling. As the canoe drew closer we were surprised to see that the woman wore some kind of dress that covered her breasts. Our surprise turned to astonishment when we were hailed from the canoe in English or a variant of it.

'Halloa, the ship,' one of the young men called. 'We are Eenglish, are you Eenglish also, pray?'

'What in God's name is this?' Tarpone muttered as the paddlers steadied their craft, standing off from the *Emerald* the approved and polite distance.

'American,' Tarpone shouted. 'What manner of people are you?'

'We are Eenglishmen with mothers from Otaheite. May we come aboard, captain?'

There were three young men in the boat and we saw no signs of weapons. 'Speak to the woman in the island tongue, Corkill,' the captain ordered.

I enquired whether they were castaways or the victims of a shipwreck, but her answer was vague. She pleaded to be allowed to board the ship and added something about Christ, our Lord and our leader.

The young men nodded emphatically and clasped their hands together as if in prayer. Ever wary, Tarpone gave the order to allow one of the men on board. The canoe drew closer and the one who had acted as spokesman leapt up, grabbed a rope and hauled himself nimbly aboard in a matter of seconds. He was tall, about six feet and of slender but wiry build. His face was longish with distinctively European features, although his skin was scarcely any lighter than those of the islanders we had encountered.

He bowed low before the captain and extended his hand. 'Thursday October Christian at your service, sir.'

Usually completely in command of himself, Tarpone almost gaped. 'Christian, you say?'

'Yes, sir. You are not British? You will not take our leader back to be hung?'

Tarpone collected himself and shook his head slowly. 'Indeed we will not. You are the son of Fletcher Christian?'

'I am, sir.'

'Extraordinary. So this is where they ended up. What think you, Corkill?'

'I am amazed, sir. My understanding is that nothing has been heard of the vessel for fifteen years or more. I thought it must have gone to the bottom and the mutineers with it.'

'Just so. Are any of the . . . crew here? Is Fletcher Christian still alive?'

'Alas, no. Only John Adams remains.'

'I don't recall the name. Well, I'll be damned.'

Young Christian almost recoiled. 'I trust not, sir.'

'Just an expression, and a poor one. I would dearly like to meet your Mr Adams.'

As this exchange was going on I was putting together in my mind what few facts I could recall about the mutiny on the British ship *Bounty*. I knew that in the course of scientific expedition of some kind to Otaheite she had been seized by mutineers under the command of Fletcher Christian. Her master, named Bligh, had been cast adrift in the launch with a number of companions and had made a remarkable voyage across the Pacific to Timor in the East Indies. I knew little more except that Christian and his followers had never been found, despite serious efforts by the British. Here was the solution to a mystery of many years and a chance for Tarpone to achieve the fame he so desired.

Christian said that he would be happy to escort the captain to John Adams and that the whole crew would be welcome ashore. Tarpone smiled at that and said that a party of three would suffice, selecting Finlay and myself to accompany him, needing our acquaintance with the island language. He told me, as we were readying ourselves and a boat was being lowered, that he wished us to talk to the woman in the canoe and any others to learn their side of the story. Finlay was ignorant of the *Bounty* story. It is a remarkable fact that most of the sailors knew nothing of it, many of them being illiterate and most not interested in affairs in the world at large.

Tarpone was a good-natured man, but not one to cross when his mind was made up. His eagerness to visit John Adams had blinded him to the fact that a storm was brewing not far away. Normally he would have noticed the change in the weather. Although I, too, was keen to go ashore I did not fancy the idea of being in that small bay with rocks aplenty in the midst of a tropical storm. So it was with some hesitation that I drew the captain's attention to the state of the wind and the sky.

He gave the conditions barely a glance. 'We'll make it a short visit. Lower away!'

NINE – Pitcairn Island and its people. John Adams, Fletcher Christian and me. A rapid departure. Our luck turns bad.

WITH FOUR SAILORS AT the oars, each with a musket concealed in the boat and under instruction to stand guard while we were ashore, we pulled for the narrow beach. The canoe breasted the waves easily and landed before us. By now there was a goodly collection of people on the sand, mostly women and children in a range of ages. After we landed – having followed the canoe through the less treacherous channel – and the sailors' instructions were reiterated, Thursday Christian introduced us to his two companions who went by the names of Adams and Quintal – their first names I forget. Like Christian, they were tall, well-made fellows with European features and islander colouring.

The cove – it was little more – had been, we were told, named Bounty Bay, and the path up the cliff was called the Hill of Difficulty. We made the climb, Finlay and I casting anxious looks at the sky, and Tarpone questioning the men and women continually. When we reached the top we found a flat area of perhaps fifty acres, cultivated with native gardens and boasting substantial houses, the whole set out something like a normal village, with a flagpole and straight running paths that had been swept clean.

With the sky darkening by the minute, we were escorted to a large house at the head of the clearing. From it emerged a man, well on in years, to judge from his grey locks, but by no means old, who greeted us by removing his hat and making a gesture somewhere between a salute and a tug of the forelock.

'Greetings, your honours,' he said. 'I am John Adams, late of His Majesty's armed ship *Bounty*. May I enquire your names and what brings you to our island?'

As we drew closer he stared at me so hard I began to wonder if my face was dirty or my clothes unbuttoned. Eventually he desisted. We obliged with the information he wanted and he invited us to sit at a bench in front of his house. A woman brought cool coconut milk in tin cups. Tarpone questioned Adams closely about the mutiny and subsequent events, but the man seemed reluctant to speak, still casting sidelong glances at me.

Tarpone attempted to assure him that, as the mutiny had happened many years before and some of those involved had been executed, he was sure the British authorities considered the matter closed, especially if he could confirm that Fletcher Christian was dead. This Adams did, but he seemed restless and spoke vaguely in unrelated snatches of his history so that it was difficult to follow. Finlay had wandered away and tried to speak to the women as the captain had instructed, but he did not succeed, partly because his attention was taken by the freshening wind and darkening sky. He returned in an alarmed state and Adams confirmed that a severe storm was on the way. Women brought woven baskets containing fruit on Adams' instruction and it was clear that he wanted us gone.

Tarpone shook hands with Adams and indicated that we should leave, the urgency now apparent to him. We turned to go but Adams called me back and went inside his house. Tarpone and Finlay, too concerned about the weather to notice, went on their way.

'You're a Manxman, surely,' Adams said as he emerged.

'My father.'

'And of the clan of Christian I'll warrant.'

'Not as I know, sir.'

'You're the living image of Fletcher,' he whispered. 'The image of him.'

'No one else here remarked it.'

'The boys scarcely remember him and then only as sick and careworn. The women hold their tongues. Here, take this!'

He thrust a thick, bound volume at me and buried it under the fruit in my basket. 'Good luck to you and tell them we have a God-fearing people here now, whatever our past. Now go!'

He spoke fiercely and just briefly I saw the man he might have been when the mutiny was afoot – stocky, of powerful build and, adding to the formidable appearance, much pockmarked. I obeyed him and hurried to catch my companions up who were by now almost running. We went as quickly as we could down the steep path to the beach, signalling to the sailors to get the boat ready. The sky had taken on a purple hue and the wind was gusting strongly. We shook hands again with the three lads and hastened to launch the boat. The waves were high and contrary currents were running but our men were equal to the task and soon brought us to the ship where all was in readiness for our departure under the instruction of the bosun.

There was much to do, but I found a moment to go below and stow the book in my chest before returning to the deck and helping get the ship underway. It was no easy task, for the wind was at gale force, threatening to drive us towards the rocks. With our full cargo we were heavy, slow, and low in the water, and the high seas broke over the deck as we beat our way to the open sea. A sudden roaring gust of wind tore a topsail, the vessel lurched and I'll swear

I felt a jolt and that the foremast bent like a bow staff. The helmsman called for help and it took two men to bring the *Emerald* back on course.

After what seemed like hours but was probably less, we got clear of the bay and the rocks and the currents and were able to run south before the wind. The sky continued to darken and rain lashed from above as the sea lashed us from below. All hands were required to man the ship and, with water washing across the planks and gushing in the scuppers, we knew we were in for a damp period below deck as well as above. All thoughts of my strange encounter on Pitcairn went out of my mind, as I worked, as befitted my rank, as hard as any man aboard to see our ship to safety.

The wind drove us south and east for some days with no sun visible to permit readings and such a pitching, rolling deck as to make such an operation useless. When the wind slackened and the sea calmed, every man aboard was exhausted and Tarpone ordered short watches and extra rum. I found myself caring more about my rum ration and indeed allowing myself an extra measure as was my right than I ever had before. When the captain summoned me to his cabin I was a little unsteady as I joined him at his chart table.

'Ye seem to be working both sides of the street, Corkill,' he said.

'I apologise, Captain. I've a weak head for spirits and I fear I've had a dram too much.'

He put his hand on my shoulder, a rare gesture. 'Ye did sterling service and it's no more than your due.'

'Still, something to watch.'

'Aye. Have you spoken to anyone aboard about our discovery on Pitcairn?

'No, sir.'

'Good. I think it best it remain a secret between us until we decide how to reveal it to the world, or indeed whether to do so.'

The captain experienced another of his coughing fits, but I fancied he had a crafty look before the convulsions took him. I had no doubt he would make the most of the discovery and trumpet his name about loudly. It was at that moment I decided to keep the journal as my secret. I reckoned it had been given to me and me alone and with a curious dedication from Adams. His words were fixed tantalisingly in my mind.

Tarpone continued, 'We'll talk of it again. Now I wanted to apprise ye of our position, which is such as to pose a question.'

'And what is that, sir? Or may I guess?'

Receiving his nod, I continued. 'Do we try the Horn?'

'That's it. Our location is such that it's the shortest way home.'

Although a little befuddled, I could see his reasoning. A long and successful voyage would be best served by a quick passage home. It was a tempting prospect – home in a matter of weeks with money in the pocket and stories to tell in the taverns. Or, in Tarpone's case, to the senior persons in maritime's high circles.

I was struggling to frame an answer when the carpenter, Finlay, privileged as the man in oversight of the condition of the ship, burst into the cabin after the briefest of knocks. 'Captain,' he announced, 'I fear we sustained damage below clearing that damned rock. We're taking on water.'

Inspection revealed that brushing against a rock when the ship had been buffeted by the gust of wind, had opened a seam in the side a little below the water line. At first the damage was thought not to be great and that the pumps could cope with the inflow of water, but a closer look showed that one of the ribs was cracked and creaking ominously as it came under pressure.

'Your assessment, Finlay?' the captain asked.

'She'll not weather heavy seas, sir. There's many a mile left in her in calm water.'

'No guarantee of that anywhere,' Tarpone muttered with disappointment in his voice. 'Plot us a course via the Cape if you please, Mr Corkill, and take over. I'm feeling poorly.'

The world suddenly seemed like a bigger place to me as I assumed command of the ship. I gave orders that the leak should be slowed as much as possible with the lashing of a canvas sheath and the pumps maintained in good working order. I instructed the helmsman to take a northerly track while I plotted our course. The captain had retired to his bed in a small compartment off his cabin and I could hear him snoring as I spread the charts on the table and did the calculations and measurements. As I did so, thoughts of Fletcher Christian came to my mind for the first time since leaving Pitcairn. Was it possible I was related to him? I'd not heard he was a Manxman, but, if so, the chances increased. Dark complectioned he must have been, possibly for the same reason as myself – the Spanish blood.

As I stared at the chart, I noticed that Tarpone had placed Pitcairn in its true position and I wondered how Christian had found it, for he must have been searching for an uninhabited hiding place. Perhaps by accident as we had. What sort of a navigator was he? And what had happened to the *Bounty*? There was no sign of any such vessel at Pitcairn and no mention of the ship's fate. Perhaps she had been wrecked on what Finlay had called that damned rock. I abandoned these vain thoughts and set to plotting a course. Our most dangerous stage was the present one – the southern ocean waters could be hectic at any time of year, especially for a damaged ship, and we could not expect plain sailing until in the forties and heading for the Cape. Happily, Tarpone's charts were of the highest standard, incorporating as much information as was then available. I plotted a course for the Cape of Good Hope where we could expect to make repairs and take on supplies. Our voyage would yet prove a success.

Many times over the weeks that followed I had cause to regret our chancing on Pitcairn Island. The damage to the ship caused endless trouble in high seas and the timber that had been used to re-house the mast on Rangiroa proved less hardy than was needed, causing Finlay considerable anxiety. However we continued to make progress although more slowly than I would have wished. Some distance short of the Cape, Captain Eli Tarpone died. He was fifty-five years of age, not old, and a strong man but the fever that struck him down as we left Pitcairn never abated and he wasted away until he could neither eat nor drink. He was buried at sea with as much ceremony as we could muster.

As acting captain I took over the running of the ship formally although it had already been my role during Tarpone's illness. I kept the log very much as he had done, restricting myself to comments on the weather and the state of the ship. Among his effects, I found his private log which was evidently meant to be the basis of a book. It covered several voyages previous to that of the *Emerald* but the captain had no great feeling for words or ability to describe people or events. I doubt that his book would have been a success. It was gratifying to read a description of myself as 'experienced beyond his years and utterly reliable'. Hardly fulsome but, as I have said, the captain was no wordsmith. I read with interest his assessments of other members of the crew and found nothing to dissent from and little to learn.

The *Emerald* was limping by the time we reached the Cape and I made the decision to sell her cargo there, dock her for repairs and discharge those members of the crew who did not want to wait for a passage back to New Bedford. I hoped that the owners and financiers of the voyage would support these decisions but in truth there was no alternative. The price secured for the oil was good and I was able to pay the discharged sailors in full and maintain the others on half pay until the ship was repaired. I had signed bills of credit that would be honoured in New Bedford and the owners would be presented with a vessel ready to work for them again. I wrote letters to the owners (omitting all mention of Pitcairn) and to my family and despatched them on a ship leaving the Cape before we were ready. I also sent off Captain Tarpone's effects to his family in New Bedford along with letters of credit accounting for his entitlements for the voyage.

When the *Emerald* was afloat again I recruited some hands to replace those who had left but was unable to find a suitable replacement for Rufus Finlay, the carpenter, who had formed an attachment to a well-provided-for widow in Cape Town. With his wages and share of the cargo price and his wife's capital, he was able to set up in business as a boat builder and carpenter and was assured of a prosperous future. I wished him well. As I took the *Emerald* out of the harbour at Cape Town, I reflected that I was the only man who had been ashore at Pitcairn placed to broadcast the news of the fate of the *Bounty* mutineers.

TEN – Return to Boston. Fletcher Christian's journal. My plan and the means to accomplish it. An alarming almost encounter.

I BROUGHT THE *EMERALD* safely back to New Bedford and gave an account to the owners of all that had happened, supporting in person what I had written from the Cape. Remembering my father's condemnation of the British Navy and the Pitcairners' fear of their leader being discovered and punished, I forbore to mention the island. I had a fancy to keep the knowledge a secret, although with more and more ships sailing the Pacific the secret could not be kept forever. Happily, they approved of my actions and were satisfied with the outcome of the voyage although the repair of the ship had eaten into their profits. I paid a call on the captain's widow and found her well provided for, Tarpone having invested his earnings shrewdly over the years. She had two sons and a daughter in the town and, though grieving, was relieved to hear that her husband had not died a violent death.

'I always feared a whale would kill him, Mr Corkill,' she said, 'he having slain so many.'

I gave her Tarpone's log and charts but she seemed to take little interest in them and I suspected they would find their way to the attic and be a prey to silverfish.

I returned to Boston and boarded with my sister Sarah while I waited for a ship, the owners of the *Emerald* having promised me an appointment, if not as captain then as mate with a rise in pay. It was during this sojourn that Isabelle told and convinced me of our mother's Iroquois ancestry. I related to my sisters how the islanders at Rangiroa had thought me a kinsman and they were amused. I showed them the tattoo on my breast but not, of course, the black stripe across my behind. Neither of them was a puritan but I forbore to speak of my sexual adventures out of common decency.

At no time had I forgotten the book John Adams had vouchsafed me, but the business of bringing the vessel home and accounting for its fortunes had driven it from my mind. In truth, the strain of becoming an acting captain had tired me and I was looking for nothing more than a period of quiet and comfort in the company of my kinfolk. Isabelle's revelation, however, put me in mind of the book again and Adams' query about my family.

I drew on my pipe and took a sip of rum. 'Isabelle, do you recall our father ever speaking of relatives on the Isle of Man?'

My sisters exchanged looks and both shook their heads. 'Never,' Sarah said. 'He spoke very little of his early years, so painful were they. Why?'

I considered, then shrugged. 'Nothing. A man I met on an island wondered about my possible kinship with a Manxman he knew.'

'What man? What island?' Isabelle said. 'You're being evasive, brother Henry.'

I smiled, knocked out my pipe into the hearth and finished the drink. 'It is the way with we sailors, sister.'

I went up to my room and took the book, which I had scarcely touched since it came into my possession beyond wrapping it in oilcloth, from my sea chest. It was not old and in good condition with the binding secure, the covers firm, and a heavy clasp closing it.

I undid the clasp and opened it. The first leaf bore a sketch of a three-masted vessel, nicely done, and but five words written in a firm, somewhat flowery hand. Words one to three I failed to understand, but the following words were plain to read – 'Fletcher Christian'. I turned a page and discovered that the writing continued in the language that had defeated me utterly. It took little imagination to conclude that it was Manx. As I have said, I knew a few words in that tongue but had no notion of how it was written. At that moment I decided that I would make it my business to travel to the Isle of Man and learn more of the notorious mutineer whom I apparently resembled so closely.

In preparation, I read all I could find about the *Bounty*, including William Bligh's *Narrative of a Voyage to the South Seas,* his exchange with Fletcher Christian's lawyer brother and newspaper accounts of the trial of those mutineers brought back from Otaheite by Captain Edwards. Also of the execution of three of the unhappy fellows. The several versions of the story varied so much I found it impossible to decide who had been to blame for the mutiny, Bligh or Christian. I was surprised to learn that Christian had been tattooed while on Otaheite with a star on his chest and a mark on his buttocks.

I was taken on as mate of the *Emerald* and completed two more voyages aboard her, one to the north and one to those waters east of South America where I had begun my seagoing career as a sealer. Both ventures were successful and my share of the profits plus my mate's wages added to my capital, although I was still far short of the amount needed to buy a substantial interest in a vessel. I wanted a good ship, nothing second rate, and I fancied a cargo run between America and Europe and perhaps, one day, with enterprising investors, a trading expedition to the Pacific Islands.

In pursuit of this scheme, and in furtherance of my plan to investigate my possible connection to Christian, I looked for a berth on a ship bound for England. I found one aboard the schooner *Liberty*, transporting timber, good Massachusetts hardwood, to Plymouth. The year was 1807, three years after my brief visit to Pitcairn. I had kept the bound book safe through that time. I had thought of trying to find someone who could read Manx to translate it for me, but on closer inspection I discovered that quite long passages were written in what I took to be, from my acquaintance with the tongue, Otaheitean. Many of the words the writer employed were unknown to me, at least as they were spelled. Translating the book was clearly a task for an expert and the most likely place to find such a person – both for Manx and Otaheitean – was in England.

The *Liberty* quit Boston on December 20 and made a smooth crossing in twenty-eight days. We sailed up the Channel to Plymouth on the south-west coast in the county of Devon and unloaded our cargo at Plymouth Dock – the voyage having been without incident of any kind. I had made it known to the owners and the skipper, one Matthew Synge, an Irishman with no love of the English, that I planned to remain in England for a time on family business and this had been an acceptable arrangement.

'Take care you are not pressed,' the skipper advised as I shouldered my seabag preparing to leave the ship. 'I look forward to working with you again, Mr Corkill.'

We shook hands. 'Surely my mate's ticket would protect me from anything such. Plus my manner of speech which is not much like that of an Englishman.'

Synge shook his head. 'Strike one of those bastards in a pressing mood and nothing would protect you. Take care to hide the tattoo on your chest. It marks you as a Pacific sailor, and there's nothing the

British navy likes better, despite the *Bounty* and that bastard Fletcher Christian.'

I was careful not to respond to this. Mutiny was a crime on a level with murder to ships' captains, perhaps worse, and I understood their aversion. There can be but one voice in command of a ship. All would hope that the authority is exercised wisely with due consideration for the varying interests and capacities of all aboard. But any challenge to that authority throws the ship out of balance as if she has lost a mast or sprung a leak and no good can come of it.

These thoughts were much in my mind, as well as strange sensations associated with a return to the part of the world whence the Corkills had sprung, as I walked down the gangplank to the dock. I was thirty-two years of age, not far short of thirty-three, but full of health and vigour. My skin had paled in the northern winter but retained its olive hue and I wore my dark hair tied back in a sailor's knot as ever.

Knowing nothing of the town I looked first for somewhere to stay for the night while I pondered how to set about my quest. I found a hostelry on Forte Street and deposited my seabag in the room I was allotted. I had a drink or two and set out to explore the town, curious about it for, as all those born in Massachusetts knew, Plymouth was the last English port for the pilgrims who first settled America. I was slightly affected by liquor and decided to walk briskly to counter its effects. As I did so I heard rapid steps behind me and spun around, anticipating I knew not what. A man in an officer's naval uniform was rushing towards me crying out a name.

'Fletcher!'

In my confused state I felt suddenly afraid. I knew of my physical resemblance to Fletcher Christian and of the certainty that, had he ever returned to England, he would have been hanged without doubt. Although I could establish my identity from documents in my seabag, I had nothing about me that moment with which to do so and that bag also contained Christian's journal. Who knows what construction might be put on that? Fear seized me and I increased my pace away from the naval officer who did likewise. I was strong and fleet of foot and I began to run and take the first turn I came to and then the next and the next. Within a few minutes I had lost him.

ELEVEN – I take stock. The origins of this journal. I modify my plans.

WITH SOME DIFFICULTY I found my way back to the inn where I had taken lodging. I fear I may have looked furtive, afraid that some other might mistake me for Fletcher Christian and accost me. No one did and I concluded that the man who had challenged me must have been an acquaintance of Christian's and that the chances of meeting another such were slim. Nevertheless, I remained apprehensive of meeting him again, although the inn was not of a kind likely to be frequented by a naval captain, being more of a match for ordinary sailors and dock-workers. I ordered a pint of ale and settled down with my pipe to contemplate my situation.

My father had filled me with a curiosity about the English but also with a great fear of them. He had painted them as ruthless and harsh, ruled over by aristocrats and monarchs who thought nothing of grinding the faces of the common folk into the dust.

'They will hang a child for stealing a crust of bread,' I remember him saying. No doubt an exaggeration, but a fearful indictment even so.

As I smoked and drank my ale – poor stuff I thought it – I realised that I had not learned enough about the British attitude to Christian and the mutiny. The matter was now twenty years in the past, but memories can be long. I had read that William Bligh had been promoted. Perhaps he was now an Admiral and a powerful figure. From what he had written in his *Narrative*, I thought it unlikely he had forgiven Christian. More probably, he would hope for vengeance for as long as he breathed. Perhaps the British authorities felt the same. My father had said that naval service was a living hell with mutiny never far from men's minds, being only held in check by the fear of informers and the drop from the yardarm.

These thoughts filled me with storm of conflicting emotions as I drank steadily. I wished I had never travelled to the South Seas, never been tattooed, never had a leather-bound book pressed upon me by a *Bounty* mutineer. But, as the fug of ale and tobacco mounted in my mind, I had something like a vision of Tahuata and Pakolo and the black beach of Rangiroa and I sensed that it had been my destiny to sail those seas and pick up the pieces of a man who, for all his faults, had made his mark in the world. I ate a supper of salt pork and boiled potatoes and felt like a sailor again. As my mind cleared, I made decisions. I was ten years younger than Christian, yet the naval officer had mistaken me for him. Even allowing that he might discount the time since he had seen Christian, the physical resemblance I bore was too dangerously close. I resolved to cut my hair and grow my beard.

Furthermore, I determined to keep, like Christian, a detailed journal of my life. My thought was that it would amuse my sisters and nieces and nephews some day and that, should I be mistaken for Christian in some serious way, the journal would help to acquit me of being the *Bounty* mutineer in person. Thus this account, drawing on my earlier scanty logs, which I always kept with me, was begun. I bought a slim octavo pocket book for the purpose.

I resolved to quit Plymouth as quickly as possible and did so after having my hair trimmed and buying some clothes that did not stamp me as a sea-going man. I had it in mind to travel north to Cumberland where I knew Christian had been born and thence to the Isle of Man. I went by coach, in easy stages, going to Bristol and Birmingham before going west to Liverpool. I stayed a night or two in each place, acquainting myself with the English and their ways of doing things. I had never had a heavy beard and my effort to disguise myself in this way was less than effective. But what diverted me from my purpose was the misery I saw in these cities. The filth and overcrowding into mean slum houses was unlike anything I had ever seen and it brought my spirits down.

I took to drinking more than was good for me, and smoked too much tobacco into the bargain, so that I might blot out some of the fearful sights I saw – starving children while men and women rode by in carriages sniffing at handkerchiefs, the price of which would have fed a child for a month. I became angry, spoke out of turn and was involved in fights that did nothing but cut and bruise me and make me wish I had never set foot on English soil.

So oppressed was I by the cities that I thought to look at those parts of England celebrated by the poets, such as William Wordsworth with whose works, thanks to my sisters, I had a nodding acquaintance. I took a coach north and spent some time walking in the wild country known to the English as the Lake District. Parts of it reminded me of rugged sections of Massachusetts and the walking cleansed my body and my mind. I encountered people who looked at me and looked again, but received no challenges. I had no reason to think that Christian was known here. Besides, my appearance was now much altered. I concluded that the curiosity was occasioned by nothing more than my dark skin, sailor's gait and manner of speech.

I returned to Liverpool to await a ferry to the Isle of Man. Again the dismal city and its many stunted, starving denizens caused me anguish. In addition, the weather turned foul and winds whipped the Irish Sea into a frenzy that no ferryman would challenge. For several weeks the storms raged until I gave up in despair, fearing to fall into the destructive habits again, and departed for the south with its milder climate and more prosperous air. March found me in London, safe from any false identification in such a teeming city, and likely to find a berth on a ship back to America.

I was downcast at the failure of my mission and slightly ashamed of my fears about being mistaken for Christian. My father's disgust for England had worked on me along with a powerful aversion to the sights I had seen. At a seaman's inn by the London docks I took stock. Many a man before me had reached such a turning point in his life and often times it was religion that had provided the stimulus. No so with me; I remained a free thinker. Clear headed, indulging in nothing but a pot or two of ale each night and an occasional pipe, I resolved to return home. I would put fanciful thoughts of the Pacific Islands, bare-breasted women and Fletcher Christian behind me. It was time to buy an interest in a serviceable schooner, find a good wife and live the life of an American. I would be free of the chains that bound the people of England and made them slaves to their unfeeling masters like the blacks brought from Africa to the plantations in the southern states of my homeland.

On May 1 1808, I boarded, as second mate, the *Boston Belle* – a vessel taking immigrants to New York. Just as it was a new beginning for them, I felt it was for me, and I make this, my last entry, in the journal which I began only a short time ago. Henceforth I will tell my sailor's tales to my children and grandchildren and finish each by letting them known how lucky they were to have been born in America.

The Journal of
FLETCHER
CHRISTIAN,
Gentleman

Pitcairn's Island, 15 January 1790

THE SEA IS IN MY BLOOD and in my bones, and more than once I have thought that the sea might be where my bones would rest. From the first day I went to sea, aboard HMS *Eurydice*, bound for the Far East, I resolved always to be a gentleman. No easy resolution I found, for within days I discovered how a sailor's life differs from all others and the obstacles that are placed in the way of gentlemanly behaviour – principally the character of the master of the vessel. In my experience this applies, whatever trade the vessel may be engaged in and whatever character he may bear to the world at large. Put a man in charge of a small world and the chances are he will, at least once in the course of a voyage, play the Emperor.

I experienced something of this myself as the *de jure* commander of HMS *Bounty*, being forced to play the tyrant to keep order. But a good captain can keep to a minimum the damage occasioned by such acts of authority if he will but observe one rule: let him never draw too close to any one of his minions nor ever play favourites. For such will surely bring havoc down upon heads. Men's heads, like their pricks, are ruled by pride, and in both instances pride is a source of both power and joy and incapacitating weakness, as I have all too much reason to know.

And now I have come to dwell on Pitcairn's Island in the South Seas with some members of *Bounty*'s crew and a number of natives; some volunteers, some pressed. Although I am addressed as

'Mr Christian' by most of the whites and as 'Titreano' by all the natives, I have no legitimate authority now that the ship is no more. Such authority as I have will soon diminish as our lives take shape here and I can no more predict what will happen to us than I could have foreseen the events that brought us here, where no man has trod for many generations.

I was never a great one for reading newspapers or listening out for the latest gossip on this and that, but I confess I have a powerful curiosity to know how the news of the mutiny on *Bounty* will be received at home. Of course, all will depend on the bringer of the news. Should B— (I cannot bring myself to write his damned name) encounter a vessel at sea, make a safe landing on an island and be picked up or even make his way to Botany Bay where a convict fleet is headed, and be the messenger, my name will be blackened forever. Should it transpire that B— and his companions are lost and the news comes from those we left behind at Otaheite, the case could be different. Fruitless to speculate.

My account, I fear, will never be told in person. At least I hope not, for if I am discovered here I will surely choke at the end of a rope. I hope to die here, full of years, with my children around me and my good name intact, at least as far as it is known on these few square miles. And yet, I begin this journal, not to acquit myself of mutiny, of which I am surely guilty, nor to justify my actions, but to explain how it all came about. As I have intimated, I expect to die here and this account can assume, though in long anticipation of that event, the character of a dying testament. A melancholy thought, one such as has been a plague to me in the past and no doubt awaits me still. For I have dark moods and angry spells and am not always in charge of my passions. Indeed my spirits can soar to heights of joy from the pit of despair with the hour.

But pride rises to the surface once more. I would leave behind my life in words, so that a child, a grandchild or a later yet fruit of these loins, might know something of whence he comes and how he assumes the character he has. For in my mind's eye I see him as brown-skinned as his mother, and sturdy, like an Englishman, or rather a Manxman. Here on this rocky island, I am compelled to view myself as an islander from the start – born of those Norsemen who occupied the Isle of Man – to the finish.

I am under canvas scratching, with a sea chest as a desk, and a candle for light, but in time we will have palm leaf roofs and wooden furniture and oil lamps. We will, with our own hands and hearts, begin in a small way a new chapter in the story of man's movement across this mighty world. I am suddenly filled with hope. I trust it lasts. I fancy the keeping of this journal will buoy my spirits. Apart from my midshipman's logs, which merely record details of the ship's progress and the weather with few other remarks, I have never essayed such a writing as this. I will have to recall conversations and describe scenes which are fresh in my memory but perhaps erroneous in detail. I will do my best to be accurate, but as a keen reader of the works of Squire Fielding and Mr Smollett, I may be tempted to embellish my account. What does it matter? I write for my own peace of mind as much as for the reasons I have stated above. I lay down my pen knowing I have a hundred tasks before me, but resolved to continue, as time permits, my tale, for in truth I believe it to be one of the most curious since the world began.

Before *Bounty*

I LOVED THE FIRST BOAT I saw – a wrecked skiff, slowly sinking beneath the river mud at Cockermouth. Something about the wood, the lines, the way it seemed to still defy the water even though time, and probably rocks and shoals, had defeated it. In my childish way I think I wanted to be part of that struggle of man against the sea. This was not surprising as I spent my youth not far from sight and sound of the Irish Sea and crossed it to the Isle of Man many times to visit family who had property there, and later my mother. That good woman had had the misfortune to lose her husband while her children were yet young and suffered, as well as this grief, financial reversals that forced her to take refuge from her creditors on Man.

I will not dwell on this painful period as it hurts me to consider what her mental state might be now, given my apparent disappearance off the face of the world. Her pecuniary position I know to be secure as a result of my brother organising an annuity to keep her in reasonable comfort. But I am straying, being no experienced pen and ink narrator. As I say, I crossed to the island many times and more than once had the responsibility of bringing the boat to safe harbour, albeit under the watchful eye of a true boatman.

My crossings were made in calm weather, but squalls blew up sometimes and the passage became hazardous, for the rocks and shoals threatened at the best of times and more so in mist, wind and rain. But I was never seasick in my life and, with keen eyes, a strong arm and a willing heart, I was useful in these circumstances from an early age.

'You'll make a sailor, young Fletcher,' old Claud Corkill, a kinsman and a boatman for fifty years, said in the Manx tongue and I glowed under his approval and bent my back to whatever task he allotted me.

I should account, at this point, for writing my story in the Manx tongue. I learned it young from the likes of Claud Corkill and also my father and older brother, Edward, who took an antiquarian interest in it as the language of our ancestors. There were signs around the island written in Manx and my father had documents in it that I perused with interest on days when the weather kept me indoors. I would not guarantee that my rendering of it is always accurate and some words and phrases escape me utterly. For this reason I will no doubt venture into English at some points and a sort of Otaheitean at others. My object is plain – to prevent others reading what I have written, for I plan to tell the truth about events and people and some may not like my depiction of them. How many of my fellows can read I am not sure, but Ned Young and Will Brown for certain and Alex Smith can at least read the Bible. Perhaps others as well.

Looking back over what I have written, and to my shame have much amended so as to be scarcely readable in parts, I see I have not made my character clear. Can any man do this with certainty? I say I could handle a tiller and master a language. What manner of man is this? Probably one who might come to glory or disaster, I fancy. To make plain; I was a fair scholar and stayed at school longer than most for want of a chance to do aught else. But I was a boy for the open air – for sports at which I held my own with the best and, I must admit it, a large measure of that pride of prick I spoke of above. Above all, from being out on the water and climbing high in the Lake District,

I had a sense that the world was big and the way to see it, bird flight being impossible, was not on foot or by horse or carriage but by sea.

So it was that, with my older brothers prospering in the law and medicine and my mother, sister and younger brother provided for, I left school trained for nothing in particular. But with one ambition – to go to sea. England was at war and needed seamen. I joined the navy as a midshipman and served in the Far East upon the *Eurydice*. There was no seafaring tradition in our family and various members told me I would hate the navy.

'It's a brutal life, Fletcher,' my brother Charles, the nearest to me in age, said. 'Harsh discipline, filthy food, villainous companions. You're a good horseman. Why not think of doing something in that line?'

Indeed I was a good rider, but currying, mucking out and tending to colicky nags had no appeal to me.

In many ways, Charles' prediction was right. Life in the junior ranks at sea was hard. Farmers may complain about their work but on wild, wet, windy days they will mostly be found indoors whilst we seamen are out on deck. A midshipman could be flogged which was a worrying thought because I made several mistakes early on which would have incurred this penalty among the lower ranks. Luckily, such a punishment was rarely invoked on the gentlemen. Villains there were many on board among the officers, sailors and marines, but good fellows too, and food I never much worried about.

What Charles knew nothing about was the thrill of travelling to places the landlocked people never saw and feasting my eyes and memory upon Madeira, the Cape colony, Madras and the coast from Goa to the southern tip of India. The sight of the coolies labouring in the rice fields under a burning sun I can conjure up still, and it comforts me to think that our natives, however discontented they may sometimes be, endure nothing as harsh as those poor, black devils. Sitting here under a palm tree with a sea breeze at my back I remember Fort St George at Madras and the hectic activity taking place all around – the trading, the carrying, the shouting – and I am glad of the quiet. Madras, I learned, was a place fought over for years by other nations before Britain held sway. I wonder how many died there in its feverish climate.

A memory from this time comes back to me. I sat on a verandah after enjoying the favours of a Madras hoori, drawing on a cheroot and taking a peg of brandy, when I was approached by a strange figure I took at first to be an Indian.

'Good morrow, young sir,' he said, removing a stained and faded wide-brimmed hat. With his face thus revealed, I saw him to be a white man, though browned by the sun, and wearing the sandals, loose shirt and pants of a native. 'Have I your permission to sit?'

I signalled no objection and he sat in a cane chair opposite my own and fanned himself with his hat. He had a face as old as any I'd ever seen, but keen blue eyes with it and, although his teeth were stained by the plant the natives chew, they looked sound. His thin hair was white and he wore a neatly trimmed white beard.

'A mariner,' he said.

I nodded.

'As I was myself once. A drink?'

His tone made his words somewhere between a request and a command. In my happy state I was amused and gestured to the hovering servant to bring two more brandies. His name I have long forgotten and much of what he said, except that he warned me against becoming entrammelled by a woman in foreign lands.

I remark this memory now because in time to come, if the story of the mutiny on *Bounty* is told, I may be accused of precisely this failing. It was not so. The matter goes far deeper.

The great thing about the sailor's life is that he may sample these strange sights, indulge in the local vices if he pleases, buy unusual items, and yet still return to where all is familiar, comfortable and safe. Not so now, although it is not to my purpose to entertain that thought lest it bring on the melancholy to which I am sometimes subject. The *Eurydice* saw no action on that voyage yet, as a ship of war, there were drills and exercises, and I gained some sense of what fighting at sea would be like. I yearned to experience it. On the voyage home I was given a watch, a rare honour for a midshipman on his first voyage.

So it was with great disappointment that I found myself land-bound again on my return to an England at peace. When questioned by my family about how I had endured the discipline and hardships, having been known as a rebellious and headstrong youth, I replied that it was easy to become respected, liked, even beloved on board ship – be ready to obey a superior's orders and be kind to the men.

24 January 1790

I HAD THOUGHT TO TELL my tale from its beginnings to the present in this journal, but I find myself forced to write now of a fact which will shape all our lives for ever, whatever that span shall be. *Bounty* is no more. Our ship has burned and sunk. We worked for a full week, dawn to dusk, stripping her of everything useful for our island life and it was in my mind to run her aground and let her break up that we might use more of her structure. And yet, I do not know if I would ever have accomplished this act of finality to the beautiful vessel that, cursed as she was by the purpose to which she was put, served us so well.

Discussion there was little. All knew that a passing ship catching sight of *Bounty* at anchor would be the end of us. Some were for leaving her afloat a little longer but by midday on the 23rd she was a hulk and I eventually gave the order to raise the anchor. We'd let her drift ashore and see what happened. It was a powerful heave needed for a small band of men, some of whom were drunk on liquor from the ship, to get the anchor up, but we succeeded and prepared to abandon her by boarding the cutter being held alongside.

The anchor was scarcely out of the water when I heard a shout of fire and turned to see smoke pouring up from the main hatch. I swore and chocked the windlass as she drifted towards the rocks.

'No use, lads. To the cutter!' I shouted and all raced towards the side where we'd hung ropes down to the cutter. We gathered there for a last look and I saw Mathew Quintal, staggering drunk, come across the deck.

'What have you done, you scoundrel?'

For an answer he flung the top of a pitch barrel over the side. 'Best to be done with her,' he shouted over the noise of the fire and the pounding of the surf, 'else the Indians would have killed us in the night and taken her.'

McCoy staggered into view through the smoke carrying a liquor barrel. With some help from others he lowered it to the cutter by rope. Then a roar came from below as the fire devoured all before it. Quintal was the first down a rope, shoving others aside. The heat was intense and the natives shouted in panic as they swarmed down the ropes. I was the last to leave the ship and the deck was blistering around my feet as I swung myself over the side.

I steered the cutter through the rocks with smoke billowing around us and the parting ship's timbers cracking like gunshots. Will Brown told me later that the flames leapt to half the former height of the masts. We could hear the wailing of the women on the beach and they rushed into the surf to what purpose I know not; Jack Williams had to jump over the side with the grapnel and line and push them aside lest they attempt to board and swamp the boat.

That night I ate little and slept less. I stood on the beach and watched the ship being consumed by fire. Sparks shot into the air visible to a great height through the clouds of smoke until at last there was a long, loud hiss of steam as the vessel sank beneath the waves.

Writing thus has relieved my feelings somewhat, but I fear the black pit that could open in my mind. I accepted a stiff tot of rum from McCoy's cask, needing something to soothe my soul's chill. I would that my wife, Mauatua, now comforting the women, was with me to warm me with her love. I will have more to say of her.

Resuming at a later date

WITH MY TASTE FOR THE sea and travel whetted I was desperate for a berth. As is the way of things, my chance came through family connection. B—, on half pay from the navy in a time of peace, had used his own family connections to secure the captaincy of a trading vessel, the *Britannia*, transporting sugar and rum from the West Indies. Through a member of the Taubman family, with whom the Christians had close connection, and likewise the wife of B—, I heard of B—'s escape from the doldrums of half pay and asked him to put my name forward. My hopes were dashed at first when B— replied that he had a full complement of officers.

Nothing daunted, and very anxious to sail with the man who had been sailing master to James Cook, I wrote directly to B—, asking that he might reconsider. I represented myself as a gentleman midshipman, not likely to pull a rope but prepared to do so if the occasion demanded. I recall roughly the words in my letter: 'Wages are no object. I wish to learn my profession, and if I may mess with the gentlemen, I will willingly go as a foremaster, until there may be a vacancy among the officers.'

Captain B—, for so he may be styled as master of the *Britannia*, though not aboard *Bounty* when he was a mere Lieutenant, appeared to think I had written in the right vein for I was accepted as an able seaman, although messing with the officers. I made two voyages in the West Indies trade and liked them well, although, money-making being what it is, there was more haste and less time to spend enjoying foreign places. The women, black and mulatta, were fine, but there was not much else to enjoy in the Caribbean, the weather being hot, sticky and stormy. Nevertheless, like many another traveller, I acquired a liking for warm climates and the feeling of freedom and health that comes from shedding heavy clothing.

I can recall no happy meetings. The work all being done by slaves, the white men almost without exception were fat, arrogant and grasping with pretentions to gentility that set my teeth on edge.

I found favour with the captain who singled me out to my surprise. 'I understand, Mr Christian, that you are a Manxman,' he said on our first meeting.

'In all but name, sir,' I replied. 'My family's history . . .'

B— was ever impatient for a conversation to go in the direction he wished. 'Yes, yes. D'you speak the language?'

'After a fashion, sir.'

'A quaint tongue. My wife has some acquaintance with it. Well, there's many a good Manx seaman by instinct. You should try to acquire the science.'

To this end he instructed me in navigation, to good effect as it turned out, and registered me as a gunner on the second voyage.

'Don't worry,' he said when I showed my concern. 'A filthy task. You'll do no gunnery. 'Tis merely a contrivance to formalise your standing as an officer.'

I flatter myself I was equally valued by the other officers and men, although the mate and I had words on occasions about personal matters. No voyage is without its frictions, but the captain held sway throughout in the proper manner, never abusing his authority nor going beyond the acceptable language of command and reprimand. It may be the place to say that B— on these voyages was in excellent health.

We were much together on the second voyage of the *Britannia*, B— and I. His instruction in navigation and all matters pertaining to seamanship continued. We dined together more often than not and he gave me the key to his liquor cabinet so that I might help myself as I pleased, a privilege I was careful never to abuse. For all that, I found him a difficult man. He was passionate in his opinions and in his language when in private and apt to make mountains out of mole-hills. Given to bursts of melancholy and hilarity as I am, our natures did not fuse, but I believe there was mutual respect between us.

'Don't be tiresome,' he said once after I'd made a remark about an accomplished Manx ancestor. But he said it with a smile. If B— was jealous, as I sometimes thought, of the distinguished lineage behind me, I envied him his voyage with Cook and his skill at map drawing and navigation and the way he had elevated himself from humble beginnings.

HMS *Bounty*

HOW TO SPEAK OF THIS vessel that has determined the course of my life from the early age of twenty-three to whenever it may close? *Bounty* was a beautiful ship before it was desecrated by the purpose to which it was put. Had it accommodated the right complement of men and officers, each class with the appropriate comforts, things might have turned out very differently. As it was, reconstituted to hold a thousand of the accursed breadfruit plants, few men aboard her could call a decent space their own. Least of all B— who, instead of having the great cabin as befitted his rank, was crammed into a fraction of the room he needed for work, associating with his officers and for private reflection. Neither were the other officers, nor the men better served. Cabins the midshipmen and petty officers had none, rather canvas flaps over cupboard-sized holes. Cabins were for the clerk, the carpenter, the gardener and so on. Huggan, the drunken doctor, had the best of it and did nothing to justify his comfort. The men had barely space to sling their hammocks and only canvas between them and their betters. A vessel a mere 90 feet long and 25 feet at its broadest, provisioned for a long voyage and carrying the wherewithal for a large garden, had not the space for nigh unto fifty men.

Before we sailed, I heard one of the men muttering to his mates in an aggrieved tone. I drew closer to listen and the man, who I later knew to be Alexander Smith, seemed not to care whether I heard him. A midshipman has to earn the respect of the men. 'A ship is a ship and a garden is a garden and it is against nature and unlucky to turn one into the other,' he said. His mates joshed him, saying he knew bugger all about gardens and not much about ships. A mild scuffle broke out which I suppressed, although I was amused by some of the jibes and said so which helped keep the peace.

And yet, we owed the voyage and the prospect of sailing in the wake of Cook to the fabulous South Seas to that very gardening plan, and I for one resolved to put any adverse feelings about it out of my mind.

To say I was full of hope when I learned of my appointment to *Bounty* would be to understate the matter. I celebrated by walking seven miles along the cliff tops, gazing out to sea and feeling powerful in body and mind. In the past I had sometimes stood on a cliff feeling a mystical tug, a wish to drop like a stone to the bottom, but not then.

My appointment, I knew, was at the behest of B— with whom I was on the most mutually respectful of terms. On past experience I had reason to expect promotion in the course of the voyage and a Lieutenancy on its successful completion. B— must surely earn a post-Captaincy for his efforts. We might make discoveries in that vast ocean, and for certain would see sights that only those with the skill and courage to sail to the ends of the earth earned the right to behold.

It is fair to say that I boarded *Bounty* in a state of high excitement, being greeted warmly by B—. 'Welcome aboard, Mr Christian. I trust the skills I have imparted to you have not been lost?'

I had visited him at home and played with his children but seamanship had not been discussed. 'No, sir. Have no fear.'

'Oh, I have no fear and neither, I assume, do your fellow officers.' He then introduced me to John Fryer, the master, William Cole, the bosun, the young midshipman John Hallet, and particularly acting midshipmen Peter Heywood, a Manxman and therefore almost kin, and Ned Young, he of the quick wit, dark skin and bad teeth. Of the others I will write as the occasion demands.

Such was my excitement and high expectation that I suffered several attacks of black melancholy during the weeks we were laid up awaiting our orders, and then through the numerous times the weather forced us back into the Channel having failed to gain the open sea.

'This will go hard with us, Mr Christian,' B— confided to me. 'I fear we will be too late to tackle the Horn on account of this delay. The Admiralty has let us down shamefully I regret to say, and allowed fair weather to go to waste.'

'But we'll try the Horn, sir?' I replied.

B— nodded but I could see that his spirits were low. Mine continued to ebb and flow as we attempted to begin our voyage only to be turned back. When lodged back at Spithead I had the opportunity to spend time with my brother Charles, who, despite his earlier warnings, was trying his hand at sea by serving as surgeon aboard the East Indiaman *Middlesex* which happened to be moored near *Bounty* on her return from the East. I was given leave to go on board, dine with my brother in the officers' mess and spend the night there.

We had much to discuss, family matters principally, including the sad death of our only surviving sister, Mary. Our youngest brother, Humphrey, four years my junior, was shortly to go a-trading in Africa which, given his delicate health, caused us some alarm.

But Charles also spoke of mutiny. After all that has happened I can still nearly enough record his words. 'The trouble began in Madras when the captain unlawfully confined an officer on the ship. Only the intercession of the Governor released him and the ship was in a troubled state thereafter.'

Here Charles paused and I could see that he would next venture something about his personal involvement. The names have slipped my mind, but the upshot was that a seaman presented a pistol to the captain's breast when that officer was of mind to once again confine members of his crew for what he saw as their failings. To his credit, my brother sprang forward in defence of the men being so unjustly treated and so was named by the captain, who had his way in the end, as a conspirator.

'A conspirator I never was, Fletcher,' Charles said. 'I felt a surge of passion at the injustice and feel I acted as a gentleman, although I fear the Company may not think so.'

I endeavoured to comfort him although his tale struck a chill in me, as I well knew that such an act as threatening a captain with a pistol was a hanging offence in the navy and likely to bring the same penalty down on any who supported it. Although my moods can be black, I fancy I have a knack of lifting the black moods of others and I attempted to cheer Charles up by recounting stories I had heard of the charms of the women of the South Seas.

He would not be cheered. 'What of Isabella?' he said and my spirits, lifted by food and wine, sank somewhat. Isabella Curwen was the ward of my uncle, John Christian. She was an heiress, close to me in age and I found her alluring. I had hopes in that direction, not entirely scuttled by the lady, but they were brought to nothing when my uncle married her. In a careless moment I had said to Charles that our uncle, being middle-aged, and not of long-living stock, might soon die and leave the field clear for me.

But I shrugged the feeling off. 'I was sore hurt as you know, Charles. But I have lifted my eyes to greater things. I am to travel ten thousand and more sea miles with a man who reads the sea like a book.'

'Pray God he reads men as well.'

'He does. He esteems me greatly.'

We laughed at my conceit, but I went on to say I knew that every mile would bring new thoughts, ease old pains, make a new man of me. We finished the bottle and prepared to sleep, but Charles had a last shot to fire.

'This voyage has cured me of the sea, Fletcher. I trust yours will do the same for you. It is an uncertain life.'

We parted on the best of terms in the morning. I surprised Charles by baring my right arm and swelling its muscle.

Charles was pale after the night's drinking and looked drawn and sick so that my demonstration was tactless. 'Brawny,' he said. 'May it serve you well.'

I said to tell our mother about it and how I could perform any duty on a ship including those requiring considerable strength. He nodded but again muttered something about being cured of the sea.

True words I think now as I write them and prepare to blow out the lamp. I wonder where Charles is now and what he is about. He told me he had borrowed money to trade on the voyage, but the markets at Canton and Madras were adverse and he made a loss. The Christians are not lucky in commerce. I trust he is doctor ashore and prosperous. And he was right; I am cured of the sea but it has been a painful physic.

Resuming, I make now an observation on a peculiarity of *Bounty* that was to have a bearing on events. By order, and unlike any other ship I ever went on, she had no cat. The reason for this, I suppose, was a fear that a cat might piss on the breadfruit plants and do them harm. And so it might. That left the problem of how to deal with the rats, mice and cockroaches that invariably infest a ship. The solution was to distribute arsenic powder between the decks. Thus the dead vermin stayed where they died rather than being consumed by the cat. This gave rise to a noxious smell which was much complained of, but this was not the main consequence of the presence of arsenic as I shall relate.

With Christmas almost upon us, the skies finally cleared and we fought clear of the Channel into the open sea. The weather immediately turned foul, and we were hit by squalls and heavy seas. I was on deck when Jim Valentine fell from the top gallant and saved his life by grabbing a stay not far above the deck. I had him brought down and B— came on deck at that moment.

'How does he, Mr Christian?'

'Much shaken, sir. But unhurt, I think.'

'Relieve him of duty and detail an extra ration of rum for one, nay, two days. He's a useful fellow.'

B— had the sails close-reefed and hatches battened and we weathered the blow, losing some sails and a yard. B—'s seamanship was demonstrated hourly and was rewarded by a lull in the weather on Christmas Day so that all hands enjoyed beef, plum pudding and rum.

The storm blew up again immediately after and huge seas threatened to swamp us while sleet and rain made handling the ship difficult and dangerous. I remember that I had to reprimand James Morrison, the bosun's mate.

'This is an unlucky bloody ship,' he said after losing skin on his hand from a flapping rope.

'We're with Cook's sailing master, Mr Morrison,' I said. 'Think on that.'

'I do, sir,' Morrison said. 'And there are those who say he contributed to Cook's murder. Not that I was there; I merely report it.'

'Nonsense,' I said, but Morrison was a man of education and experience, although bold and loose-tongued, and what he said lodged with me.

The storm drove in the makeshift windows in the great cabin and flooded it, so if we had had breadfruit aboard not a stalk would have survived. So much water found its way into the ship that some casks of rum and supplies of fish and bread were ruined. But the wind dropped to something we could run before under some sail and something approaching the usual activity resumed. B— ordered clothes and blankets to be washed and aired and fresh clothes and extra tobacco were handed out to which all took kindly.

The first week of the new year found us safely moored off Santa Cruz in Tenerife, the largest of the Canary Islands. The weather was warm but damp and I wondered that the snow on the top of the island's mountain did not melt. B— called me into his presence.

'I have a mind to make you Acting Lieutenant, Mr Christian. I have a sense that I will be forced to issue unpopular orders on this voyage and I'll need a popular officer to see them carried out.'

That was a two-edged sword if ever there was one, but promotion cannot be refused. Still, I had a concern. 'What of Mr Fryer, sir? You would be placing me effectively as second in command.'

'I am aware of that. I said I had a mind. The promotion is somewhere in the future, depending upon circumstances and, of course, can be rescinded at any time.'

B— directed me to go ashore and pay our respects to the Governor, which I did, after donning my best uniform. Despite my misgivings, I decided to take the allotment of this task and the captain's talk of promotion as signs that I continued in his favour and was glad of it. I admit I enjoyed being rowed ashore looking my best and being respectfully greeted by the Governor's aide who spoke English.

'My captain will salute the Governor provided he is returned a salute by an equal number of guns,' I informed the Governor, a tired-looking little man in somewhat dowdy surroundings. It was explained to me that the Governor could only salute a person of equal rank so that was let pass. My request for us to be permitted to repair and provision our ship was graciously acceded to. So my first diplomatic mission ended and gave me no taste for more.

After several days we got underway again although disappointed at not being able to replace the ruined stores, only some inferior beef, pumpkins and potatoes being available for purchase. Once at sea we were struck again by rain and squalls and here B— made two decisions which, on reflection, show the contradictory side of his nature.

In order that the men might have eight hours rest between watches, he revised the system to three watches instead of the usual two, which involved four hours on duty and four of sleep. This was welcomed by all and I was made officer of the third watch and Acting Lieutenant. Against that, he announced to a full muster that he was reducing the ration to two-thirds of the usual allowance of ship's biscuit to make it last through what could be a long battle at the Horn. He thus expressed doubts in a manner unlike his usual confidence and underlined them with a degree of hardship.

As all who have taken ship know, food is of great importance on a voyage. Time can hang heavy and the meal breaks afford a rest, a change in routine, an opportunity to talk and to enjoy the simple act of eating. A wise captain feeds his crew as best he can; in this matter our captain was not wise. When a cheese was found missing from a cask he cursed all and sundry and threatened to flog Jack Williams, the man who ventured that it had been removed before we sailed and conveyed to the captain's house. Cheese stuck in our throats for some time after this. Worse, when the pumpkins taken on at Santa Cruz were found to be rotting, B— ordered pumpkin substituted for bread to prevent waste. Sailors value their bread over and above its role as food, and by depriving them of it the captain wronged them sorely.

Still, this might not have mattered as sailors must needs have something to complain about. But when the men refused to eat the pumpkin, the captain summoned all hands and had his clerk call on a man from each mess group to accept the pumpkin. When Quintal, on whom the choice first fell, hesitated the captain's voice rose almost to a scream. 'You damned infernal scoundrels! I'll make you eat grass or anything you can catch before I have done with you!'

At this, Quintal took the pumpkin and the trouble subsided for the time. But over the next few weeks I heard complaints that when a cask of beef or pork was opened the prime pieces went to the captain's mess and the contents were never weighed as was the correct procedure. I attempted to placate the men by permitting McCoy, who claimed to be a good shot, to attempt to shoot sharks. After McCoy enjoyed only moderate success, B— forbade the practice and again addressed the company saying he had got wind of complaints about the food and its distribution. His words are etched in my memory: 'I am the first and only judge of what is right and what is wrong aboard this vessel. I will therefore flog severely the first man who dares to complain. Flogged, I say, from shoulder to arsehole and left to piss blood and stand in shit.'

To those who did not know the captain, some of his practices seemed eccentric. He insisted on a weekly inspection of the men's hands and clothing and severely reprimanded any who appeared dirty. A second offence brought a stopping of grog. Likewise, he had the ship swabbed out with vinegar so that she should smell sweet and not harbour disease. Also, sweet wort or malt extract was issued and required to be consumed as a preventative of scurvy.

'I'll have no teeth dropping from soft gums on my deck, Mr Christian,' B— informed me when I expressed a distaste for the stuff. 'Cook lost not one man through scurvy and I plan the same. Besides, a sick man causes work for others.'

I took his point but he might have borne it in mind when making a period of dancing compulsory each day. Michael Byrn, a half-blind Irish fiddler, scraped the music with little skill and no joy. The dancing was hated by all, reminding them of the absence of women, and not a few twisted ankles and knees causing them to lay up and be unable to perform their duties.

'So much for improving theories,' someone remarked – Peter Heywood perhaps.

Although I and others attempted to conceal it from the captain, it soon became apparent that Surgeon Huggan was a sot who could not spend an hour without a dram and was thoroughly drunk by midday. He spent most of his time in his bed and was useless when out of it. This enraged B—, who used the strongest language to and about the surgeon, all to no avail. It gave us a taste of what his tongue-lashing would be like if we incurred his wrath and all were in dread of it. He did not content himself with damning and blasting but 'scoundrel' and 'villain' were brought into play as if the surgeon's behaviour were a direct attack on the captain himself.

In hot, sultry weather we crossed the line, and those of the ship's company who had not done so before were obliged to perform the ceremony, or a version of it. It was an odd, levelling business with the uninitiated officers and men daubed with tar, shaved with the edge of a hoop iron and required to give a rum tribute to King Neptune – the role assumed by those of us who had crossed the line before. B— permitted no ducking as he considered it dangerous to health. Old hands muttered about this, but were content to receive extra rum and forgo the pleasure of seeing others distressed. I would not say *Bounty* was a happy ship as she crossed the line – the short rations and constant washing and airing of our selves and our clothes and the cleaning out with vinegar were regarded by some as onerous and unnecessary.

'God help us when we have the plants aboard,' Ned Young remarked. 'If water were to run short I'd wager the breadfruit would get the best measure.'

'Mayhap he'd swear at them to help them grow,' said Peckover, the gunner, who thought himself to be ignored by B— except for those occasions when he felt the edge of his tongue.

The day after crossing the line was a Sunday and the captain performed a long and tedious divine service, which had the men sweating and aching where they stood. B— read from the Bible and used the most delicate language as if drawn from a different dictionary from the one he customarily used. Some days later we fell in with the whaler *British Queen,* bound for the Cape. Like others, I despatched letters to my family in which, also like others I daresay, I made light of difficulties and expressed confidence in the success of the voyage. It is a sad thing to send a letter and never know if it arrived.

As I write this I can see the light in Mathew Quintal's house across the square and see his lurching shadow as he prepares, drunkenly, for bed. Quintal is a Cornishman, a troublesome fellow, as I will have further occasion to report. Sufficient here to say that he was first man flogged on *Bounty* in consequence of behaving insolently and contemptuously towards John Fryer, the master. My good opinion of Fryer was by now much abated. Though Quintal's language was foul and his manner unpleasant, a better balanced person than Fryer would have been able to bring him into line without the necessity of flogging. I did so myself a few times. Nevertheless, with the offence recorded, the captain could do no other than order twelve lashes, a light penalty in truth.

James Morrison administered the flogging with the whole company present, and though he appeared to lay on weightily, Quintal's skin was not broken. Out of curiosity I attended Quintal in the sick bay and asked him how he did.

'Bless you, sir, I had worse from my own father. Will you thank Jem Morrison for me. He has a rare skill.'

When I attempted to say something about the captain and master he turned his head away and spat. Thereafter he harboured no love for Fryer or B—, as he was later to show, and little enough for me. The flogging was a sorry prelude to what was to be the greatest test of the ship and the men so far encountered – the rounding of the Horn.

I had heard sailors' tales of the Horn but the reality exceeded any story. For three weeks we attempted to beat our way south far enough to round the Horn and were continually thrown back by gale force winds and mountainous seas. At times the ship carried only staysails as any more canvas would certainly have been torn away. The surgeon fell and damaged his shoulder; the cook broke a rib and several men went down with rheumatic complaints caused by the cold and wet. I remained strong and in good health, although greatly fatigued by the constant work and lack of sleep.

B— ordered porridge served with butter and sugar for a hot breakfast and potable soup added to the pease for a solid dinner. But with all areas below decks awash and the pumps working without let up, the discomfort never abated. Quarrels broke out among the men and tempers became short among the officers, myself included. The sailors had to climb the rigging to reef and reset and reef again, all in sleet and biting wind and at great risk. With men out of action, I climbed and handled sails myself more than once, with hands raw and ice in my eyes. Young Tom Ellison, handy with sails in normal conditions, at one time spent hours aloft unable to descend. When he finally reached the deck he had to be wrapped in blankets and held near the galley fire. I tried to comfort him.

'Well done, Tom. You've got grit, boy.'

'Answer Mr Christian,' Fryer growled.

The boy just stared out of blank eyes and we realised that he had lost, for a time, the power of speech.

The taking of readings was impossible on many a day due to the sleet, rain and cloud but B— apprised me of our position when he was able to determine it. His skill in this matter bordered on the supernatural, so it seemed to me, and immensely proud of it he was. However, when our most southerly reach was 60° 14' and, after a struggle worthy to be recorded in the annals of the sea, we were at 59° 05', even our proud captain had to admit defeat.

The decision came hard to him and he spent much time weighing it and moving it this way and that in his mind. I attended on him when he was in the extremity of this mood and his anguish was painful to watch. Never one to drink more than was wise, he took several glasses extra upon this occasion and was red-eyed when he looked up from his charts.

'I will succeed in this venture, Mr Christian, and let no man hinder me, though this adds ten thousand miles to our voyage.'

'Aye, aye, sir,' I said and knew he meant every word.

On the morrow he summoned the crew and in a quiet voice, which I am sure not many heard above the wind, he thanked them for their efforts. I caught only snatches myself.

'. . . British Navy . . . gallant ship . . . long voyage . . . bear away . . . Cape of Good Hope.'

His words were passed back from those closest and when their import was clear they were greeted with shouts of joy, but I fancy there was a tear in B—'s bloodshot eyes.

To Otaheite

TAKING A LEAKING SHIP HALF full of sick men a quarter of the way around the world was no easy task but B— managed it, ably assisted, I would claim, by those of us who were fit for our duties. No fewer than a dozen men were rheumatic invalids who did not improve in the damp, squally condition *Bounty* experienced all the way to the Cape. At least the dancing was suspended. The captain remained moody during the voyage and I sought his company less and less. I drew closer to Peter Heywood, with whom I shared a feeling for Cumberland and the Isle of Man and indeed, on discussing family members and stretching our limited knowledge of our forebears, we concluded that, however distantly, we were related. I instructed him in navigation and mathematics and we discussed those of the classical authors with whom we were both familiar. B— overheard one of these sessions and was scathing about the ancients.

We anchored in False Bay, across the spit from Cape Town and remained there for over a month while the ship was repaired. Torn rigging was mended and reset and new ballast replaced, that which had been cracked and ground down to dust in the struggle to round the Horn. Supplies of bread and meat were taken on board, all at great cost, of which B—'s clerk kept a scrupulous accounting overseen by the captain. Such accounting was of great interest to B—. I approached him for an advance of money.

'Neither a borrower nor a lender be, Mr Christian,' he said, the only time I ever heard him quote from literature.

'I have a need for it, sir, and who better than you to know that it will be repaid.'

'Indeed it will, sir, and with interest, although the interest will not be too heavy.'

I took this as a joke, but, on reflection, considering his later conduct, I am not sure it was a joke. Well, it is one debt I will ne'er repay and interest he will ne'er collect.

I journeyed into Cape Town on horseback several times along rough roads but with magnificent mountain scenery to take the eye of one who loved climbing high and looking down. My purpose in having money in my pocket was to buy presents for my mother, writing materials and a notebook that I might keep an account of the voyage, and to avail myself of some of the pleasures of the town. Here, castaway as it were, it is not fitting that I should lie about my habits. On occasion I took strong drink, and after so long at sea with only male company (never being inclined to indulge in those practices whereby men eased their wants with each other) I frequented the best-mannered brothels of the town and so disposed of B—'s few guineas.

On board ship I found Peter Heywood composing a long letter home detailing all he could recall of our voyage thitherto.

'You have a chapter of a book there, Peter,' I said after a cursory glance at a few pages, 'and right well writ too.'

'Thank you, Fletcher. But I plan no more than a letter home. If someone should choose to allow it to be seen by a newspaper or magazine . . .' He gave a shrug of his shoulders.

'You're a sly devil, Peter, and no mistake.'

Equally sly, I concealed my intent to write a journal. But, as luck would have it, Tom Ledward, the hard-pressed assistant surgeon, had begun a journal but he remarked on it to B— who informed him that naval regulations required all such writings to be turned over to the Admiralty at the completion of voyages. B— was firm, close to abrasive on the point, and his purpose was clear – the only account of this voyage to receive an official imprimatur was to be his own. Ledward, somewhat cast down, told me that he had abandoned his journal on receiving this intelligence, and I made not a single entry in this notebook until installed on Pitcairn.

We midshipmen were required to keep logs of our voyages to be submitted when we presented for the examination for Lieutenant. These were merely records of duties performed, observations made, navigational points and such. They contained nothing of a personal nature and reflected nothing of the reality of life aboard ship. Mine was destroyed in circumstances I will relate. B—'s log I never saw, but I would give much to have read it. I have no doubt he put himself in the best light, little that it availed him in the end.

Our time at the Cape was a pleasing interlude but no more than that. The weather varied and was frequently overcast and damp. The sojourn started badly with a sailor being given a dozen lashes for neglect of duty in taking the soundings. As far as I could see, no harm resulted, but the sentence was carried out nonetheless. The men and the ship healed equally well and I know that B— enjoyed himself in the company of the master of the East Indiaman *Dublin* and the Governor of the Dutch colony. I was invited to enjoy the festivities aboard the *Dublin*, but I reneged, being struck down by one of those bouts of melancholy that surfaced in my mind with no warning and rendered me powerless, almost mute, like Tom Ellison when he descended from the frozen rigging.

The men were well and the ship was repaired but still we lingered at the Cape while B— haggled over the price and quality of supplies. He was the purser and any profits to be made by buying cheap were to go to him and he was assiduous in his pursuit of same. For my part

I was anxious to reach the Pacific, to experience what we white men still had cause to think of as another world where all manner of things were different. It was sameness that weighed me down, that and boredom and inactivity. A ship at rest is not a ship at all to my mind, and the men aboard her not sailors.

At last we left the safe billet and took to the sea again, making the passage to Adventure Bay in Van Diemen's Land in seven weeks. Once again, B—'s navigation could not be faulted nor his handling of the vessel.

'Ropes across the decks, Mr Fryer,' B— ordered. 'A positive spider web of ropes.'

'I don't understand, sir.' Fryer replied.

'Damn you, I don't require you to understand. Just to obey orders.'

Fryer dithered and I directed three men to tie ropes across the decks as best I understood B—'s instruction. The efficacy of it became apparent when the storm threw lightning bolts about us such as to terrify a man into grabbing whatever was to hand, and even more when a wave from hell almost pitched us on our beam ends. The ropes saved men's lives at that moment.

Van Diemen's Land was an unlovely place with nothing to recommend it in the way of scenery, weather or inhabitants. B— had been here before with Cook and found us a safe anchorage. But Adventure Bay proved no adventure for many of us, including John Fryer, William Purcell, the carpenter, the other officers and me. We were despatched about various duties and I was in charge of a party filling casks with water, cutting stove wood and conveying it to the ship. Will Peckover was a useful companion in this work, made difficult by the heavy surf and the rainy weather.

'It reminds me of the north coast of Scotland,' James Morrison remarked at one point. 'I had not thought to come this far to be rained on and chilled.'

I made no comment, feeling a similar discontent. But the work proceeded well enough until Peckover and I were forced to construct rafts to get the wood to the ship. When the first of these arrived, admittedly wet, but a goodly load that would dry in time, B— raged at me.

'God damn you, Mr Christian! Have you joined the miserable inhabitants of this island in your contrivances? Raft indeed, sir. Have we not boats?'

I tried to explain that the task of loading the bundles of wood onto the boats was made nigh impossible by the height of the waves, but he dismissed my explanation with a curse I barely heard but which seemed to consign all Manxmen to perdition. Peter Heywood, I knew, had earned a dressing down for some minor neglect of duty and it now seemed that we were lumped together in the captain's mind as incompetents. I bit my tongue and prepared to return to my duty when I heard B— order a boat lowered. 'It seems I must supervise everything ashore as well as aboard,' he said.

We went ashore in separate boats although there was no need to put another in the water. William Purcell was supervising the cutting of billets and B— found fault with them. I was nearby and heard the captain say, 'Those damned billets are too long, Mr Purcell. Do you not know your business?'

'I do know it, sir, and I believe you have come here looking for something to complain of, though why I cannot tell.'

'How dare you question my motives? Your insolence is unsupportable.'

'No more than your interference, sir. I bid you begone and allow me to proceed.'

'You'll not proceed another stroke, damn you. I order you back to the ship. Your duties are suspended.'

Purcell spun on his heel and approached the boat I had come

ashore in. 'The man has lost his senses, Christian,' he growled. 'But I'm damned if I'll bow to him.'

I said nothing but B— came storming towards us, struggling stumpy-legged in the mud, his normally pale complexion a flaming red. With water running down his face, for it was raining throughout this exchange, he looked a sorry sight. 'Do not engage in conversation with this wretch, Mr Christian. I've a mind to Court Martial him.'

At this Purcell let out a guffaw. He signalled to the boatmen to pull closer, waded out a few yards and swung up into the boat, his back turned to B— the whole time.

'Would you take his part, Mr Christian?'

'No, sir.'

'No, sir. And better for you, sir. Never forget you are in my debt.'

He signalled for his boat, cursed when it could not quite draw up on the beach, and thoroughly wet his boots getting aboard. The cutting party and my men drifted off to find some shelter and to smoke, their superiors having obviously left work in suspension. I was left standing on a grey, windswept, rain soaked beach on an island that had the appearance of being forgotten by god and man. Like the captain, my face was aflame, but at the insult he had offered me by referring to the advance of money combined with his criticism of my work. I fancy that at that moment I had an intimation of the troubles that might lie ahead with a man of such uncertain temper as B—. Charles' account of what had befallen him aboard the *Middlesex* came to my mind and I felt a shiver down my back not due to the wretched weather. Had the forest presented a more friendly face, I verily believe I might have walked into it, leaving B— and his moods and fancied grievances behind.

But at that moment a group of natives stepped out from the cover of trees and presented themselves to me in an attitude hard to determine. There were four men and two women with a child of perhaps ten years. They were naked except for some skins worn around their loins. The men's faces were daubed with paint that resisted the rain and their skins were black, although from the stench and the way the water ran off them I fancied some of the colour might be merely grease and dirt. The men stood no taller than an inch or two above five feet and the women did not make that mark. With crinkled hair, stuck through with sticks and feathers, they were uniformly ugly, yet possessed of a quiet dignity difficult to describe.

I was unarmed yet unafraid. I raised my hands in a gesture of conciliation, at which they stepped back and the spears the men carried were lifted. I shook my head and smiled. I was desperate to summon the sailors who had moved out of sight, but fearful that a call or a wave might bring forth aggression in the natives. I leaned back against a tree and tried to appear relaxed as they conversed among themselves in a soft, almost musical tongue with much nodding and hand gesture. At length, one of the men stepped forward and held out his hand.

I took this as a request for tribute which, given we had trespassed upon his land, I considered fair. Having gone ashore merely to super-vise work, I had very little about me beyond a tobacco pouch, a pipe, matches and a clasp knife for shaving the tobacco plugs. Removing these from the pockets of my jacket, I took a step forward, not wanting to show cowardice or inferiority, and placed them on the ground just beyond the reach of the supplicant. He spoke briefly to his fellows, then took up my belongings and the whole party melted back into the trees without so much as a glance in my direction.

The wood-cutters came back into view just as the natives departed and I signalled to them not to follow or offer any offence. We resumed the business and continued to raft the wood to the ship although I knew I risked the captain's displeasure. Deciding that enough wood had been procured I was careful to make an inventory of the tools and took a boat back to the ship, now straining at the anchors under a blow. As the boatmen battled the waves, I thought about my encounter with the Van Diemonians. They appeared to be a mild people, rather ugly and certainly dirty. But something about their calm manner impressed me and I had a sense that they were happy enough in their primitive state. As I boarded the ship I was a prey to conflicting emotions. One part of me wanted to travel not one mile further with this master who had power over us all. Against that, the meeting with the natives had rekindled my enthusiasm to get to the islands of the Pacific where, by all reports, the natives were of a far more interesting and impressive character.

But the *Bounty* I re-boarded was a very different ship from the one I had left so little time before. An ill-used man will talk and Will Purcell had said his piece to a number of others and enlisted some sympathy. B—'s mention of a Court Martial had revealed the limitation of his authority. He had no officers aboard of sufficient rank to hold such a court and, as one holding the King's warrant, Purcell could not be physically disciplined. He was ordered to assist John Fryer in his duties and when he refused B— ranted and roared about confining him until he could be dealt with under the Articles of War. An empty threat as everyone knew, because Purcell's skills were needed almost daily.

The result was talk and more talk and the citing of precedents and jokes about marooning, as the masters of vessels used to do with undisciplined men. In the end B— ordered that the carpenter be given no provisions of any kind until he agreed to resume his duties. This sufficed but left burning resentments in its wake.

Soon after, I was on deck and intending to smoke. I had a second pipe and I commented that it was not drawing as well as my old one.

I then borrowed Ned Young's knife to shave tobacco. Unknown to me, B— had overheard this exchange.

'What happened to your pipe and knife?' he asked in no friendly manner.

I explained how I had come to be parted from them and he gave a sickly smile. 'Funk, Mr Christian,' he said. 'Pure funk.'

Moments of this kind continued on the passage to Otaheite. Once, during a period of calm, I was taking part in some sports during an off time. I demonstrated my ability to balance a musket, no light object, on my palm at the end of an outstretched arm, for as long as I wished. This brought forth a quiet applause and yet more when I showed how I could leap from one barrel into another, the two being placed about a yard apart. My legs, though slightly bowed, had a powerful spring to them and I could perform the trick with ease, having been a great jumper for breadth and height in my school days.

'Lose a musket overboard or damage a barrel, Mr Christian,' came B—'s piping voice, 'and the cost will be entered along with your other debts.'

But so contrary was the captain's nature, that he continued to request me to dine with him every so often and behaved most mannerly at table, only to make some thrust at a later date. He still occasionally offered me some navigational instruction and once suggested, not unkindly, that I pass it on to 'my young friend, Heywood'. I knew he had formed an antipathy to Peter, on account, I think, of his somewhat proud bearing and manner of speech, so the remark surprised me as did almost everything about the man as we pushed into those but recently charted seas.

The captain's usual dining companions, apart from when I or another officer was invited, were the master and the surgeon. But he spent the remainder of the passage to Otaheite dining alone as he fell out with both. First John Fryer refused to sign off on the books the captain kept about the provisions and such, unless B— signed a certificate testifying to Fryer's good conduct. B—, enraged and swearing, refused and ordered the master to sign, having read the Articles of War which gave him the authority. The master signed, but spoke up loudly. 'I sign in obedience to your orders, but this may be cancelled hereafter.'

Opinion about this conflict was divided among us. Since my promotion, Fryer had exhibited no friendliness towards me and had grown ill-tempered and nit-picking, but the captain had our sympathy in his dealings with Surgeon Huggan. The man was a drunkard and the death of the seaman James Valentine must in part have been due to his incompetence in treating him, for Valentine had been a stout fellow until he took sick after Adventure Bay. Bad enough to spoil the captain's perfect record of never having lost a man, but worse was to follow. The surgeon diagnosed several men as suffering from scurvy, a disease B— prided himself his ship was free of and would ever remain so due to the diet of sauerkraut, portable soup and malt extract.

He called Huggan into his presence, not caring that other officers and not a few of the men were close by. 'You, sir, are a drunken sot and a disgrace to your family, the navy and England.'

Huggan summoned a drunk's dignity. 'I protest, sir. I . . .'

'Protest all you like, you incompetent rascal. I have examined those men and they suffer from the prickly heat, this being the twenties. Nothing more. This you might know were you not snoring drunkenly when not eating, pissing and shitting.'

In this he was no doubt right, but to disgrace an officer so in the presence of the men was unwise. As it was again when John Mills, the gunner's mate and somewhat older than most, and William Brown, the gardener's assistant, complaining of rheumatics, refused the evening dance and the captain stopped their grog. This caused more mutterings and, I am sure, an amount of malingering. In a ship the size of *Bounty*, with all hands crammed together, no detail of dispute and disagreement among the officers escaped the notice of the other hands. All were affected by it – the turbulent spirits like Quintal and Ned Young mocking authority and neglecting their duty, and others, like me and Charles Churchill, the Master-At-Arms, falling prey to gloom.

Even the prospect that we were nearing our destination failed to lift my spirits. My dignity was considerably offended by an inspection, cursory, almost laughable though it was, of our private parts by the surgeon. Huggan had somehow managed to lift himself from his bed where he had lain in a stupor for days, so that the captain had had his cabin searched and his private store of liquor confiscated. Thus deprived, he was sober enough to perform this duty and to declare every man free of the pox.

'But what of himself and the captain?' Ned Young observed as we shared a meagre meal, the two-thirds ration of bread having been reintroduced, to much annoyance.

'The surgeon is too pickled to harbour the pox,' I said.

Ned speared a mealy potato. 'And the captain?'

I bit back a bitter remark and shook my head.

'He made you an officer aboard the trade ships and Acting Lieutenant early in this voyage, Fletcher. Whence now his disdain?'

'I'm damned if I know, Ned. It's a hellish mystery to me.'

With the Tropic line crossed we were close to Otaheite and I made a point of questioning Will Peckover, the gunner, who had sailed with Cook, about the place and particularly the language.

'Best ask the captain, Fletcher,' he said. 'I heard Mr Nelson, the gardener, giving him lessons in Otaheitean. I have forgot much.'

'The captain has much else on his mind.'

Peckover took my meaning – that I, like many others, was out of favour with B—. He told me what he could about the manners of the islanders and wrote down, in crude fashion, his version of as many of the words in their language that he had picked up. I did the same with Joe Coleman, the Armourer, who was similarly experienced, and acquired some more information and vocabulary. Peter Heywood came upon me studying these notes.

'You think to become an Otaheitean, Fletcher?' he asked, jokingly.

'One can never tell, Peter. Say the ship is wrecked on a reef and we're forced to stay there?'

Peter shook his head. 'Say the captain's behaviour continues so strange and we're forced to desert.'

I looked around quickly, but we were alone and out of earshot of any others. 'Easy, Peter. It has been a trying voyage and he is stretched close to his limit.'

'As he stretches you, me, and others. You were his favourite, Fletcher. Can you not go to him and beg him to view us and the enterprise in a better light? I fear I shall go mad if I am checked and criticised at every step.'

I agreed to make representation to B—, not of grievances, but of our loyalty and determination to see the venture through to success to his greater glory and our own.

That night, with the expectation of raising Otaheite on the morrow, I went to the captain's cabin, knocked and opened the door. The ship was running before a breeze and creaking and he evidently did not hear me. The light was dim but enough to see by and I saw our captain in his cramped quarters opening one of the packets of arsenic that had been provided for the killing of vermin. This task fell properly to the assistant surgeon and I could not understand what he was doing. Almost afraid, I held the door ajar and peered through the gloom. B— took a spoonful of the powder, carried it to a small bowl and added a lump of sugar. He crushed the sugar, mixed the two ingredients together, and placed a small amount on his tongue. This he repeated three or four times.

As I sit here, on this island, which has a history no man knows, I see clearly my mistake. How dearly I and God knows how many others have paid for my failure to act then and there on my certain knowledge that the captain of *Bounty* was an arsenic eater.

A ship under sail is not quiet due to creaking timbers and flapping sails and I was able to close the door and retreat without being heard by B—. I went to my bunk with a mind sorely troubled. I knew little of arsenic save that some whores used it to whiten their skin and stimulate themselves to perform their duties. B—'s complection was pale to the point of translucence and his mood and behaviour varied between hectic activity and interference in everything and an indifferent lassitude. I had no doubt the drug ruled him and thereby might rule us all.

I longed to tell someone of my discovery and share the burden. But who? Not Huggan. Peter Heywood? I could not. Why burden another, especially one so young and green, with something that had happened to me alone and by chance and the consequences of which were so uncertain? I slept scarcely at all that night and the matter preyed on my mind continually.

I spoke of it to nobody until much later when the die had been cast. It proved a heavy burden and I dreamed about the matter that, in the nature of troubled dreams, always ended bady.

Otaheite

TO GO BACK TO MY narrative – we reached the Society Islands on my watch and I was the first, through my spy glass, to espy Otaheite. As we drew nearer and the light increased, the island appeared like a massive green mountain rising out of a blue sea. I dropped the glass and it almost fell to the deck but, cricketer that I was, I caught it before it suffered damage. I brought it to my eye again and swept across the waves to the white breakers off the black beach and the trees beyond with smoke rising from the natives' huts. In the distance I could see cascades of water as a mist enveloping the land lifted. I was struck dumb by the island's beauty and majesty as never before since climbing in the Lake District and coming upon some wild vista.

The lookout's cry came soon after and other eyes now gazed on the scene. I knew that the island had been much visited by our people, but still I had a powerful sense of being the first to see it in its best guise – as a mountain rising from the sea. It may be a fanciful invention, but I recall all my senses being alerted at that moment. I smelled the land as well as saw it and heard it – the thunder of the breakers and the bird cries – and I knew I would never look at the world in the same way again. Ever the free thinker, I had no impulse to think of Otaheite as an Eden, rather as a place where work and play might not be too distinct.

This elation relieved me of the burden of the terrible secret I had stumbled upon, but not for long.

'You look sad, Fletcher,' Peter Heywood, who'd joined me on deck, said. 'Why so? We're here.'

'A slight headache,' I said. 'Of no consequence.'

In truth, I was dwelling on detail. I wished I had knocked louder, not pushed on that door. But it could not be changed. Another thought troubled me. It seemed to me that I had closed the door and retreated without the captain being aware of my presence. But what if I was wrong and B— knew that I knew? What changes might I expect in his behaviour towards me, already hard to tolerate, if that was the case?

To my surprise, B— came and stood close to Peter and me and conversed with us most amiably. His usually pallid face had a little colour and his eyes were bright. Encouraged by this, I ventured my opinion that Otaheite looked like a mountain arisen from the sea.

'That is a perceptive remark, Mr Christian. It was James Cook's belief that the island is volcanic and has indeed risen from the sea.'

B— always spoke of Captain Cook thus, as if to claim a better acquaintance with him, though not such as to use his first name alone.

Peter remained silent, still fearful of B—'s tongue. But the captain touched him on the shoulder and extended a finger, which did not tremble as I had seen his fingers do on occasion. 'That is Point Venus, Mr Heywood, where James Cook made his observation of the transit of Venus.'

'Did you observe the phenomenon yourself, sir?' Peter ventured.

'No. I was busy with other duties, damned busy, as I, and both of you, will soon be here. Look! They are coming!'

He hurried away to give his orders and left Peter and me to gaze upon the flotilla of canoes heading out towards *Bounty*. The waves were high and strong and it seemed impossible for these craft to manage them but manage them the paddlers did through their infinite skill and courage and, I dare say, experience running back many generations.

B— ordered sails taken in, the anchor lowered, all small loose items on deck stowed away and larger objects securely lashed down. It was busily supervising these tasks that brought me within earshot of the captain and the master.

'They are born thieves, sir,' John Fryer said, 'to the last man, woman and child as you have observed yourself.'

'Perhaps so, Mr Fryer, but less when temptation is not placed in their way. Haphazard trade between the ship's people and the natives is a curse and I plan to bring it strictly under control.'

'I wish you well, sir. Captain Cook could not do it as I recall.'

'I will benefit from his experience in this as I have in other matters.'

As *Bounty* rode the swell, the canoes drew alongside and our deck was almost instantly aswarm with brown bodies. The natives climbed aboard the heaving ship as though walking along a street and sprang over the rail with many inches to spare.

The captain had shouted greetings to them when they were within hailing distance, no doubt welcoming them aboard and they took him at his word. But they did not come empty-handed – baskets of plantains, coconuts and cooked pig meat soon covered the deck accompanied by garlands of flowers which the natives draped over protuberances and distributed to any willing to accept them. I was nothing loath, since B— seemed to be exercising no discipline at this point, and was soon bedecked. Likewise Peter, Ned Young, George Stewart, the Orkneyman, and many members of the crew.

Will Peckover, whose knowledge of the language, despite his claim to have forgotten it, was greater than that of anyone else on board including Nelson and B—, stood beside the captain and helped him to set matters aright with the natives. I have no knowledge of what passed between them at that time and I imagine all was of a formal nature. I was told later that the gardener, Nelson, who had a smattering of Otaheitean, had introduced B— as the son of Captain Cook – he who embodied British power and prestige – and that this son sought to conceal from the natives that their fellows in the Sandwich Islands had killed Cook. Later, when my knowledge of the language increased, I found that these stratagems occasioned much mirth among the natives as a ship calling earlier had told them of Cook's death. Luckily, they put not the same stress on the literal meaning of the word son as we do, and did not accuse B— of lying in that regard, although some resented his deception about the death of the great man Cook.

Everything I had heard about the beauty of these people proved to be true. Although those in their middle years and later were corpulent, all in the prime of life were slim and muscular. There were few elders aboard initially so the physical impression they made upon us was strong. Like every natural man aboard, my eyes were drawn to the women who were tall and full breasted, wide of hip and entrancing with their brown skins and hair and teeth like the finest white marble. My own teeth were good; I had a clear skin tanned by the sun and a full head of dark hair, but many of my fellows were pockmarked, gap-toothed and balding and suffered by comparison with the least handsome of these people.

They all wore flowers in their hair and their skins were fragrant and shining with the oil of some flower or tree. The men exhibited the greatest friendliness, bringing their faces close to ours and touching nose to nose while smiling widely. The women, wearing nothing but some kind of native cloth around their loins, pressed themselves against us, inviting us to stroke their shoulders and fondle their breasts. I saw Will Peckover smile as I turned one of the women around and cupped her breasts, pinching her dark nipples with my fingers. She rubbed her buttocks against me as she pressed my hands harder against her luscious flesh. Then she danced away and plunged into the crowd until I could not distinguish her from a dozen others.

Peckover still wore the smile and I approached him, gently dismissing other hands.

'Will,' I said, 'I know you've been here before and witnessed this scene, but what amuses you so?'

'Look at your right hand, third finger, Fletcher.'

I did as he said and saw that a ring I had worn, a gift from someone I esteemed, was missing. 'I'm damned,' I said.

This theft made me look on the scene through somewhat different eyes. The natives' friendliness seemed genuine enough and I fancied that, if one could speak with them, comradeship and more intimate association might be possible. But without that facility, and remaining dependent on gesture and facial expression, the possibility of misconstruction could be endless. As I have written, I had learned a few words of Otaheitean and I resolved to set about using them and learning more. I pushed my way into the crowd uttering the words I knew and pointing to people and objects and inquiring by look and gesture the local word in use. I listened hard, repeated the words until I had them set and lapped up the approval the natives, male and female, accorded me.

This free association between the Otaheiteans and our people lasted several hours with fruit being eaten, coconuts split and the milk drunk, and small amounts of our foodstuffs being dispensed as well as presentation of glass beads and trade goods to the few dignitaries who had boarded. In a lull in the hubbub I found Peter Heywood, massively garlanded with flowers, busily writing in a notebook.

'It's amazing, Fletcher, the number of words they have for the sea. I have a list and I think it far from complete.'

I contributed all I could recall of the words I had been given and he wrote them down in his fine hand. As I write this now, in my script much inferior to his, I miss him and hope he has fared well through whatever has happened since our final parting. Our work on the Otaheitean tongue drew us closer together and it is sad that our friendship could not have continued until we were both grey-bearded retired Admirals, gazing out at the Irish Sea from Douglas or a Cumberland hilltop. Too sad to continue. Enough.

'Mr Christian!' I heard B—'s thin, harsh voice from the quarterdeck as I was conferring with Nelson about the island language.

I hurried into his view. 'Sir?'

'I see some of our people trading. Put a stop to it at once. I'll flog any man I find missing a shirt and put in irons anyone who trades the ship's property. See to it, Mr Christian, and work to clear the decks without giving offence. I see you and Mr Heywood compiling word lists. Very commendable. Put them to use.'

It was a peculiarity of B— that he appeared to see and overhear much more than you would credit for one pair of eyes and ears. I believe he had spies among the company, but I never found out who they were. On this occasion I sprang to and, enlisting Nelson's aid, set about breaking up the knots of men and natives who had formed for the sort of purpose the captain stated and no doubt for others. We explained by word and signs that the ship was *tapu* to them for the rest of the day until we had brought her safely to anchorage in their bay when they would be welcome again.

Obligingly, the natives departed the ship expressing their pleasure at our arrival and, so Nelson informed me, saying they hoped we would stay longer than ships had in the past. As they went over the side, climbing like the very best of sailors and dropping into the canoes with perfect balance, I tried to see she of the perfect breasts and nimble fingers but failed. Still, I could smell the heady scent of her and I rubbed my hands together at the memory of her velvet skin. Nelson gave me another of his sly smiles which I ignored.

It was remarkable to see our people clustered at the rail waving to the departing natives and then to see them falling into intense conversation, along with lewd gestures and shouts of laughter. Ordinary sailors, for the most part, converse briefly and in mutually understood grunts, unless they are in drink, when their language becomes violent and profane. At that point, however, our people were in high good humour under the burning tropic sun, well disposed to each other and the world. I heard the word paradise used more than once. As an unbeliever, I struggled not to curl my lip.

I was summoned to the quarterdeck. 'Foodstuffs to be properly stored, Mr Christian. A check on our mooring, soundings to be taken, and if all is well, appoint three lookouts. All other hands to be issued rum and allowed a two-hour rest. Then I will address the company.'

There was some grumbling that coconuts and other fruits which people had traded for buttons and, I dare say, nails and lengths of rope, were to go into a common store, but the rest and the rum smoothed these feathers. At the end of the rest period, with the afternoon drawing in and clouds building on the horizon and over the island, the captain appeared on the quarterdeck with a piece of paper in his hand. I cannot recall his words precisely but, from acquaintance with his manner of speech and the matters he dealt with, I render them as best I can.

'We are here to perform a task of great benefit to our nation,' he announced. 'Crucial to the carrying out of that task is discipline among us and civilised behaviour towards our hosts, for that is what these people are. This paper will be nailed to the mizzenmast. It sets out how you will conduct yourselves towards the natives and how all intercourse between you and them is to be conducted. The greatest care must be taken that they do not regard the ship as a kind of shop and to that end a strict control will be maintained over the smallest piece of the ship's property.'

This long address in a raised voice caused B— to run short of breath and he coughed several times before resuming.

'By necessity a party will be obliged to remain on shore to supervise the growing of the breadfruit plants and other matters. Other hands will be permitted to go ashore on the basis of a roster, but must return to the ship at night. We are thousands of miles from home and from the nearest European settlement. Our ship is our connection with our homes and must be safeguarded at all times. Those of you who do not read must prevail upon others to read the paper to you and make clear its contents. Ignorance of these rules will not be an excuse for their violation. Congratulations on having successfully carried out this first stage of the work. That is all.'

The bosun tacked the paper to the mast and over the next few hours every man aboard knew what rules B— intended to enforce. I have forgotten the wording but the import was that no one should tell the natives that Captain Cook had been killed by the Sandwich Island people; that no one should reveal the breadfruit plan until the captain had done so; that every man was to solicit the good will of the natives, not to do them violence unless in defence of one's own life; that no ship's property was to be traded and anything lost to be the responsibility of the loser and its cost to be deducted from his wages. Lastly, a person was to be appointed to supervise all trade between the natives and the ship's people and any man wishing to purchase food or curios must go through this person. The idea, no doubt good in principle, was to establish a regular market in all things with a recognised price and thus avoid disputes.

'Red feathers, Mr Christian,' the captain told me, having invited me to dine with him that night and I having no reason to refuse, 'became the price for a pig at one island on the voyage of the *Endeavour*. Rare, red feathers tendered by one foolish seaman with the result that the pig supply ran very thin.'

I nodded, taking the point. I had been observing him closely and he seemed almost a different man from the peevish individual of uncertain temper he had been of late. He seemed calm and his hands did not tremble and I had reason to hope that his arsenic eating had been a temporary aberration, brought on by the strain of the early parts of our voyage. Never a jovial companion, he nevertheless conversed interestingly on a variety of subjects and we both enjoyed the fresh pork. He was generous with the wine.

'What think you of our hosts?' he asked, tapping his bread as sailors will, although there were no weevils in it.

'I hardly know what to think, sir. They are completely beyond my experience. I have never seen a people so free.'

'Free, yes. It appears so. But do not be deceived. They are savage in warfare. Cannibalism is a ritual they embrace along with human sacrifice. It would not go amiss for you to so inform your fellow officers and those of the men you think could profit from the information.'

We ate a little more and drank and then he told me he had it in his mind to put me in charge of the party that would remain on shore. I said I would be honoured to serve in that capacity. He then rattled off some words in the Otahetian language but in a thin, piping tone utterly unlike the musical voices I had heard, so that I think the natives would have had difficulty in understanding him. Still, I complimented him on his facility.

I had thought I was back in the captain's favour and that my fears about his knowing what I had seen were groundless. Mellowed by the wine, I had hopes that the good relations we had enjoyed in the past might be restored. Knowing that my own tongue could be sharp at times, I forgave him his insults. There had been no talk of money for some while. But afterwards, on reflection, I was less sure. As was his way, he wanted to use me to convey unwelcome information to the men so that they might view me as its source and sponsor. And I suspected he had offered me a bribe in the form of the shore duty. I did not do as he suggested.

4 April 1790

ON TAKING UP MY PEN, I realise that it is a full year since *Bounty* sailed from Otaheite, laden with breadfruit. In future years, should our story be told, many will assume that events on Otaheite determined the happenings to follow. This is not entirely true as most of what proceeded resulted from my turbulence of mind, which had a number of causes. But time enough to tell of that. I resume with our initial mooring in Matavai Bay and how things fell out thereafter.

Under a light breeze but made difficult by the many canoes clustered around the ship in the bay, we manoeuvred to a secure mooring and dropped anchor. I was in charge of the launch which was to convey the King to the ship and drew the admiration of the natives by springing from the bow to the sand and arriving with dry feet – a jump I fancy of about twelve feet. Along with Peckover, I was conducted into the presence of Tynah, more the chief of the area than a King, to whom we made presents and behaved with the greatest courtesy and respect. Tynah and his consort were both impressive figures, he being well over six feet tall and well made. They gladly boarded the launch and sat most regally through the short trip to *Bounty*.

After much circling about and polite enquiry from the chief about England and his counterpart King George, B— got down to the business of explaining our mission.

'That went well, Mr Christian,' the captain observed after the interview. 'We have permission to uproot and grow the tree to the number we require, indeed I fancy he was relieved we had no other request.'

'Just so, sir.' And so it seemed, although I was later to learn that the natives regarded these visitors, some of whom had come to stare at the sky and others to acquire trees that grew in abundance, as what we would term 'touched'. However, in the days that followed we made expeditions along the coast to ensure the goodwill of an adjacent chieftain, a child, and inland to inspect the villagers' gardens and their methods of cultivation. Bivouacking, the natives performed a dance of remarkable lasciviousness and B— demonstrated his indifferent ability with his pocket pistol, shooting at coconuts from very close range. I was prevailed on to make several running broad jumps and far out-leaped all others.

After several days of such politenesses, we took possession of an area of land at Point Venus where Nelson the gardener and Brown, his assistant, were to establish the breadfruit garden. Along with them went Peter Heywood and Will Peckover, who had been appointed comptroller of trade as B—'s paper had promised, and myself as the officer in charge. In fact it was the site of Captain Cook's camp for the astronomical observations and very ill-chosen for our purpose, as I shall relate. It was situated close to the river where all white visitors, including ourselves, drew their water. We built several huts and a shed and a line was drawn around the area and light barricades erected. The place was out of bounds, except by permission, to all natives without exception and this was explained to them. Although visited regularly by B—, our encampment became something apart from the ship and its rules and regulations.

Four ratings served as an armed guard on a rostered system and right glad they were to have the duty as they had almost nothing to do and spent their time pleasantly. I saw no reason to put them to meaningless tasks, so they enjoyed their shore time very much as we did.

Another spending much time ashore was Joe Coleman, the old Otaheite hand, who won much praise from the natives, and enjoyed the favours of their women, by sharpening and re-fashioning their tools and weapons at his forge.

Peter and I consolidated our friendship still further and quickly equalled and out-distanced Will Peckover in our grasp of the language. With the gardeners busy and time to spare, we associated freely with the natives, allowing them to approach the compound but meeting with them at a short distance to eat and smoke, swim and talk. We were provisioned from the ship but ate a good deal of the native food and thrived on it as, indeed, did the whole company.

'I doubt those men had scurvy,' Peter observed after one of the supposed sufferers had delivered a heavy set of tools from the ship. 'I think that devil Huggan diagnosed them as such to annoy the captain.'

'He succeeded then,' I said. 'But in truth this climate and food agrees with me mightily. I never felt more . . .'

Peter scratched in the sand with a bare toe. He caught my meaning. 'Nor I.'

I laughed. 'Nor you! You'd done no more than squeeze a hand before this I'll warrant.'

''Tis true. But are they not wondrous free, Fletcher?'

'They are.' His words recalled B—'s warning of their cruelty but I took no heed. I had lain with half a dozen of the island women and had come to no harm. The King himself visited and presented me with a fine spear which I kept on display.

Right glad we were to be ashore for when the large cutter's gudgeon was stolen, Alexander Smith, later to be known under another name, whose responsibility the cutter's equipment had been, was given twelve lashes. I was not present but I was told by some who were that the native women were shocked at the punishment, and wept and begged Morrison to desist. B— continued to have men flogged for neglect of duty although no more than a dozen lashes were inflicted. That is for the company. It was different for the natives. One night an empty water cask, part of a compass and the bedding from Will Peckover's hammock at the camp were found to be missing.

I was for letting the matter pass over in the interest of harmony but Nelson, proving to be something of a toady, reported it to the captain. B— stormed up to the camp. 'You are a set of neglectful villains and hounds.'

I protested. 'Sir, I will endeavour to recover the items by diplomacy. In any event, they are easily replaced.'

'Diplomacy is it? By God, sir, that is another word for cowardice and slackness. I swear your native King, who shows you such favour, will bring me the thief or suffer severe consequences.'

'I don't take your meaning, sir.'

'I refer, Mr Christian, the diplomat, to the ship's guns and their destructive capacity. Good day.'

Very frightened by this threat, the chief absented himself for a time and eventually returned with a captive whom he declared to be the thief. Tynah advocated killing him, but B— had him taken to the ship and spreadeagled on a grating. He had the ship's company assembled and several score natives. Will Cole, the bosun, was given the duty and we all expected twenty.

'A hundred lashes, Mr Cole,' B— ordered. 'And lay them on.'

A hundred! I watched in horror. I doubt I could have withstood fifty myself.

B— later said that he had been merciful in not executing this wretch but he was entirely wrong. His vengeance not complete, he had the native, who had survived the punishment remarkably well, confined in irons. Tynah and his consort dined aboard that night

I was told and harmony was restored. But the wretch who, I learned later was not guilty of the theft, but had merely been nominated by the chief, broke loose from part of his shackles and threw himself overboard, still somewhat weighed down, whereupon he drowned. So an injustice was multiplied and I began to wonder if the captain had resumed his poisonous habit, his moods once again swinging so wildly.

'You bear a charmed life, Mr Christian,' Nelson said after the theft reported above was followed by the more serious one of a boat's rudder stored within our shore tent. Although a replacement was available, the theft reduced the number of spares and was therefore of concern. I had recently earned B—'s commendation for my supervision of the airing and drying of the sails, and fully expected to incur his wrath at the theft as all stores within our camp were my responsibility. In theory, as a mere midshipman, I could be flogged or, at the very least, have the cost of the rudder debited to me. No mention of any such punishment was made. This made me wonder again if B— recoiled from a severe punishment aware that I knew of his habit.

'Yet I tread on eggshells daily,' I replied.

Nelson, never heard to question the captain in any matter, surprised me by saying, 'As do we all.'

Nevertheless, the time passed pleasantly enough, especially after I made the acquaintance of Mauatua, a tall stately woman, who granted me her favours and whom I came to love. I gave her the nickname Mainmast because of her height and bearing and spent my nights with her, sometimes in her quarters, sometimes in mine, in violation of my orders. Again, tattle-tales might have alerted B— to this association but he took no action. Although others among the island women claimed to prefer fair skins, Mauatua admired my brown colouring and encouraged me to bare as much of my body to the sun as I might so that my colour would approximate to hers. This

I willingly did, finding the darker the skin the more resistant to sunburn. I also submitted to the painful ordeal of having a star tattooed on my breast. Thus we drew ever closer. She was tender and passionate and since meeting her I have sought no other, and so it remains to this day.

Many of our company were tattooed but no others, I fancy, received the stripe across the buttocks that was the mark of a warrior. I was accorded this doubtful honour, doubtful because the pain of the operation was prolonged and intense and the recovery slow, through having bested one of their strongest wrestlers. Otaheitean wrestling involves a great deal of hand clapping and foot stamping but not much fight. Although the man was taller and heavier than I, he had no notion of scientific holds or the cross buttock and I was able to use his weight against him.

As a boy, I had seen Peter Corcoran, the Irish champion of the prize ring, fight an exhibition bout at the Cockermouth fair. Although Corcoran was not reckoned a scientific boxer, he milled well enough and several of my schoolmates and I amused ourselves by sparring and attempting to copy the style of the pugs. I was the equal or better of any at my height and weight and several times, in my wrestling contest with the Otaheitean champion, I was tempted to tap his claret with a right cross. But, having seen the horror displayed by the islanders when one of the seamen punched another, I refrained and wrestled him straight.

Spending all of my spare time with Mauatua and her family and friends, my grip on the language tightened so that I could converse fairly easily on most matters. Indeed, often wearing only a loin cloth and taking part in fishing expeditions and, with increasing enjoyment, dances and other rituals – many very lewd that so shocked the puritan in B— that he once ordered a dance to be stopped – I began to think myself as near to one of them as a civilised man could become.

Living in a balmy climate with an abundance of food and the minimum of work needed to acquire it, life on Otaheite was seductive. And that is not to mention the charms of my Mainmast. But I never lost sight of my ambition to rise in the navy, make a name for myself, perhaps take prizes in time of war and restore my family's fortunes. Ambition burned with me only matched by my concern that B— might scupper all such plans should he resume his arbitrary ways towards me and provoke me into a rash act.

His moods remained uncertain, swinging from favouring the natives one day to concern for the company another. Above all was his care for the plants, which meant a care for his future. Like me he was ambitious, but when thwarted he flew into a rage whereas it was my habit to retreat into myself until the obstacle receded. I believe this was a habit acquired since my early schooldays when, bullied by a bigger boy, I lost control and thrashed him so badly he was sick for a month. I knew, or some part of me knew, that such violence must be kept in check.

Although little happened to disturb us ashore, it was not so on the ship. When the thin-skinned carpenter Purcell refused to make a whetstone for the natives because to do so would blunt his tools, the captain scorched the air with oaths and confined him to his cabin for a period. Had the captain known how his attempt to control trade, particularly in the matter of pigs, had failed, his anger might have brought on apoplexy. After a few months most of the seamen had formed friendships with natives who were anxious to supply pigs in return for items they esteemed – knives, nails, beads and the like. But by the captain's orders all pigs taken on board were seized to become part of the common pool and payment was minimal and impersonal. On a visit to the ship I found Quintal, McCoy and Mills feasting in secret on two roasted hogs. Quintal winked at me and offered me a slice which I accepted. Later I asked Menalee, one of the native men with whom I had become friendly, how the men were able to eat as they pleased.

'Oh, we wait until the captain is ashore and then bring the pigs out to the ship. We make better trade this way.'

Little by little, B—'s authority was weakened by these things and some of the natives began to mutter against him and wonder when he would be gone. He was no Cook in their eyes and his distaste for their freedom with their bodies and the arts of love they openly displayed made him the butt of much concealed humour. Whether he noticed or not I cannot say, but he was frequently out of sorts and often confined himself to his cabin for long periods, complaining of eyestrain and headache.

'That bastard Huggan,' Peter Heywood exclaimed one day as he dried himself after a swim. We were both powerful swimmers and had improved our capacity in this regard by racing each other and covering ever longer distances.

'What now?' I asked.

'He has listed me as a venereal, and you as well. We are both to be fined.'

I struggled to contain my anger. 'He has not examined us.'

'He will claim he had. I went to him some time back with a cough and you'll recall you had him give you some liniment for a twisted ankle.'

'That's villainous! The man is constantly drunk and delights in provoking the captain. I must make some representation about this. I won't have my name entered as a venereal.'

'I'm with you.'

We resolved to approach B— with our protest and schemed to find a reason to go to the ship, for our duty was to remain ashore unless summoned. A violent storm blew up at this time agitating the sea, swelling the river than ran close to our camp so that we were cut off from all communication with the ship. Such was its strength that it brought salt spray our way so that we were busy lashing canvas in place to protect the plants and keeping watch on the rising water for the time the blow lasted. Only the digging of a trench, supervised by Nelson but the work of all hands, saved the garden from devastation. Mauatua told me that the wet season had arrived and that no white people had been present on the island during it ever before.

She said that such storms were frequent and that the place chosen for our plant nursery was a poor one.

'Why did no one tell the captain?' I queried.

She shrugged. 'He chose, he did not ask.'

Throughout this struggle with the elements, I seethed with anger at Huggan's slander and had decided to go out to the ship without an excuse other than the protest itself when a summons to muster arrived. The summons applied to the whole shore party and its deliverer, sprightly Tom Ellison, stressed urgency.

'What's the occasion, Tom?' Peter inquired.

'The surgeon's dead, Mr Heywood.'

'Of what cause?' I said.

Cheeky Tom picked up a half coconut shell and mimed.

'Too late now,' Peter observed as we readied ourselves. 'We'll be entered as poxed.'

'I'll be damned if I will,' I said as I struggled into the unfamiliar clothes. 'I'll not have it even if I have to rip the page from the log.'

'Have a care, Christian,' Nelson said. 'The captain will be in a fret over the plants and the loss of the surgeon and his mind at such times is as a tinder box.'

'Just so,' I said. 'And mine the same. As for this piece of hypocrisy . . .'

'Meaning, sir?'

'Spouting gibberish over the corpse of a useless, drunken, lying scoundrel who should have been fed to the sharks years ago.'

Nelson looked at me curiously and Peter drew me away. 'Fletcher, he has the captain's ear. Do you want to be reported for atheism?'

'What care I? I've a mind to introduce each and every one of these bloody plants to a bucket or two of sea water.'

'You're over-wrought. The work of the last days and the lack of sleep have twisted your judgement. We must conduct ourselves properly at the burial and see what lies in store. Our enemy has perished. We must rest content with that.'

'Who steals my purse steals trash. But he who steals my good name, steals all that I have,' I said. 'You're the poet, Peter. Don't deny it, I've seen you scribbling. Who said that?'

'Shakespeare, of course.'

'What play?'

'I don't know.'

I laughed. 'Nor do I. One of the *Henrys* I fancy. Come on, let's bury that old bastard.'

Most of the company, apart from the sick, attended the ceremony along with Tynah and a good selection of the natives, some of whom wept although all our eyes were dry. B— conducted the affair with appropriate gravity, and the disgusting tub of guts was lowered into the black sand to rot away in a more beautiful spot than he had any right to be.

'A melancholy event, Mr Christian,' the captain observed as we left the spot.

'Yes, sir, and all the worse for it now being impossible for him to correct his errors.'

'And what is the meaning of that?'

It was on the tip of my tongue to burst forth about Huggan's slander but, seeing B—'s pale visage with a blue vein throbbing at his temple, I forbore. 'I hardly know, sir. Please forget I spoke.'

'You puzzle me, sir. Your conduct verges on the insolent and your performance on the incompetent – at times, at times. But you sometimes acquit yourself well and deserve the respect all seem to accord you.'

I said nothing as we tramped along the sand under a dark, threatening sky.

B— cleared his throat as though to dismiss our conversation to that point. 'The garden will have to be moved. I am informed storms such as the one we have endured are common in the monsoon season. I have selected a place. The plants, when Nelson deems them strong enough, will be taken to the ship and transported, landed and cared for as before. I put you in charge of this operation and need hardly tell you that the loss of a single plant will reflect ill upon you.' He increased his pace and stumped away from me.

'He's at it again, Peter,' I said, later. 'Giving with one hand and taking away with the other.'

Peter slapped my shoulder. 'Never mind, Fletcher. It will soon be Christmas and we'll show the natives how Englishmen celebrate.'

Celebrate we did with a pudding as near to a plum duff as the cook could manage with the foodstuffs to hand and a double ration of rum and an allowance of wine. Not all hands were joyous, however. Will Muspratt, the cook's assistant, had been flogged twelve lashes for neglecting his duty and a few days later we heard that Robert Lamb, the butcher, had received the same punishment for allowing his cleaver to be stolen. Again, we had reason to be glad to be ashore while such discord was going on aboard ship.

Oparre

OUR NEW CAMP, AT OPARRE, about five miles to the west of Matavai, was in a better situation than the first – well protected off a beach where the water was calm with the mildest of surf. *Bounty* rode easily at anchor in a sheltered moorage and B— ordered her to be laid up and everything moveable to be stowed below. This to prevent theft, but it also meant that the sailors would henceforth have to perform only light duties.

'Not wise,' I said to Peter when I heard of this arrangement. 'With four men flogged and others discontented they would be better kept hard at work than allowed to idle and chatter.'

'What would you have the captain do?' Peter said.

'Surely these islands need further charting. Surely there are discoveries still to be made. The ship should be at sea.'

Peter shook his head. 'He has too great a care for the plants to go discovering.'

'Exactly. He has no faith in us – in Nelson, in Brown, in Will Peckover, in you or me. He needs must watch over the garden like a nursemaid while his ship . . .'

'What, Fletcher?'

'Don't you sense it? Didn't you note it over Christmas when tongues were loosened and buttons undone and every other man wore flowers in his hair? Many among us want to stay here.'

'Do you?'

I sighed. 'One part of me does certainly. I grow fonder of my Mainmast day by day and I know she yearns to have my child. But I am an Englishman yet, and an officer in the King's Navy and I have ambition to rise and succeed.'

'Just so,' Peter said. 'I feel the same.'

'But we have prospects, careers, opportunities. What of those who have nothing to look forward to but a sailor's lot until they are too old to pull a rope, or they lose a leg to grapeshot?'

Peter scratched at a newly healed tattoo on his arm. 'They must be disciplined to their duty.'

'Aye, as our poet says, "there's the rub".'

'Your meaning?'

For an answer I pointed to the boat pulling to the shore through the calm waters. B— stood at the bow, fanning himself with his hat. The weather continued hot and steamy under a grey sky and B—, always fully dressed with his stock tied and his coat buttoned, was feeling the heat. He stumped ashore and conducted his usual inspection of the plants, plaguing Nelson and Brown with questions and one above all.

'When, Mr Nelson? When?'

'Two months, sir. Possibly three.'

'Can you not be more precise?'

'It depends on the weather.'

'The weather is damnable. The sky at night is so thick with cloud I am unable to take any celestial reading.'

''Tis very black, sir,' I ventured, 'and our *taios* tell us it is likely to remain so for some time.'

'Do they, Mr Christian? And what do they tell you about our plants?'

'Nothing, sir.'

'Nothing. Do you not think to ask about the very reason for our journey here?'

The truth was that the natives thought the garden a joke and not worthy of comment, but I did not dare tell this to the captain. 'Our plan is beyond their comprehension, sir.'

'Indeed. And evidently beyond that of some of our company. Carry on, Mr Christian.'

With that he departed. Sweat was fairly dripping from him and his hand trembled as he wiped his face, and I wondered about how he spent his time in his cramped cabin, visited only by Tynah and his tiresome courtiers, and with few orders to give.

'The man is not well,' Brown observed. 'Ledward tells me he had him bleed him, giving no reason, and that he was a long time recovering his strength. You've sailed with him before, Christian, and continue more in his favour than others. D'you know what ails him?'

Unable to speak, I shook my head. Peter was observing me keenly and, as he appeared likely to question me further, I moved away and busied myself at some pointless task.

I fretted and worried about my secret knowledge so much that I had difficulty in sleeping and would awake in the night and sometimes walk about or sit, gnawing at the problem. The ever-present sound of the surf on the reef I found soothing in my distress. So it was that on a night early in January I was on the beach in one of the black nights B— had referred to when I saw lights and activity aboard the ship moored little over a hundred yards away. I heard shouts and then a boat was lowered and came quickly towards our camp. I ran back to the tents and hut in my nightshirt and scrambled into my clothes. James Morrison came striding along the beach carrying a lantern and I went to meet him.

'What's amiss, Jem?' I asked.

'You're wanted aboard immediately, Mr Christian. You and Mr Heywood. Those damn fools Churchill, Millward and Muspratt have deserted. They've taken the cutter, muskets and ammunition. Those relieving the watch found them gone.'

'Jesus! Who was the officer of the watch?

'Mr Hayward. He was asleep.'

'God help him. The captain . . . ?'

'Icy calm, sir. Icy calm, and every man aboard with an itchy back. The captain wants you and Mr Heywood, as the best speakers of the language, to join him for his meeting with the King.'

'How so?'

Morrison shrugged. 'Not my place to say, sir. Where's Mr Heywood?'

Nelson and Brown had risen on hearing our voices and were pulling on their clothes. Peter was with his woman in the village.

'He'll do his duty. Where and when d'we meet the captain?'

'At Matavai at first light. I'm to convey you.'

'Stand by your boat, then. We'll be along in good time.'

'Aye, aye, sir.'

There was cheek in Morrison's salute and manner, but he was a subtle cove, impossible to pin down, and I had learned to let his insolence pass. I informed Nelson, Brown and Peckover of what had happened and despatched Peckover's *taio*, who had spent the night in our camp, to locate Peter.

'My only surprise is that it wasn't Quintal,' Will Brown observed as we waited for dawn and Peter's return.

'Muspratt was flogged and Millward is weak,' I said.

'And what of Churchill? As Master-At-Arms his duties are not onerous. Whence his grievance?'

At that I held my tongue. Charley Churchill, a hot-headed fellow, had come to our camp a few days previously during his shore leave and had brought with him several bottles of wine which he had filched from Surgeon Huggan's store. It being some time since we had enjoyed any wine, Peter Heywood, Will Peckover and I drank the wine in Churchill's agreeable company and, under its influence, our tongues wagged. Charley revealed that he was much enamoured of a woman ashore and for two pins would stay with her. In the course of our discussion Peter and I revealed similar attachments, but declared ourselves ready to desert the women rather than the navy and advised Charley to do the same. It was a light-hearted talk as I thought then.

Peter returned to the camp as dawn was breaking and hurriedly donned his uniform, or as much of it was clean. We went to the boat and were conveyed back to Matavai where the captain stood on the beach together with three seamen armed with muskets. B—'s calm manner was almost more alarming than his rages. His eyes were tight slits and he licked constantly with a yellowish tongue at the corners of his mouth.

'I have sent word for Tynah to meet us,' he said. 'We will proceed to the village in tight formation. Our attitude, I will remind you, is one of sternness. There will be no exchanges between our party and the natives, whatever their blandishments. Is that understood?'

We assented and marched across the beach and along the paths to the village. The sun, scarcely visible through thick clouds in recent days, broke through, swiftly replacing the slight chill of early morning by a sullen heat.

The village was astir and we approached the King's hut to find him seated in front of it, flanked by several of his advisers. B— made the appropriate obeisance and then turned to me. 'I wish you to convey to His Majesty our distress at the desertion of our men and the loss of the cutter and arms. Tell him that Captain Cook experienced similar desertions and it was his judgement that the deserters must have had cooperation from the natives. Doubtless this is so in the present case. Therefore, I hold him responsible for the return of the men, the cutter and the arms and, unless this is achieved, I will visit a terrible punishment upon his people.'

I bowed. 'Sir, that is a complicated proposal and I would defer to Mr Heywood whose command of the language exceeds my own.'

B— waved his hand in exasperation. 'So be it, Mr Christian. I am surprised to find you so modest, but Manxmen in my experience stick together. Proceed, Mr Heywood, after fastening a few more of the buttons on your disreputable clothing.'

Peter blushed and attended to his uniform which indeed was stained and ill-buttoned, revealing one of the tattoos on his wrist. He proceeded to state the case to Tynah in Otaheitean that appeared to me to be fluent with many words and phrases I did not know. I knew Peter had out-stripped me in this way, but I had not realised by how far.

Tynah discoursed with his courtiers with Peter paying them close attention. The king then spoke at length in a sorrowful fashion.

'His Majesty wishes to know,' Peter said, 'whether you intend to take him and others as hostages pending the return of Churchill and the cutter. This, as you would know, was the practice of Captain Cook.'

At this, B— drew himself up to his full height and the smile on his thin lips had nothing of humour in it. He spoke in rapid, if halting and somewhat childlike Otahetian, torturing the language with his unmusical tone. He told them that he was glad they remembered what Captain Cook had done twenty years before but that he had no such plan. He would leave them to think what was in his power to do should the deserters not be located.

The king assured the captain that it would be done and the meeting ended with the customary politenesses.

'That was cunning of the captain,' Peter said on our return to camp. 'His words will prey on their imagining and they will endeavour to avert his wrath.'

'In the meantime, what faults will he find in the rest of us miserable souls?' I said. I could feel myself falling into a dark mood.

The following day, Peter and I were summoned to the ship. We had cleaned our clothes and were able to present most respectably, somewhat to B—'s surprise. 'I must ask you gentlemen to explain a singular discovery among Churchill's possessions – a piece of paper with your names and that of another written in Churchill's hand.'

Peter and I exchanged glances. 'I can offer no explanation, sir,' I said. 'Churchill visited our camp a few days ago and passed the time of day.'

'Speaking of what?'

'General matters – life here on Otaheite, our tattoos . . .'

'Ah, yes. You are both much tattooed. Peckover sailed thrice with James Cook. Is he similarly disfigured?'

'He is tattooed. Yes, sir,' Peter replied.

'I don't mince my words, Mr Heywood. It is a barbaric practice.'

'Perhaps Churchill was compiling a list of those who are tattooed,' I suggested.

We were in the captain's cabin, standing while he sat in the cramped space with his knees drawn up uncomfortably. 'Why?'

'I know not, sir,' I said.

'Convenient. Well, we will see when these miscreants are returned for, make no mistake, I will have them back. You are dismissed.'

We left the cabin and stood on deck waiting for a boat. Peter had a brief conversation with Samuel, the captain's clerk, and learned that Tom Hayward had been stripped of his rank and confined in irons.

'Poor devil,' I said. 'Confinement below in this weather would be hellish, but nothing compared to what might befall us.'

Peter almost yelped in alarm and, seeing that others were nearby, he asked me what I meant in Otaheitean.

With melancholy descending upon me I answered him in Manx. 'Churchill must have listed us as would-be deserters.'

'God's blood! Why? We stated our loyalty.'

'We were drunk and so was he. Who knows what construction he put on our words? We must be careful, Peter.'

'You alarm me, Fletcher. I scarcely know now whether I want Churchill taken or not.'

'He'll be taken. The captain will not have deserters besmirch his record.'

In the two days that followed I noted the *taios* of Churchill and Millward skulking close to our camp. I bade them be gone but they persisted. Knowing that Nelson would report their presence to B—, I devised a way of driving them off. Slipping away from the camp when the others were occupied, I went to a sacred grove and cut a branch of an oil-nut tree. This I tied to a post supporting our hut. It had the desired effect of making our camp *tapu* to the natives. If B— noticed it on his next inspection, he made no comment.

The nursery continued to thrive but I remained wary and strove not to attract B—'s attention over any matter. He raged when he learned that a native, reputed to be involved in the desertion and taken on board, escaped by diving overboard and swimming to shore.

'Why was he not confined instantly?' George Stewart later reported the captain as saying. 'And why not pursued?'

None dared tell him they were obeying his order not to be violent towards the natives and he berated Elphingtone and Ned Young, employing his favourite epithets of rogue and villain.

'Ned will not take kindly to that,' I said, and Stewart agreed that Ned had coloured deeply beyond his usual dark hue and appeared to be on the point of protesting.

'He held back with an effort,' Stewart said, 'and drew blood from his palms from the clenching of his fists.'

'Then he should trim his nails,' Peter said.

I shook my head. 'It's no joke, Peter. Ned Young is a fractious fellow and the captain has no love for him. With Hayward confined and us under a cloud he may feel he has no officers he can trust. How stand you with him, George?'

Stewart, short and slight, mimed shrinking himself. 'I dread putting to sea with him again and the starvation rations he favours.'

'None of this is good,' I said to Peter after Stewart had left. 'I fear what could happen when we put to sea with such a ballast of grievance and insult.'

Peter nodded. 'What next, I wonder.'

We found out soon enough. B— discovered that a set of sails, not previously used, were mildewed and rotting. Declaring he had ordered them to be aired, he ranted at everyone in sight as incompetent and criminal.

'Criminal?' I said to Morrison who had conveyed this intelligence. 'He used the word?'

'He did, sir, threatening to turn all officers before the mast.'

'An empty threat. And I recall the order to air the sails. I carried it out, and it applied only to those that had been in use.'

Morrison said nothing and I regretted speaking for Nelson overheard me. Nothing followed however, and I wondered again why B— did not hold me to blame in his anxiety to find a culprit. The knowledge I had was like a weight on my chest. I considered consulting Ledward, the Surgeon's Mate, now Acting Surgeon following Huggan's death, but he was a very private creature, difficult to estimate. I doubted that he would have the backbone to take action against the captain.

These thoughts were much in my mind when, after about three weeks, news was brought of the whereabouts of the deserters. They had abandoned the cutter in favour of a large canoe, tried a nearby island but ended up at to the east at Tettahah, a mere five miles distant. Although it was a dark, windy night, B— set out with an armed party of whom I was one in the launch. The deserters had taken shelter from the rain, failed to hear our approach and surrendered without a fight. Their native companions slipped away and the captain made no effort to apprehend them.

Churchill looked me in the eye as irons were being applied to his wrists but he made no remark. We recovered the muskets, which were rusty and the ammunition wet, and the cutter, it having proved of little use due to a worm infestation of its planks. B— spoke not a word to the deserters, left them in charge of the Master, the armed sailors and myself, and returned to the ship.

Fryer abused Churchill and the others all the way back to the beach and the cutter, telling them they could expect fifty lashes each and confinement for the duration of the voyage. Churchill was defiant.

'He'll not cripple and confine three men, mad though he be.'

'Shut your mouth,' Fryer said. 'He can do as he pleases.'

'Do you agree, Mr Christian,' Churchill said, 'that the captain can do as he pleases?'

'He can, consistent with the efficient running of the ship.'

'That's what I meant.'

Fryer turned to me. 'Would you take his part?'

'I take my own part, Mr Fryer, as every man must, sooner or later.'

Fryer said nothing and the next minute we heard Muspratt swearing foully. 'My back's still tender from my last flogging. I don't think I could take fifty.'

'You should have thought of that before you deserted,' Fryer said.

Muspratt summoned his courage and spat near the master's feet as we tramped along. 'I was thinking of it, Mr Fryer. He'll flog every man he can before he's done.'

The next day, in pouring rain, the captain read the Articles of War and sentenced Churchill to twelve lashes and Muspratt and

Millward to twenty-four, the punishment to be repeated within a fortnight. With the King and sundry other natives present, the punishment was administered, each man bearing it bravely. As on all such occasions, the natives expressed deep sympathy, especially when Muspratt's back bled copiously.

Ned Young told me later that he drafted a letter for the three, thanking the captain for his clemency, pledging their future good behaviour and requesting that the second flogging be not given.

'But his base blood was up,' Ned said, 'and he spared them nothing. Cole laid on so that Muspratt fainted away and all three were in the sick bay for days afterward.'

1 May 1790

As I set down this account of suspicion, desertion and punishment, I am in hopes that here we may have a happier existence, free of the divisions, inequalities and jealousies that infect society at home – nay, I must not write thus for England is home no more – and on board ships whether in the navy or the merchant service. We have laboured hard to bring our stores and provisions up to the flat land in the centre of the island, with only the heaviest of the ship's timbers still to be raised.

All hands set to the work in a comradely fashion and the natives, although unused to heavy labour, took instruction well. We used ropes and pulleys from the ship's tackle to raise the heaviest loads and great was my Isabella's (for so I have named her) glee when she discovered a path cut by previous inhabitants of the island. The spirits of the natives, men and women both, lifted when they saw that others of their kind had lived here. On further exploration they found breadfruit and other plantations and *maraes*, though much overgrown and decayed, such as they themselves revered. Why these people abandoned the island no one can tell, for it appears to have all that is needed to sustain life – fresh water, cultivatable land, birds and abundant fish in the sea.

I called a meeting and proposed that the habitable portion of the island be divided into nine equal parts between us where we may build our houses and cultivate our gardens with the natives to help us, they to be allotted small plots for their own use. In this way we may hope to build a happy commonwealth with each person free to live in his own way. Our bond could not be tighter and must override any differences of manners and temperament among us. We must keep constant watch and extinguish all signs of habitation should a ship venture near, for our bond is this – discovery means death.

Departing Otaheite

THE WEATHER CONTINUED FOUL, overcast and wet through the rest of our time at Otaheite, so much so that Peter, for one, said he'd be glad to be gone, despite his attachment to a native woman. My own feelings were mixed – I knew the bad weather would pass and give way to those blissful days when the island seemed touched by magic and my feelings for Mauatua grew ever deeper, although I struggled against them. And yet, and yet, ambition still drove me although not as fiercely as before for one reason: I was sure B— would give a bad account of each and every one of his officers so that our chances of promotion would be lessened.

Indeed, there was much to provoke him. Only a few days after Muspratt's back had been laid open, the bower cable holding the ship at anchor was severed and she drifted towards the rocks and was only saved by a favourable current and the stern cable holding firm.

'I'll have the hide off the villain responsible for this,' the captain raged, 'though he be white or black.'

So fierce was his anger that Tynah and his consort burst into tears and exhibited the greatest distress when the captain refused them his company for some days. No culprit was found and it only emerged later that Tom Hayward's *taio*, one Wyetoa, had cut the cable with the intention of keeping his friend on the island. What is more, this native had witnessed the flogging of Churchill and the others and resolved that if Hayward were flogged he would kill the captain.

So, as we began our preparations to depart, did things get slowly out of hand. Distressed by the obvious signs of our leaving, the natives began to thieve more boldly. When a compass was stolen the captain flew into a passion and once again threatened Tynah with dire consequences if the thief was not produced. The King and his consort had recently failed in their attempts to persuade the captain to take them to England, and there was evident friction between them and B—. Mauatua told me Tynah was terrified that the other chiefs on the island would attack his people to loot the things they had gained from our presence.

'He will do anything for guns,' she said.

So it proved, for, when the compass was recovered and the thief identified, the King told B— to kill him. This the captain did not do, but ordered him to be given a hundred lashes and confined in irons. The native survived this punishment, which has been known to kill a man, and retained sufficient cunning and strength to pick the lock of his irons and escape by swimming ashore.

B— vented his fury on George Stewart, officer of the watch at the time the native escaped, but included all of us in his curses and condemnation. Nor did the successful loading of the plants, a difficult operation carried out under my supervision, gratify him. He fussed and interfered, driving the gardeners, and Brown in particular, mad.

'Should one of those plants die, Mr Christian,' Brown confided, 'I fear for the captain's sanity.'

I said nothing in reply although I shared his fear for another reason. B—'s behaviour and appearance showed all the signs of his having renewed his destructive habit. His pallor was ghastly and he fell to clasping his hands behind his back as he moved to prevent them shaking. But not at all times – for hours, even days, he was his steady, forceful self, only to become hectic and tremulous when baulked by even the smallest matter.

Many days were spent overhauling the ship from stem to stern, re-calking her planks, strengthening her rigging and sweetening her bilges. An immense body of stores for the return voyage were stowed so that the ship could scarcely carry another coconut. The island cats and dogs that had come on board were cleared out which took time and was done reluctantly, as seamen love to have cats aboard.

To Brown's fury, we loaded three hundred more plants than originally planned, thus insuring the captain against loss. 'A false assumption,' Brown told me. 'The more to care for the greater the risk.'

At this point I was offered an insult scarcely to be borne. In front of Tynah and his queen, B— dissented from the King's opinion that B— was lucky to have me as his second in command. It was reported to me by Fryer, who was present, that the captain said, 'He does not hold that office. He is no more than one of the people.'

On 5 April I farewelled Mauatua sorrowfully and waded through the waves to the boat with my eyes brimming with tears. I had regained my composure by the time I reached the ship and was able to join with the captain and the other officers in farewelling the King and Queen. B— had presented them with two muskets and two pistols together with powder and shot. Purcell, no doubt hoping to curry favour with the captain, added a musket of his own. Their majesties requested that our guns be fired to mark the departure but B— refused on the grounds that the shaking of the ship might disturb the plants. So did the blasted breadfruit take precedence over all else. The royal party boarded the cutter and were taken ashore. They had to content themselves with three British cheers as we followed the buoyed channel out of the bay. Some claimed they heard the cheers responded to from the beach but I did not.

I supervised the re-stowing of the cutter and turned my eyes to the island for what I thought would be the last time, at least until another voyage some time in the unknowable future. The rain had eased but the sky remained heavy and seemed to weigh down upon the island, the ship and the sea itself. My melancholy was intense, almost unbearable, as if I had some forewarning of the unhappiness that lay ahead.

Nor' nor' west from Otaheite

MANY HEARTS WERE HEAVY AS we watched the island drop below the horizon. But, equally, thoughts of home helped to lift the spirits and, as the days passed, my melancholy began to fade. Surely, I thought, B— will do everything in his power to contrive a happy ship with a contented crew for the perilous days ahead. For we were to pass through the Endeavour Straits following Captain Cook. In happier days, B— had told me of these waters.

'Treacherous, Mr Christian, treacherous in the extreme, with shoals and uncharted reefs.'

'Yet you are determined on this course, sir,' I said.

He tapped the table in front of him and the side of his head. 'Aye, I have James Cook's charts and my own memory and that will see us through.'

Had I been given to prayer I would have prayed that this confidence would have stayed in him, and with it a determination to communicate it to all hands by way of decent treatment. Unlike most others aboard, his health appeared not to have benefited from the time on Otaheite. But, with the difficult and delicate parts of his undertaking behind him – the diplomacy and the gardening – I had hopes that henceforth only his seamanship would be called upon. In that area he was unsurpassed and I could not imagine that he would be in need of dangerous stimulants.

And indeed this seemed to be so through the first week. When we neared an island, the name of which I forget, and could not land because of a reef and heavy surf, the captain greeted the natives who came out in their canoes most graciously, gave them presents in return for talking with him of the weather and other islands in the vicinity and allowed the men to take women below. Thus some, but not I, consoled themselves for the loss of their Otaheitean sweethearts.

But in the aftermath of a squall that blew up after we left this island, B— accused me of having allowed the sails to be damaged. They had suffered no ill that I could see and I said so whereupon B— gave me one of his black looks.

'You forget yourself, sir. I am master here.'

'I do not deny it, sir, but . . .'

'Your manner denies it though your sly mouth may not.'

With that he stalked away leaving me fuming at the injustice.

Worse was to come. We next made for Anamooka in the Friendly Islands where B— had spent time ten years before under the command of his hero, Cook. On reaching the island I was put in charge of a watering party. The captain stressed that the arms the men carried were to be kept on the boat and not to be used unless in the defence of our lives. I faulted myself later for not questioning this order and making clearer its intent. As it was, the natives clustered close around the boat and behaved so threateningly that I ordered the task abandoned when less than half complete.

On re-joining the ship and reporting this occurrence B— shook his fist in my face. 'Damn you for a cowardly rascal! Are you afraid of a set of naked savages and your party well armed?'

I struggled to maintain my temper and dignity. 'The arms are of no use when your orders prevent them being used.'

'You mistook my order. You are a coward.'

'You will withdraw that, sir.'

'I will repeat it. It is Adventure Bay over again.'

At this point there were too many witnesses to his injustice and he adopted his usual method of finishing a discussion by walking away.

The next day I went ashore again to complete the work and by gesture and threat managed to keep the natives at bay at the watering place although they carried weapons and shouted insults. The work went slowly under these conditions and came to a halt when Fryer joined us. He was red in the face and out of breath.

'A native attempted to knock me down,' he gasped. 'And would have but that Quintal alerted me.'

I nodded, turned away, and then heard a shout from Fryer. I spun around to see a native hefting a long spear and apparently attempting to gauge this distance between us. As I moved aside a shower of heavy stones fell among us, and Fryer and I gave the order to take the casks, empty or full, back to the boat.

Here, against my strict instructions to hold the boat off with the oars, the sailors had released the grapnail and were allowing the children to play around the boat. Children they may have been, but they were clearly under adult instruction, for one dived down, released the grapnail from its ring and was assisted by others to make off with it.

B— was apoplectic at the news, and at our meeting I became sure that he was once again under the influence of the arsenic. He was pale, hectic and sweating and his lips had a blue tinge.

'God damn you for an incompetent wretch!' he raved. 'Was ever a man set about with such lubberly officers.'

'I admit ...' I began.

'I don't want your beggarly admission, Mr Christian. I want ...'

His attention was distracted by spots of blood on the deck. 'What is that, Mr Fryer?'

Fryer pointed to Quintal who was groaning and lifting a rag to his head. 'Quintal was struck by a stone, sir.'

B—'s eyes appeared to glitter though it may have been a trick of the light. 'Have him wash the deck, the whole deck.'

Now the loss of a grapnail was serious but hardly threatening to the success of the voyage there being spares in store. But the captain's behaviour in response to the loss, and then its consequences show how far he had slipped from a rational code of behaviour. First, he surprised us all by encouraging the natives to come on board and breaking out some of our remaining stock of metal goods for trading. Soon, with all hands trading furiously in curios such as weapons, mats and carved objects, the decks were piled high and even the boats were filled, particularly with yams and coconuts as provisions for the voyage.

B— drew out several of the chiefs among the natives and paid them special attention, requesting them to send the remainder back to the canoes. Anticipating B—'s anger at this state of untidiness, I was attempting to have the decks made orderly when I realised that the anchor had been raised and that the ship was moving. The chiefs wailed and beat their heads as they saw the canoes and their island receding. Ignoring this for the moment, B— proceeded to once again abuse his officers.

'A more useless, lubberly set of rascals never set sail,' he ranted, and I fancied he looked directly at me. 'I can trust you to do nothing right. Well, see how this piece of thievery is managed.'

He turned to the chiefs and in his thin voice, made even harsher by his fury, he told them that they would be held until the grapnail was returned. The chiefs burst into cries of distress and informed the captain that the object had surely been carried far away by now.

'To treat people thus,' Ned Young growled, 'over a piece of iron. I'll warrant there are half a dozen grapnails in the stores.'

'Four at least,' George Stewart said.

'Mutter would you?' B— said. 'Mr Christian, pass up the arms and guard these fellows.'

The chiefs scarcely needed guarding, such was their distress. Several beat themselves severely around the eyes with their fists. What could they do? The canoes continued to follow the ship, but whether the natives knew why their leaders were detained no man could say. It was a futile exercise – a dull-witted strategy to recover a piece of metal lost in the vast Pacific, a piece that could easily be replaced. I felt foolish in charge of this senseless guard, and when the captain's attention was diverted, attempted to reassure the chiefs that no harm would come to them.

'I can scarce understand your chief,' one said. 'His voice is so high and harsh. This was a child's game only. Are we to die for this?'

The theft was undoubtedly planned and skilfully executed, but I pledged that no one would die over it and I believe that if any such order had been given, I would have refused and countermanded it. B—, however, was not so far gone in his passion as to commit murder, and near sundown he ordered the helmsman to slow the vessel and had me gesture for the canoes to come alongside.

Making no reference to the theft, he presented the chiefs with a hatchet, a packet of nails and several knives, and permitted them to leave the ship. Several attempted to make thankful speeches but were prevented by the more self-respecting ones, who took the gifts and dropped down to their canoes with faces as black as thunder.

'God help the next vessel along in these waters,' George Stewart murmured.

I said nothing, but I thought – Amen.

We had had good sailing since leaving Otaheite but, as we departed Anamooka and headed north the wind dropped so that the ship was close to being becalmed. This appeared to have an effect on the captain's mood for, when he came to the quarterdeck, he cast about in that manner we had got to know – to find something amiss. I was not on deck and the following was told me by Churchill. B—'s eye fell on the coconuts piled up between the guns. He sent for Fryer and asked him if he thought the pile had been reduced.

Fryer said, 'They are not so high as when I last saw them, for they neared the height of the rail. But the people may have walked on them and so made them look less.'

'A likely story,' B— said. 'Some have been stolen and I will find out who has taken them.'

Churchill was then sent to request all the officers with coconuts stored privately below to bring them on deck and account for them.

'What madness is this?' Peter Heywood said. 'Has he taken leave of his senses?'

'Long ago,' Ned Young said. 'Well, I have a small store of the damned things. I'll humour him. It might be amusing.'

The other officers seemed to be of the same mind and went on deck with their nuts in bags and baskets and paraded before the captain. I went up but took nothing with me.

'Mr Young, how many nuts did you buy?'

'I don't know, sir. A certain number. What I had room for.'

'And how many did you eat?'

Ned could scarce suppress a smile. 'Again, sir, I kept no tally not thinking it would become a matter of such interest.'

'Interest!' B— proclaimed. 'Interesting it is indeed when I am thieved.'

He interrogated each of the officers with similar unsatisfactory answers until he reached me, standing at the end of the line with no baggage. 'And you, Mr Christian. How many nuts did you buy? None?'

'I do not know, sir, but I hope you do not think me so mean as to steal yours.'

B—'s face flushed and a vein throbbed in his temple. As I say, the ship was almost becalmed and there was little sound from her planks or rigging so that everyone present heard his words. 'Yes, you damned hound, I do. You must have stolen them from me or you could give a better account of them.'

'I took one only during the night because I was thirsty. I thought it no matter.'

'You lie, you scoundrel. You have stolen the half of them.'

I protested passionately but he continued to rant and rave until, knowing that he could not sustain such a charge, he vented his fury on us all. 'God damn you scoundrels, you are all thieves alike, and combine with the men to rob me. I suppose you'll steal my yams next, but I'll sweat you for it, you rascals. I'll make half of you jump overboard before you get through Endeavour Straits.'

He then ordered Samuel to cut our allowance of yams and stop our grog until the coconut thief was revealed. I was in a rage and would not have cared whether I ever ate or drank again. It passed through my mind to take the captain in my arms and leap overboard with him, a thing I could easily have accomplished. Then the absurdity of such an action struck me and, despite my anger, brought a smile to my face. B— saw me thus and ordered our dismissal in a voice trembling with passion.

I fear I lost control of myself at that point and suffered a bout of uncontrollable laughter interspersed with a kind of weeping. I damned the captain and did not care who heard me. I vowed I would endure such treatment no longer, and would sooner die than continue the voyage. Peter Heywood and others calmed me down lest word of my threats reached B— After a time I collected myself, helped by a few tots of rum and I was about to attend to one of my tasks when I was instructed to go to the captain's cabin.

'I believe you are speaking mutiny, Mr Christian.'

'Not so, sir. But I believe you have spies who would tell you so.'

He seemed to struggle to accept this but did so and poured two glasses of wine. 'I suggest we put our differences behind us and attempt to complete our journey in amity.'

He moved one of the glasses towards me across the table that stood between us and I became immediately suspicious, not only because of the deliberateness of his action, but at the change in his manner. B— was no actor, and his friendliness was such as you might see on the stage by one who had no business to be there. He raised his glass. 'Drink, Mr Christian, and let bygones be bygones.'

I raised the glass and caught, faintly but distinctly, a smell that never arose from a Madeira. I poured the contents onto the floor. 'God help the cockroach that drinks that,' I said, 'and God help you, sir, in your arsenic madness.'

He drained his glass and stared at me with his pale eyes inflamed and starting from his head. 'We are a long way from Portsmouth, Mr Christian,' he whispered. 'With much rough water and weather still to come.'

I put the glass on the table and left the cabin. I went to my own quarters and rooted out a bottle of brandy I had bought in Tenerife and had barely sampled. I took a couple of decent swigs and sat down to consider my position. To my amazement John Smith, B—'s servant, came up and said the captain requested my presence at dinner. This had happened before after we had disagreed over one matter or another and the meal had served to smooth our feathers, but after the insult and threats I had been offered on this occasion it was not to be endured.

'My compliments to the captain,' I said. 'But I regret that I cannot oblige him as I am indisposed.'

I heard later that the same invitation was issued to the other officers, all of whom refused except Hayward who must have been endeavouring to win his way back into the captain's favour after his punishment at Oparre. I found the circumstance so astonishing that

I fell into a kind of mad mood so that I scarcely knew what I was doing. I began to distribute the curios I had bought among my friends and went on deck where I shredded some of my papers and threw them overboard, along with my log. Encountering Purcell, the carpenter, I asked him if he would provide me with the means to make a raft as I intended to leave the ship. Of course I had no such intention and was, if not exactly joking, saying the wildest things I could think of in my distress.

George Stewart overheard and took me seriously. He pressed the pig I had ordered roasted for our mess upon me and offered to help me prepare myself for the desertion. Purcell offered some planks and nails and suggested I make use of the launch's masts. Whether he was joking or not I could not tell, so wild was my mood. The night was hot and the air below decks was stifling but I did not dare go topside, lest I encounter B— and do what I had threatened – drown him and myself.

I could not eat or sleep and I continued to drink brandy until it rose in my gorge. The heat and the liquor and the turmoil in my head brought phantasmagoric images to my mind. I saw the captain succeed in poisoning me, or ordering me to perform some hazardous duty and contriving my death, of bribing one of the men to throw me overboard or provoking me to strike him so that I would certainly be hanged on returning to England.

Returning to England was no longer a happy prospect. At the very least, the captain would find some charge to level against me which would bring disgrace or worse. With this thought in mind, Otaheite, and the love I had experienced there and the abundance and simplicity of life, as I then understood it, took hold of me.

A man who joins the navy knows that he has put his life at risk, daring the fury of the elements or war with his country's enemies. For that I was prepared. But this risk to my life was different. B—'s threat to cause us to jump overboard was made in a blustering passion and had no real force, but now I knew his secret and could not be permitted to live. His attempt on me and threats for the future were coldly made and deliberate, though his mind was disordered. I had no doubt he meant to kill me and had the means to do it.

Mutiny

WITH LESS THAN AN HOUR until my watch I lay sleepless in my bunk. I had a feeling of hopelessness such as I had never experienced before, even in my blackest moods. In those depths there had always been something to cling to, some glimmer of hope that eventually grew brighter and allowed me to emerge from the despair. Now I felt that my life was a worthless thing that could be snuffed out by a madman. And who might be next, should his madness take a hold? Peter Heywood, lumped together with me in B—'s mind as a Manxman? Or George Stewart, to whom I had drawn closer in recent days, as the captain's injustice impinged on us all? Or Ned Young with his fierce temper, tolerated by B— for his aristocratic connections but despised by him for his West Indian blood?

In the night both George and Ned had come to dissuade me of the desertion, an act I had never seriously entertained. As my head cleared I thought of telling George what I knew of B—'s disorder but to what avail? Nothing would change. Ledward would not consent to any move to constrain the captain on grounds of incapacity and for all I knew B— could have disposed of any evidence. He would certainly resist such an action with the full weight of his authority, which would tell on all but the most resolute of his enemies.

As my thoughts drifted in this direction I was acutely aware of the danger of these notions. Mutiny was a hanging offence in any navy in the world and brought shame and ignominy to its perpetrators.

I recalled my brother's fears about the consequences of those actions aboard the *Middlesex* which had tended in that direction. Mutiny at sea meant divorcement from all comfort and solace from society, but what other choice lay before me with an early death or certain disgrace in the offing? And, having endured the injustices and witnessed the cruelties I knew that the captain had a number of enemies within what he fancied as his little kingdom.

George Stewart, on pushing back my canvas screen to leave me in my turmoil, had said that the over-crowded, mis-aligned ship was a powder keg ready to blow. He whispered something like, 'Should you act, Christian, most would be with you.'

His words lit a fuse that was already prepared for lighting. I saw a way to save my life and that of others, to assert my manhood and reclaim my honour, at least in the eyes of those who had seen what injustice had been wreaked since this voyage had begun. I felt a surge of energy through my body as I resolved to take the fine ship from a man who was unfit to command her.

Normally, when going on watch, I would tidy myself and my clothing, put on a jacket and perhaps a hat, but I did nothing of that kind on this occasion and went on deck in my breeches and unfastened shirt with my hair loose about my shoulders. I cared nothing for my appearance, only for becoming master of my own fate. All appeared normal as I relieved Peckover and his watch and saw some of my men come on deck. There was no sign of the midshipmen Hayward and Hallet, absences not surprising. Both were notorious shirks, apt to sleep through half of the watch and near to useless anyway. Young Tom Ellison took the helm, an easy duty as the ship was scarcely moving. The spurting volcano on Tofua, to the west, was the only light showing as the moon had set and it lacked two hours or so until sunrise.

When all seemed quiet, I cut a length of rope with one of the leads attached and looped it around my neck. A lead weight at the end of rope makes a formidable weapon. I approached Quintal, who had been flogged, and Isaac Martin, who bore the captain no love.

'Matt,' I said, 'I plan to take the ship. I have Mr Stewart and Mr Young with me. We can endure the captain's madness no longer. Are you with us?'

Quintal answered immediately. 'Aye, Mr Christian, body and soul.'

'Martin?'

Martin was slower to reply. 'Who else, Mr Christian?'

I numbered them on my fingers. 'I feel sure of Charley Churchill and Will Coleman . . .' I swear I had not thought of it before but it came to me that Coleman had the keys to the arms chests, Fryer being sick of the responsibility. 'And Will can provide the arms.'

The mention of the weapons excited Quintal and seemed to decide Martin in favour of the scheme. 'Will McCoy is surely with us,' he said, 'and Matt Thompson and Alex Smith.'

'And Jack Williams, I'll warrant,' Quintal said.

I shook each of their hands and took comfort from their hard grips. 'That's enough. First, we seize the arms, then the captain and any who offer resistance. We arm ourselves to the teeth, lads, and make as much noise as possible when I give the word. Not a second before. Surprise is the thing. Not all will be with us, but I doubt many will die for the captain.'

'None,' said Quintal, 'and only milksops will speak for him.'

'There's to be no murder though,' I said. 'There's to be no more injustice aboard this ship.'

Martin inclined his head at Charles Norman, the carpenter's mate, who was staring at the sea. 'What of the loony?'

'Ignore him. He'll give no trouble.'

I despatched Quintal to rouse those he thought would be with us and to secure the keys to the arms chest. After a few minutes he came back on deck with the keys but also a problem.

'Mr Christian, Mr Hallett is asleep atop one of the arms chests and Mr Hayward on the other.'

I fancy I almost laughed, or perhaps I did. 'God damn them for useless fools. They should have been on watch an hour ago.'

'They have played into our hands by not being alert,' Quintal said and his statement was true, although he did not yet have the courage to act decisively against officers. Seeing that my authority was needed, I went below and shoved Hallett off the chest, which I opened with Coleman's keys. Hallett made no protests. By this time Burkett, Lamb and Thompson had appeared. We armed ourselves; I took a musket with a fixed bayonet, a pistol, a box of cartridges and a cutlass, an encumbrance I soon discarded. I ordered Thompson to stand guard over the chest and to arm those who were of our party and put the fear of God into any others.

On going to the other chest I found that Hayward had left it. I opened the chest, gave more weapons to Mills, McCoy and Churchill and re-locked it. Going on deck I found Sumner, Alex Smith and Hillbrandt all armed by Thompson and ready for action.

The ship was now partly astir with a chopping sound coming from the galley and Michael Byrn uttering his usual curses as he struggled in his blindness to dress himself. Without being sure of the numbers, and uncertain of the whereabouts of Ned Young and George Stewart, I felt that I now had a strong enough contingent to take the ship. At that point Hayward appeared and challenged me with a courage I would have credited him with.

'What is the cause of this act?'

'Hold your tongue,' I said, the first harsh words spoken since the mutiny began. Hayward then questioned Mills, who replied rudely and threatened him with a bayonet. Hallett appeared and I deputed Martin, who was fingering his pistol, to stand guard over the pair of them.

'We are taking the ship,' I said. 'And no man will receive a scratch who obeys our orders.'

Little Tom Ellison leapt forward, begged a bayonet from Mills, and flourished it in Hayward's face like a toy. I saw terror in Hallett's eyes and knew the reason. In the half-light the band of us, armed to the teeth and excited, must have looked like the most desperate set of pirates afloat. I put my finger to my lips, indicating that the time for noise was not yet, and, with Smith, Churchill, Quintal and Burkett, went through the hatch and down to where B—'s cabin was situated on the starboard side.

As I write, it surprises me how clearly everything comes to my mind. As my foot hit the bottom rung of the ladder I hesitated, but it was far too late to retreat. Conspiracy to mutiny is as much a hanging matter as mutiny itself, and there was no chance of turning my heavily armed comrades from their purpose. Besides, I did not want to change course. I was full of energy and resolve and felt as if the course I had set was the only one possible and no power on earth could move me from it.

We stepped inside B—'s cabin. He lay on his back, snoring. I took hold of his shoulder and shook him awake.

He threw off the cover and struggled to sit. 'What is the meaning of this violence?'

'Hold your tongue, Sir. We are taking the ship.'

There followed a fusillade of oaths from B—, and from the men.

'You mutinous bastards! You foul buggers!'

'Shut your mouth, you pig,' Mills said. 'Bugger you, Mr Bligh. Bugger you.'

Quintal called him a flogging bastard and a thief and the others did likewise. I pulled him from the bunk and he stood with his nightshirt flapping, a ridiculously small figure in his nightcap and bare feet, towered over by Martin and myself.

Suddenly B— yelled in his piping voice, 'Murder, murder!'

This brought a laugh and the men joined in shouting, 'Murder, murder, murder!' No need to give a signal for noise. The shouting could be heard from bow to stern and it was time to direct matters firmly lest the hot-heads carry things further than I intended.

'Secure Mr Fryer,' I directed Quintal and Sumner. 'Keep him below. We'll take the captain on deck and show him so that all may know how things stand.'

B— and I continued to stare at each other while Churchill shouted for rope to be handed down to secure the captain. This was done and Churchill tied his hands, catching the hem of his nightshirt in his haste so that B—'s pale bum was exposed, further robbing him of dignity.

The ship was in uproar with men shouting and jostling and only those of us who had acted knowing what we were about. John Fryer must have seen us pass by his cabin with B— under guard for he shouted, 'What are you doing with the captain?'

Sumner shoved him down on his bunk for I heard his head strike something hard. 'Damn his eyes. We'll put him in a boat,' Sumner said, 'and see how long he can live on ten ounces of yams a day.'

Fryer continued to shout his protests and Sumner yelled abuse at him but I paid it no heed as I herded the captain up on deck. The sun had risen and with no one at the helm the ship was wallowing with noisily flapping sails. I pushed B— along, holding the end of the rope as if he were a dog on a leash, until we reached the mizzen mast, whereupon I detached the bayonet from my musket and pointed it at his chest.

'God damn you, Christian, for a black mutinous bastard. I'll see you hanged and everyone you have infected with your poison . . .'

I attempted to silence him by placing the bayonet near his throat. With the shouting and the wind in the sails none could hear me as I hissed in his ear. 'Be silent, sir. You are not one to speak of poison.'

To give him his due, he spoke up bravely. 'By my honour, you are a dead man.'

That was too much. I shouted, 'You have no honour, sir. None. I have been in hell these past days! In hell!'

It was B—'s turn to hiss. 'I'll send you there, by God. One way or another.'

I jerked on the rope and put the bayonet to his chest, silencing him for the moment. Fryer was still shouting from below but some order was forming on deck as those who had taken up arms pushed those who had not into a group. I gave orders for Fryer to be allowed on deck as it was time to deal with him and the captain and sundry others in the same manner.

Now began what I look back on as a sort of country dance with B—, Fryer and myself all shouting, moving back and forward while Quintal, Burkett and others showed their weapons. I turned aside to order the small cutter or jolly boat lowered and men sprang to do my bidding. B— began shouting and swearing and and I eventually seized him by the shoulder and shouted in his face.

'*Mamoo! Mamoo!*'

The others took up the cry and shouted this word, Otaheitean for silence with a suggestion of threat, and the volume of it from so many stilled the tongues of Fryer and the captain. As that cry went up I knew in an instant what was in the hearts of my fellow mutineers and the same wish swelled up inside my breast – to return to Otaheite. It was a siren's call and could only be temporary, but I muttered the name and it was sweet to my ears. The sun climbed in the sky and the air grew warmer by the second. My gaze was still fixed on B— but I had a keen awareness of what was happening on deck. The cutter was being lowered and Peter Heywood was holding a musket. My heart leapt at the thought that he was with us but, strangely, I could see no sign of George Stewart or Ned Young, both of whom I had thought would be active and in support of my authority.

It is strange to consider how men act in times of danger and distress. Like Tom Hayward, who I would not have thought capable of courage, John Fryer showed bottom by ignoring my blade and speaking up.

'Mr Christian, consider what you are about. You and I have been friends on this voyage. Give me leave to speak. Let the captain return to his cabin and I have no doubt we will all be friends again in a short time.'

Bravely said, but nonsense, and one glance at B—'s face was enough to give it the lie. I burst into laughter, echoed by Mills and Burkett.

'Shut your lying mouth, sir,' I said. 'You have been no friend of mine since this villain made me second in command over you and failed to honour me in the post. And he would forgive and forget nothing. Not another sound or I swear you are a dead man. I have been in hell and this is my escape.'

Seeing my passion, Fryer changed his tack. Looking towards the davits he said, 'At least give the captain a chance. The cutter's bottom is worm-ridden, as you well know.'

'Aye,' I said, 'and good enough for him.'

Fryer then moved closer to B— and muttered something I could not hear. Their eyes drifted about the deck and I guessed they were considering the possibility of re-taking the ship. This was confirmed an instant later when B—, in a voice that was fast losing its little power, screamed, 'Knock Christian down! Knock Christian down!'

The only man to move was Fryer and, brave though he was showing himself to be, he was no threat. I swung the bayonet in his direction and he raised his hands in surrender.

'Take Mr Fryer below and keep him safe and silent,' I ordered. 'He has thoughts of re-taking the ship and every man here with a weapon in his hand knows what that would mean.'

Millward, who I had not realised was with us, and Quintal who was and showing unheralded qualities of calm and purpose, escorted Fryer away. 'Keep him in his cabin,' I instructed, 'away from the gardener and the clerk and the like for he fancies himself a plotter.'

I caught sight of Smith, B—'s servant, standing in the crowd near the quarter-deck and ordered him below to fetch drink for all men under arms and also the captain's clothes. Smith moved to obey me and, on passing B—, he pulled his nightshirt free of the rope so that his bum was covered. I saluted him for this kindly act.

Smith returned with several bottles and a tray with glasses and tin cups. Strong measures were poured and all who wished took a drink and then drank again, myself included. Smith helped B— pull on his trousers and shoes and draped his jacket over his shoulders. He accepted a glass but said nothing as he watched the last of the coconuts and yams being removed and the jolly boat lowered to the water.

'She's sinking, Mr Christian,' one of the men called.

'Bail her,' I ordered.

But it was no use. The boat's bottom was like a sieve and I gave orders for the large cutter to be lowered. It was a well-made craft and would give B— a fair chance of making land, but on looking about and making a rough head count I could see that, by their absence or attitude, a good number of the crew remained loyal to the captain. To hell with them, I thought, I can sail the ship with ten men if need be, but in practical terms the cutter would not suffice. I ordered the work on the cutter to cease and for the longer vessel, the launch, to be lowered. Cole spoke up for the launch but I had already decided on it although there were dissenters among the men who had sided with me.

Cries of, 'It's too good for him,' and 'He'll sail the damn thing to England,' were raised so that I feared for a moment that I might lose control. B— was encouraged and cast about for support but found none. There were evidently those willing to take their chances with him but not to go against their armed and aroused shipmates. I smiled to myself thinking how B— would castigate them for this on every league of their journey, however long or short it might be.

The appearance of Ned Young, armed with a musket with fixed bayonet, and the thought of being rid of B— once and for all and those willing to suffer him energised me. I gave orders for all who wished to get into the launch. Some obeyed immediately, stepping briskly down the gangplank, while others rushed below to collect belongings.

'Will you send me in no more than what I stand up in, Christian?' B— said.

I cut the rope tying his hands. 'I wonder what you would do in my place.'

'I'd throw you over the side with a cannon ball for company.'

'Just so. Well, I'll show you more mercy than you deserve.'

With his hands free he was able to pull on his jacket and no one offered to help him. For the moment he was quiet and apparently reconciled to his fate but still I kept a close watch on him. At the same time I had to watch the loading of the launch lest B—'s supporters take arms and mount a counter-attack or smuggle aboard other items we might need. Purcell, no lover of B— but evidently resolved to go with him, ordered McIntosh to load two saws and other personal items and then turned to me.

'I want my tool chest, Mr Christian.'

Churchill had the chest on deck for what reason I know not, perhaps to taunt the carpenter. 'On no account,' he shouted. 'The bugger could build them a boat to take them safe.'

I could see the sense of that but, as I saw good men enter the launch carrying their meagre belongings with fear in their eyes, I relented. It mattered not whether they made it safe to some port or not. Henceforth I knew that mutiny would be spelled with the name of the ship or perhaps with my own. As Fryer got into the launch along with Purcell I thought of the stories they would tell, if they survived, when B— was court-martialled for losing his ship. Humiliation enough, I reckoned.

I waved to Linkletter to lower the carpenter's chest but Churchill continued his protest and got down into the launch to retrieve the chest. He was encouraged by Quintal, who had abandoned his guard duty and was now considerably drunk.

'Damn them. They'll build a vessel in a month. Grab all you can, Charley.'

Churchill punched a man who had attempted to restrain him, opened the chest and tossed a number of tools up to Quintal to the cheers of those of our party.

There was no stopping the flow of goods into the launch and in any case my heart was not in it. A cask was lowered along with other provisions. Cole carried his compass with him and Quintal attempted to stop him.

'Damn you, what need have you of a compass when you're in sight of land?'

Cole said, 'You can spare one when there are nine more in store.'

Burkett laughed. 'Let it go, Matt. They can trade it for coconuts.'

In truth coconuts were being thrown into the launch along with other items like a grapnel and line and it was sinking ever lower. I was surprised to see Hayward come on deck with a bag and his flintlock. I gestured to Quintal, who wrenched the gun from him, causing Hayward to stagger.

'Damn you, you'll not have that.'

Samuel came on deck carrying bags and papers to be intercepted by Churchill, now very drunk, who snatched some of the things before allowing Samuel to board the launch. B—'s eyes rested on his clerk and the things he had managed to retain and I could guess at what he was thinking – how could he face the tribulations ahead without the drug? And there was nothing he could do to obtain it.

Things were approaching the end. The launch was near full to overflowing with men and materials and there were yet more to board her. Isaac Martin, in a change of heart, dropped down into the launch and was immediately repelled by Purcell.

'If ever we get to England I'll hang you myself.'

Quintal and Churchill looked at me and I gave them an order to train their muskets at Martin and order him back aboard the ship.

That left Cole, Fryer, Hayward, Hallet and the captain and perhaps others. With so much to keep watch on I was losing count. The launch could not take many more. I ordered Hallet and Hayward, who was now in tears, to go down the gangplank. And saw Nelson and Peckover hurry to join them. Fryer's courage had finally deserted him on seeing the condition of the launch and he begged to be allowed to stay. It was almost funny. Those in the launch obviously did not want him and neither did I for he was a disagreeable complaining fellow.

'We can do very well without you, Mr Fryer,' I said.

B— looked at me and I could see that here was our last clash of wills. 'You are to remain on board, Mr Fryer,' he said in a voice that had recovered some of its strength.

I put the bayonet to the master's chest while Ned kept his eye on the captain. 'Board, or I'll run you through.'

That settled it. Fryer entered the launch with a bowed head. Only B— remained, and I wondered if his nerve would hold now that he could see there was no hope of his authority being restored. I hurried him to the head of the gangplank, where he stopped and turned, as if to cast a last look at the ship he had lost.

'Come, captain,' I said as gently as I could, 'your party is in the launch and you must join them.'

B— stood stock still.

'If you resist it's your death, sir.'

'Consider what you are about, Mr Christian. For God's sake, drop it. I'll give my bond never to think of it again.'

I smiled at that, a complete lie, and said nothing.

'I have a wife and children in England and you have danced my children on your knee.'

'Aye, many of us have family in England and you have so arranged matters that we will never see them again.'

'I?'

'You, sir. Damn you to hell where I have been these many days.'

I saw in his eyes and the droop of his head that he knew my meaning. 'Can there be no other method?'

'None.'

Cole stepped up the plank towards the ship and said something in support of B—'s plea but I waved him down. B— caught sight of Ned Young. 'This is a serious matter, Mr Young.'

'Yes, sir. Starvation is serious. I wonder how your fat belly will tolerate it.'

B— shook his head as if to throw off the insult and the accusation. As we gazed down into the launch I fancy we were suddenly of one mind, though for different reasons.

Coleman, the armourer, and McIntosh and Norman, the carpenter's mates, were useful men I could not spare and I ordered them out of the boat. B— confirmed the order in a confident voice as though he were still in command.

'Don't overload her. Some of you must stay on the ship.'

The three reluctantly came back up the gangplank and we prevented others from taking their place.

'Do you consider this treatment a proper return for the favour I have shown you in the past?' B— said.

'That is a long gone past, sir, and you have swept it away by your own actions. Board!'

B— walked down the plank with much dignity and took up a position amid the chaos in the launch, bumping alongside the ship, secured by a line in a rising swell. Someone threw chunks of salt pork down but some fell in the water. I ordered Mills to fetch my sextant, which he did and I directed him to take it down to the launch.

'There,' I said to B—. 'That is sufficient for your purpose. You know it to be a good one.'

He gave no acknowledgment and busied himself trying to bring order to the launch. His kingdom had shrunk but he was its ruler still. Churchill lowered a set of cutlasses to the launch but Cole's request for muskets brought a roar of laughter.

McCoy levelled his musket at the captain. 'For two pins I'd blow your bloody brains out, but you ain't worth the powder.'

The sun had now been up for over three hours and it was very hot. Sweat streamed down my body and ran into my eyes from my hair. My vision blurred and I saw and directed the rest of the action as if through a screen. Skinner, who was very drunk, levelled his musket at the launch and appeared about to fire, so I cuffed him and wrested the gun away. I ordered Cole to cut the line. The launch's oars were shipped and the two vessels began to part company.

All was noise and confusion on deck with bottles being lifted and men scuffling with each other, some seriously, some not. I heard Byrn weeping but could not determine what he said. Something about his blindness no doubt. Coleman shouted for all to bear witness that he took no part in the mutiny. Quite true. Through it all the words of Jem Morrison stuck in my mind and I can hear them to this day – If anyone asks for me, tell them I am somewhere south of the line.'

I wonder sometimes what has happened to him.

And through all the sound and fury I heard, faintly but clearly, the last words I would ever hear from the captain. 'Never fear, my lads, I'll do you justice if ever I reach England.'

Morrison was standing not far off. 'What does he mean by that?'

The launch was now moving quickly away from us. 'You know bloody well what he means, Jem,' I said.

Huzza for Otaheite

I COULD HAVE EMBRACED THE men who cried, 'Huzza for Otaheite' as the launch moved swiftly away with six men at the oars while we were almost becalmed. I ordered Tom Ellison to loose the topgallant to get us underway and instructed the helmsman, whose name I forget, to steer west-nor'-west. Some might think I paid no heed to the call, but I guessed that B— would believe that a set of tattooed rebels, crying out in a heathen tongue, would have no thought but to return to the land of plenty and such was not my intention.

At that moment, seeing in the distance that the launch was now masted with a sail hoisted since she was out of reach of our guns, I had a feeling that the captain would survive the ordeal before him. Was I glad or sorry? So much has happened since that I hardly know. His kindnesses had been many but none had been so great as his cruelties.

As we caught a slight breeze and began to move, I surveyed the decks where the crew milled about in confusion, some drunk, some sober, some hostile, some resigned. It would be a formidable task to control them but I was filled with a kind of exhilaration – a feeling that this had been my destiny since first I went to sea. This feeling was bolstered by a thought that made me proud. There had been many mutinies in the army and navy, but had any been conducted without a single shot fired, a single drop of blood shed or a serious blow being struck? I doubted it. Whatever might be said in the future about our mutiny, no murder was done. I resolved to conduct myself and manage matters so that this would continue to be true, whatever hazards we might encounter.

I found myself strangely calm although in truth the condition of all aboard *Bounty* was perilous. Quintal, Burkett, McCoy and Sumner were drunk and possibly anxious to settle old scores with some of the officers. Many of the company were unwilling to be there and would have taken their chances with B— and the others if there had been space in the launch or if I had not had need of them. Glancing around, I saw that Ned Young was resolute and calm.

'We did what was necessary,' he said to a group around him, 'and will continue to do so, as free men.' George Stewart seemed meditative, deep in conversation with Morrison. The drunkards were rowdy, brandishing their weapons and bullying those who they saw as enemies. I had to find a way to direct their energies.

I thrust my bayonet in the air and then drove it deep into the mast. 'To the great cabin, lads,' I shouted, 'and let's be done with his bloody floating garden.'

There was a roar of approval and a rush to get below to the cabin. The ship was still scarcely moving and needed little attention, the light breeze and current keeping her safe from any drift towards Tofua. I followed the crowd to the great cabin. There we found Will Brown assisting McCoy in opening the window and throwing the pots of sprouting breadfruit into the sea. I threw a few myself to show willing and then drew Brown aside as the throwing and shouting rose to a crescendo.

'I did not see you under arms, Brown,' I said. 'Whence this show of support?'

'I'm with you all the way, Fletcher.'

I was surprised at his use of my first name, but I knew that he had been in the navy before becoming a landsman and had served as a midshipman and been under enemy fire – a scarred cheek and drooping eyelid were the legacy of his service.

I was cautious, aware that there were some aboard who might harbour notions of re-taking the ship and rescuing the captain. 'I welcome that,' I said. 'But also would welcome an explanation.'

Brown sighed and moved a few pots to the cover of a sheet of canvas. 'We may have need of these, unpalatable though I find the stuff to be.'

I laughed. 'I'm with you there. I doubt that the slaves for whom it was intended would take to it unless under the whip.'

Brown nodded. 'You know I served in the navy before this. I never met a man less fitted to command a ship than the one you have set adrift. I think some madness must have entered into him when we failed to round the Horn. I've seen it before – men turned to monsters by being unable to carry through their designs.'

'Just so,' I said.

Brown let out a cheer as Quintal heaved one of the biggest pots through the window. 'Besides, I've had enough of the sea and there's nothing awaiting me in England but a shrewish wife and a hard life. I fancy, Fletcher, that we'll fetch up on an island somewhere with native women and the chance to grow things the like of which frost-plagued English gardens have never seen.'

'I hope so,' I said. 'I hope we all have a mind to enjoy freedom for the rest of our days. We have a chance here to be . . . equal.'

'I had not taken you for a republican.'

'Nor am I. The story in my family is that a good many of us were Clubmen – those who kept King and Cromwell at bay in the civil war.'

'I'd not heard of them, but I fancy I might well have been of their party.'

We clasped hands; there was no more to be said, but Brown's honest and straightforward support greatly encouraged me for the tasks that lay ahead. I celebrated by drawing the cork from a bottle I had picked up on my way, spitting it through an open port and taking a drink. I handed the bottle to Brown and joined in the riotous jettisoning of B—'s precious plants.

I now faced a dilemma. As the one responsible for the mutiny, I felt it my duty, as well as my fate, to take command of the ship, but I did not wish to begin by imposing my authority arbitrarily. When George Stewart and Matt Quinlan approached requesting me to take command, I took a risk.

'I have no right to command you,' I said, 'and I will act in any station I am assigned to.'

A heated discussion broke out in which all of those who had acted with me took part. The result was that they unanimously voted for me to become captain. I agreed and gave as my first order the tidying of the decks.

'What about the dancing, Mr Christian?' McCoy, who had hated it more than most, asked.

'Anyone who wishes to dance may do so and welcome, but no man will be compelled.'

This brought a cheer and they set about their work with a will. I drew Stewart aside. 'I know you had no active part in the affair, George, but now that it's done you'll agree order must be maintained.'

Stewart nodded.

'I propose to make you second in command and I suggest you go armed at all times because we still have fellows aboard who may have ideas.'

'I accept, Fletcher, but I would know your plans.'

'To find an island where we may be safe. The Navy will search the seven seas for us and the captain, if he survives, will damn us all.'

'Except those you took from the launch and Coleman.'

'His memory may fail him.'

'You hate him.'

'Yes, and pity him.'

'Why?'

'I can't tell you. Perhaps when we are safe. Now I'm going to look at the charts and find our haven.'

'The men expect to go back to their *taios* and women on Otaheite.'

'They are to be disappointed then. Another reason for us to be on guard.'

I went down the hatch to B—'s cabin which I intended to make my own, and found Peter Heywood seated there, staring dumbly at the chaos Samuel had left behind on securing as many of the captain's possessions as he could muster. I leaned on the edge of the table looking down at him. He had conducted himself well in the business of the ship and had behaved in a manly fashion on the island, if a trifle too enthusiastic in the matter of being tattooed. I knew that he had compiled an extensive Otaheitean dictionary and I was sure I had glimpsed him on deck at some point carrying a musket.

When he lifted his head to look at me, I saw at once that I had been wrong in imagining him to be a supporter.

'How could you do it, Fletcher?'

'How can you ask?' I said. 'The man was . . .'

'Our captain, duly commissioned by the Admiralty, and therefore by the Crown.'

It was a sharp-edged moment, not only between the two of us, but to do with my position in the world. I felt myself to be a true Englishman in many ways. Had the French or Spaniards or any other foreigners invaded our island, attacked our shores, I would have gladly given my life in the defence of my country. And yet, there was a side of me that leaned towards those Norse ancestors, those raiders and conquerors who defied authority and carved out territories of their own.

'He forfeited his commission, Peter.'

'It is not for you to say.'

'Those who have the power to say support only those who exercise it in their name.'

'You sound like . . . I cannot put a name to it.'

'Don't bother. Mutineer will do.'

'God help you, Christian.'

I laughed. 'Nothing from that quarter I fear, for me or anyone else. What am I to do with you, Peter? We have been friends, and you know that the captain will deem you a rebel on that account alone.'

'I know. It partly accounts for my despair.'

'Do not believers count that the ultimate sin?'

'Fletcher!'

'I rejected it all long ago. Give me your parole that you will not offer armed resistance, and I will do all in my power to leave you so that you will bear no blame for this.'

Peter shrugged and the action reminded me how young he was, barely seventeen, I thought, and already having experienced more than he should for those few years. I hoped we might shake hands, but he rose abruptly from the chair, brushed past me, and left the cabin.

Some of B—'s charts had been taken by Samuel, but many remained. From force of habit I wiped my hands before unfurling them. When under pressure my hands tend to sweat, and I always keep a rag or handkerchief nearby to dry them. I sorted through the rolls, precisely numbered and labelled, and spread the ones I wanted on the table. The whole of this part of the Pacific Ocean lay before me as I took up the instruments that would help guide us to safety.

My eyes were aching by the time I had poured over the charts and books B— had unwillingly provided. Many of the Admiralty charts were annotated and altered in his own hand, and passages in the published works of Cook and others were underlined and commented on in the margins. I was looking for an island that could support life but was not likely to be visited by the ever-increasing traffic of ships into the Pacific. It should have a harbour but one that was difficult of access. Toobouai, some three hundred miles south of Otaheite seemed to be the place. It had been noted by Cook but not approvingly, and so far as I knew was unvisited as yet by white people.

I made my measurements and calculations and estimated how long it would take us to make the passage. This done, I called the crew together and announced our destination.

'You think you can find it, Fletcher?' Ned Young said.

I then made a foolish boast. 'I'll give you a date and time and wager a bottle of best wine that I'm within an hour of when I say.'

'I'll take that wager, Christian,' Coleman said.

'Where will you get a bottle of wine?' Young asked.

'I won't need one,' Coleman said, turning on his heel.

As I worked on the charts I had been thinking about leadership and the difficulties of bending men to one's will. I decided that it was a matter of fair treatment at all times and judicious rewards when appropriate. With a few others muttering support for Coleman, I ordered the goods of all those who had gone in the launch, with the exception of B—, to be divided into lots which would be drawn for by all on board. This was greeted by cheers from some and met with no opposition. Within an hour, with our course set and the ship moving under a fair wind, twenty-five piles, including sea chests, clothes, books, weapons and island curios were arranged in lots in the great cabin where the plants had been and the process began. No man stood aside.

Still, although each was now implicated in what had happened, I did not delude myself that all were prepared to spend the rest of their lives as hunted men. For some of us, that was our fate; for the others no man knew what was in their heads and hearts. It shames me to say that I employed one of the tricks B— himself had used – I set Ned Young and Tom Ellison, popular with all aboard, the task of keeping their ears open and reporting loose talk.

With the plants reduced to a few, and the watering system and pot-holding benches dismantled, I now had the great cabin in the state it was meant to be. I spent many hours there on the long run to Toobouai, and one of the first things I did was search through B—'s goods for his log or any notes he may have made on the course of his ill-fated voyage. I found nothing. I would have dearly loved to see his lies and misconstructions, but Samuel had done well by his master and removed everything of that nature.

But something damning remained of which neither the captain's clerk nor his servant could have had any knowledge. Secreted in a compartment of one of his lockers were several packets of arsenic and a set of scales that still bore traces of the deadly powder. I stared at these things for a long time, troubled in my mind as what use to make of them. I now faced a new problem. If I showed the arsenic to such as Young or Stewart I could be forced to confess that I knew of the captain's indulgence before the mutiny. What remonstrances might they justly offer? How might they reproach me for not revealing what I knew and dealing with the matter in another way? Of no avail to tell them of my turbulence of mind.

Once more, there was no one I could talk to of this and no escape again from the necessity of concealment. The night after I made this discovery I lay sleepless in the bunk where we had surprised the captain and wrestled with the matter. I came to wonder how and why he had resorted to arsenic-eating and, in my distress, I admit that I came close to trying the physick myself as a means of relieving an agony of mind. B—, I knew, had been subject to headaches and trembling of the limbs, since the time when we had sailed in the West

Indian trade. Always passionate and intemperate of speech, might he have resorted to the drug as a palliative for his headaches and the strain of keeping his outbursts of temper and insulting language under control? I wished I had Charles present to tell me of the effects of using arsenic, although I suspected that I knew what a doctor's manual might say – prolonged use likely to cause increase in doses taken and erratic movement of moods and humours.

I rose from the bunk, gathered the powder packets and scales and opened one of the portholes through which we had thrown the bread-fruit. Feeling like a thief in the night, I craned my head out to ensure there were no witnesses, and flung the stuff into the sea.

'Let the fishes swallow it and die,' I muttered. 'It'll do no more harm to good men.'

Still uneasy in my mind, I lit a candle and settled at the table to make a list of those aboard the ship and their disposition as far as I knew it. I found myself able to see in my mind's eye a great deal of the action which had swirled around me in the morning. This was a facility I had long had, although it was by no means perfect – to single out bits and pieces of events and record them accurately. It has been much in demand in the writing of this journal. I drew out a sheet of the captain's paper, sharpened one of his quills and dipped it deep, divided the page and made my list. Although the sheet has been lost I can recall it exactly:

Rebels:

Self	Matt Thompson
Ned Young	Will McCoy
Matt Quintal	Will Muspratt
Charley Churchill	Alex Smith
Tom Burkett	Bob Lamb
Jack Sumner	Jack Millward
	Will Brown

Doubtful:	Opposed:
Tom Ellison	Peter Heywood
Zac Martin	James Morrison
Henry Hillbrandt	Joseph Coleman
Dick Skinner	Charles Norman
George Stewart	Thomas McIntosh
Jack Williams	

I omitted Byrn, the fiddler, from the list, as a man, due to his blindness unable to take part in any action, poor soul. I had heard him during the mutiny weeping, but most probably for himself. He was a disagreeable creature and all parties, I am sure, would have been pleased to be rid of him.

Surveying my list, I was by no means sure it was accurate and events were to prove that I was wrong in a number of instances. Still, it gave me encouragement to think that those I reckoned to have crossed the mutiny line with me out-numbered all the others, though not by as much as I would have wished. It grieved me to assign George Stewart to the 'Doubtful' category and Peter Heywood to those opposed, but such was my inclination. It served to plant in my mind the notion that, whatever might transpire, it could be necessary to maroon some of our number somewhere, lest the hot-heads among us, such as Thompson and Quintal, thought to deal with them more severely.

About George Stewart I remained unsure. He had made some encouraging remarks to me before the mutiny yet had not taken an active part. Indeed he seemed determined to be absent while the matter was in the balance and for a time afterwards. I had need of him and, as described, thought to bond him to me by making him my deputy, and at times he seemed to embrace the role whole-heartedly and was helpful.

With a course and watches set, I found my mind filled with

thoughts of Mautaua. I had abandoned her once and was about to do so again. In a mood of pessimism, I thought that for this I must surely be punished. For the mutiny, I felt sorrow but no regret. For the future, no certainty.

'Fletcher, a word,' Stewart said from the lower deck on the morning following my restless and troubled night.

I was on the quarterdeck, approving of all I saw: the ship in good order and men at their posts, although fewer than was strictly required. Millward and Muspratt had provided breakfasts and Tom Ellison had assigned himself to me and seen that I had bread and hot rum against the slight morning chill, as I had been on deck since dawn. We were moving well under a favourable breeze. I gestured for George to join me.

'A fair morning,' I said.

'Aye. Fair enough. How did you sleep?'

I made no reply. It occurred to me that we were both armed with pistols. Was this a moment for Stewart to shoot me and take the ship? But his manner was friendly enough and he seemed not to notice that I had not replied.

'I've a thick head from yesterday's drink,' he said. 'You've definitely decided on Toobouai for our base?'

Again, I wondered what he meant. Base seemed a strange word to use, suggesting a point from which to come and go. Surely he had no thought of us becoming pirates, in the manner of those on the Spanish Main, raiding and retreating to a fortified harbour? I laughed aloud at the thought – there were no prizes to be taken in the Pacific.

'What?' he said, puzzled.

'Nothing. Yes, Toobouai.'

'What is known of its natives?'

'Little. Cook did not land or linger long but made a detailed chart which is printed in his journal. I could show you the book if you've a mind to see it. Canoes put out but he deemed them hostile. Why d'you ask?'

'I might take a look later. It sounds well. I wonder you don't want to return to your woman.

'I do, but Otaheite would be a death trap and I trust that all aboard know it. Cook wore out his welcome in the Sandwich Islands and we might well do the same, although the greatest threat is from the bloody Navy.'

He nodded and said no more.

Toobouai was sighted exactly one month after the mutiny. I consulted the glass and called Coleman to attend me with the piece of paper on which I had written my prediction. 'There is the island, Coleman, and here is the date and the glass. I bid you compare them.'

He did so and looked at me with a grudging respect. 'You're within an hour as you said. That's remarkable. I'm sorry. I can't pay the debt.'

I put my arm around his shoulder. 'No matter. It was a foolish boast and I had luck on my side. Had we encountered a storm or the breeze failed I'd be paying you.'

'Still, you have remarkable talents as a navigator.'

I opened a bottle of wine and bade him sit and share it with me. 'I had a great teacher. The captain, in the days before he . . . in days gone by he instructed me well. He was of great use to Cook. I doubt that Cook could have achieved what he did without him and I certainly could not.'

I showed him some of the annotated charts and books and he nodded. 'Word will spread about your achievement, Christian, and all will hail you as a great navigator. You have the devil's own luck.'

His words, loaded with sarcasm, brought on a feeling of gloom and I made no response.

'Great navigator that he be, can the captain take the launch to safety?'

'Probably,' I said. 'Probably at the sacrifice of half of his party.'

Coleman had drunk a glass but refused another when I pushed the bottle towards him. 'Do you regret the action that has put you in charge of this parcel of rascals and wretches, Christian?'

'No, damn you. I had no choice.'

'That is an interesting philosophy. I'll take my leave and tell everyone you took us three hundred miles to a point a mere half hour from your estimate, but I leave you with this – Quintal, Skinner, Smith, Thompson, Burkett and perhaps others have one object in mind.'

'And what is that, pray?'

'As you must know – the securing of women, and unless they succeed, you must look to the safety of Ellison, Mr Heywood and anyone else young and not too ill-favoured.'

He left and one of my black moods descended hard upon me. There were no buggers by choice aboard *Bounty* so far as I knew, but on long voyages buggery was common and something to be avoided now in the case of men who had already cast some constraints aside. There must certainly be women on Toobouai, and if our experience so far held true, they could assuage our men's lusts. Still, the thought of it was not uplifting, and as we sought the passage to the island, I found myself fighting phantasms of Isabella and Mauatua meeting and quarrelling over me. I write this not to excuse what happened but to help to explain it to my children who share the blood of those unfortunate people – the islanders all apparently deriving from the same stock – and others who may deem me a devil. I will make this clear.

We entered the sheltered harbour with difficulty, coping with currents and reefs, and I had to rage and threaten to ensure our safe passage. I thought I had all liquor aboard safely under lock and key but I must have been wrong because more than one man was drunk or near to it. We anchored and scores of canoes put out from the beach, each with a couple of natives aboard and most carrying a conch shell blower – a noise most unharmonious and unpleasant to the ear. Soon dozens of natives had swarmed aboard the ship and were busy stealing and trading, for many of the crew were willing to part with the things they had acquired from those who had gone in the launch in return for yams, coconuts and curios.

Enough of our men could make themselves understood in the native language to offer goods in the return for favours from women, not as yet sighted. It did not take Peter Heywood or George Stewart to tell me that many such contracts were entered into. After a time, I decided that this initial contact was enough and I ordered all the natives from the ship. This was only accomplished by means of severe looks, shoving and threats, some of which I administered myself. It was not a happy beginning to our Toobouai enterprise.

I spent another sleepless night considering whether Toobouai was the right place for us or not. Such was my dark mood that I decided firmly that subjugation of the native population was the only method promising success. Only strength could prevail against their superiority in numbers, their guile, and their likely apprehension that white people were creatures to be wary of but exploited nonetheless.

The next morning I saw Quintal leaning over the rail looking, eagerly in the direction of the beach.

'Expecting something, Matt?' I asked.

'Aye, Mr Christian. Women.'

His tongue was practically hanging out and I pitied the lass who offered him any resistance. I moved away and was joined at the rail by Ned Young and George Stewart.

'It's a fair enough island,' Ned said, 'And well off the charted routes.'

'The Pacific routes are not much charted yet I believe,' George said, 'but they will be. Our energetic people will hunt whales here and other things.'

'Such as?' Ned said.

George shrugged. 'Whatever's of value.'

Ned laughed. 'Like breadfruit.'

I pointed. 'There they are.'

'Jesus, it's like a floating knocking shop,' George said.

A group of canoes was churning up the calm waters. Each had two men at the paddles and four or five women aboard, who were naked apart from a bark cloth around their loins and flowers in their hair and around their necks. Their bodies were oiled and they all had lustrous hair hanging to their waists, partly concealing their breasts. They stood with perfect balance in the canoes as they neared the ship and the movements they made left no doubt as to what they were expecting. Although I read enough in B—'s books to be aware that this arrival could be a prelude to an attack, I was still aroused by the sight of the women – no normal man could fail to be. At least, I thought, it will turn thoughts from boy's bums. I had orders to give and I hurried to give them to the men I had confided in.

Once on board, many of the women, advised by their male escorts, made straight for those who had contracted to have them, and before long they were coupling on deck and below. The native men not busy negotiating the sale of their women were moving around the ship looking for things to steal. They found little as I had given orders for all loose items to be stowed away. These men carried no weapons of any kind, only serving to confirm my suspicions.

The attack came suddenly. As many as fifty war canoes, manned by expert paddlers, came surging towards the ship with the conch shells hooting, the warriors shouting and crashing spear shafts against the sides of the canoes.

Had they been allowed to board they would certainly have overrun us, even given our superior power of weaponry. In that event who knows how many might have been killed on both sides? As the canoes drew nearer I checked with the gunners.

'All loaded, lads? Grapeshot?'

'Aye, Mr Christian,' came the word from those manning all four of the short four-pound guns.

'Wait until they're in killing range and your aim is straight down. I'll give the order.'

When I called 'Fire!' the guns blasted down into those of the heavily laden canoes that were closest. The boom was followed by screams from the warriors and cries from those women still aboard the ship and the men accompanying them. One volley was enough. The natives on board leapt into the water and swam towards the canoes that had immediately turned away and were making for the beach. Through the smoke I saw many islanders wounded but had no idea of the casualties until later when it was reported that more than a dozen had died and at least three times that number were wounded. Our only casualty was Burkett, who had been wounded by a well-thrown spear.

Coleman stared at me in horror. 'You villain,' he said.

'What would you have me do? Allow them to kill us all and take the ship?'

He muttered something I did not catch and turned away. Peter Heywood, who had lately emerged from the sulks and was again taking a lively interest in happenings, stood beside me near the guns, peering through the ports.

'Was that necessary, Fletcher?'

I was tired of being questioned and rounded on him fiercely. 'I've been merciful,' I said. 'Think what the ten swivel guns could have done.'

I named the anchorage Bloody Bay on a chart I was making and took an armed party ashore to look the place over. I had to be careful in the selection of the men I took, and made sure I left enough rebels aboard to hold the ship secure. Despite the hostility the natives had shown I still had hopes of the island. It was theirs to defend, as I saw it, and no blame attached to them for doing so. History abounds in examples of the conquered and conquerors living together in peace after a time.

Most of the natives had fled inland but, to judge from the size of the villages and gardens, Toobouai did not appear to be over-populated. Fruit grew in abundance and there was plenty of land available for cultivation, although there was no livestock.

Quintal and Smith were complaining as we made our way back to the boat. 'I don't want to work like a nigger,' Quintal said. 'I want some niggers to work for me.'

'I doubt we'll soon persuade any of those women to join us again,' Smith said. 'We've put the fear of God into them. I wish . . .'

'What d'you wish, Alex?' I asked.

'I wish I had my woman from Otaheite, Mr Christian, and I wonder you do not wish the same.'

I heard a muttered agreement from others in the party and resolved to hold a meeting when we returned to the ship. A lone canoe drifted about a hundred yards from the ship. Quintal stood, levelled his musket and fired, the shot falling wide and short.

'You fool, Matt,' Brown said, 'there might have been a sweet piece ready to open her legs for a nail.'

Quintal snarled, 'About the size of your prick, gardener,' and aimed a blow which I deflected.

'Easy lads. We'll thrash everything out over a few tots when we're aboard.'

Martin and Muspratt had caught a great many fish while we were ashore and, with the yams and fruit we had traded the day before, all aboard enjoyed a meal the like of which we had had not had since leaving Otaheite. I summoned a meeting on the after deck which was attended by all except Coleman, Byrn, Hillbrandt, Millward, and to my great regret, Peter Heywood. Given the size of the vessel they could well still have heard everything that was said.

I began by pouring tots of rum all round, releasing the bottles, and then inviting anyone who wanted to speak to give an opinion of the island. Quintal and Smith voiced their objections as before. A number of those who had not been on shore spoke but they were divided on the crucial question – the women.

'They were a comely lot that first came out,' Jack Williams said. 'The one I took below knew what to do.'

A few added a similar appreciation of the charms of the women, but McCoy swilled down his drink and rapped the tin cup on his knuckles to gain the attention of the meeting. 'I didn't want to allow it but I didn't tup the one I took.'

'Why not, Will?' Williams said. 'Was she too much for you?'

For an answer McCoy lifted his shirt to show a scabbed wound running from his ribs to his navel. 'She did this to me with a shell knife and I kicked her arse for her.'

Williams scoffed. 'Only because you're so ugly.'

But others joined in and admitted that the women had bit and scratched them.

McCoy asked for more rum and I poured him a measure. 'There's our problem, Mr Christian. We'll never see England and our wives and sweethearts again, nor even the waterside doxies, and men cannot live without women.'

Brown lifted his hand to gain my attention and although others howled him down I quelled them with frowns and fierce looks so that he might speak.

'I never saw a better place for the cultivation of gardens and fields. We could grow there any food a man might wish.'

'Except tobacco,' said George Stewart who, like Ned Young and despite their weak lungs, was over fond of his pipe.

Brown smiled. 'Not so, Mr Stewart. I have with me a supply of tobacco seed, as I was curious to see if the islands might provide what now must come from the east or America. I am confident tobacco can be grown on Toobouai.'

Churchill spoke up, 'And drink made from the fruit.'

The meeting then lost form as the rum was poured and the various points pro and con were debated, with no result. Making no contribution but listening hard, I perceived that the question of women weighed most heavily with the majority and that few of the company, George Stewart and Churchill aside, had given much thought to our security. I let the wrangling continue for a time and then called the meeting to order, no easy matter, for I had no experience in such things and the men were unused to being consulted about decisions. Obeying orders had hitherto been their lot in life.

When the mutterings had subsided and I was able to be heard, I looked around and tried to catch the eye of each and every man. 'You elected me your leader,' I said, 'and right proud I am of the honour. But I called this meeting that it might be clear I want nothing to do with the kind of leadership we have endured in the past. So I have listened to what has been said on one side and another, and learned something from all who have spoken. We are desperate men in a desperate condition, and our decisions will determine whether our lives are long and happy or short and sad. I wish for the first.'

This brought a quiet cheer. I had their attention.

'My concern, as your leader, is above all for your safety. Just as Will Brown has said that Toobouai will grow all we need, I say that it is easily defended. I have no doubt we will be hunted through this ocean. A needle in a haystack we may well be, but the day could come when a ship discovers us and if it should be here we can fight. We have an ample supply of powder and shot. I have no personal experience of land warfare but I have read about it, and I never learned of a better site for a stout fort than here on Toobouai Island.'

They fell silent and then a voice was raised, slightly furred by drink. 'What about the women, Mr Christian?'

'We will fetch them from Otaheite.'

The cheer that rang out must have been heard all over the ship and out across the bay.

Toobouai

WE SAILED THE NEXT DAY for Otaheite and reached Matavai Bay a little over a week later. As before, the canoes came out to meet us and the customary exchange of greetings and goods took place. When Tynah asked about B— I told him we had encountered another larger vessel at sea and that the captain had transferred the breadfruit to it and sailed on with a part of the original crew to complete his mission. This was believed and I added that B— would certainly return to Otaheite with more gifts and that meanwhile it was our task to acquire supplies to enable us to establish settlements in other places at a distance. The chief seemed pleased with this prospect and agreed to trade with us for whatever we should need.

I allowed no man to go ashore and enlisted the certain rebels to keep a close watch lest any should try to desert. I wanted our Toobouai destination to remain unknown to all for sooner or later an English ship would come to Otaheite in search of HMS *Bounty*. The trade went well and in a very short time we had a goodly number of live pigs, goats and chickens and also the bull and cow left by Cook ten years before. I assured Tynah that B— himself would look after the bull.

'I will take any who wish to go with us,' I said. 'They will have a place of honour in our new home.'

At this the chief looked less pleased and I learned that he gave orders that none were to go with the exception of Mauatua and the women of Smith, McIntosh and Quintal, whom they had named Jenny, Mary and Sarah. Mauatua and I had a joyful and I may say tearful reunion. I took her below to the cabin and we enjoyed a bout of love-making so fierce we threatened to do each other an injury.

I well knew, however, that the number of women secured was far short of what was required and voiced my concern to George Stewart.

'I fancy we will find women on Toobouai in time,' I said. 'But randy men lack patience.'

'Aye, I have tried to persuade several women to join us but with no luck. I wish I had won a heart as you did on our previous visit here.'

'There's nothing else for it but to take some against their will or without their knowledge.'

'Some of the natives will help, given the right rewards. But it will blacken our name here for ever after.'

I shrugged. 'Our names will not be heard here again.'

At that I was wrong, but we sailed from Matavai Bay ten days after our arrival with eight Otaheitean women aboard as well as some men and boys. These people had been kept occupied by allowing them to try on pieces of clothing and to attempt to eat with spoons while the anchors were hoisted and we made way.

'God, they make a noise,' Quintal said on hearing the howls from the natives when they realised what had happened.

'So would you had you been stolen from your home.'

'Not I, Mr Christian. I'd have been glad to go from that bloody hell hole. Hulloa, who's this?'

A native had emerged from somewhere and I recognised him as Hitihiti, of Bora Bora, who had travelled far and wide among the islands with Cook. He greeted me with a cheeky grin. 'Good morning, captain.'

'You devil. Don't you know we throw stowaways overboard?'

196

His grin widened and he flexed the muscles in his wiry arms. 'Not when one can work ship.'

I had a conversation with my Isabella, as I called Mauatua henceforth, on the matter of the stolen women.

'They will be honoured to be taken by white men,' she assured me. 'And will make good wives and mothers.'

Their only fear would be of the natives on Toobouai where I told her we were going. 'Are they fierce?' she asked.

I told her they were but that we had beaten them once and would do so again if necessary. 'Then we will make arrangements with the chiefs to have some of the men work for us and so we will have a good life.'

She accepted this as normal, it being the practice of Otaheiteans to enslave their enemies. Whether she believed my story about what had happened to the captain and the missing crew I know not, but she asked no questions as we lay together as man and wife in the now spacious cabin. It was passing strange to sleep with her in a bed and with linen in the way of civilised people. It took Isabella some time to accustom herself to it and to wearing as a nightdress one of my shirts. But she was no less passionate, presenting her breasts and sweet parts to my hands and mouth and pleasuring me in the same way so that we tangled the sheets and left them wet with our sweat and juices.

A few days out on our voyage and she told me she was bearing my child. I was over-joyed and filled with hope for the future of our colony-to-be. I ordered a hog to be slaughtered and roasted in honour of this news and the ship celebrated to a man and a woman, even the kidnapped women expressing their pleasure. We drew ever closer and our bond tightened. Just as I had taken on some of the native characteristics – the tattoos and the wearing of armbands – Isabella sought to absorb our ways by dressing her hair as she saw it done in some of the books in the cabin and learning more English. Although we conversed chiefly in her language, she sometimes surprised me and others by the English words and expressions she had picked up. She has a quick mind and I consult her often on many matters.

We had taken on several dogs and cats at Otaheite and I allotted a pet to each of the seven women, two of whom had already formed attachments among our company. With the exception of Coleman, Byrn and a few others, we made up a happy assembly enlivened by generous measures of grog. Deep in his cups, McCoy confided that his woman too was with child and I toasted him with sincerity.

'What of Smith and Quintal?' I asked.

He winked. 'Working on it, Mr Christian, you may be sure.'

After that quiet start, the remainder of the passage was stormy with the ship being tossed about like a cork. The natives, including Isabella, were terrified, never having encountered a severe storm when far out to sea – or if any had had the experience they had not lived to tell the tale. We attempted to assure them that *Bounty* had endured far worse, but they huddled in misery and wailed in such a way as to test our patience. Happily, our livestock and provisions had been soundly stored so that we only lost a few hogs, a goat and the bull, who broke a leg and had to be killed. In a way I was glad of the storm, for it reminded all aboard that they were sailors yet and that discipline and hard work were required to survive at our trade in normal times and all the more so in the uncertain world of rebellion and abduction we had entered.

One Sunday, when the worst of the storm had passed and Toobouai was near at hand, Coleman attempted to recruit men for a Bible reading and prayer of thanks for our delivery. He enlisted only three, including Hillbrandt, Byrn and another whose name I misremember, and the meeting was brief. Still, it gave me pause for thought about what might be our practice in our island home. I doubted that my free thinking would appeal to all and it was a lesson of history that religious dispute pulled a commonwealth apart more effectively than any other force. I resolved to find a mild path in such matters that would adequately serve all adherents of belief and disbelief.

On 23 June we enjoyed calm weather as we sailed through the gap in the reef and anchored again in the lagoon of Toobouai Island. Detailing Tom Ellison to keep an eye on the canoes in the lagoon, I called another meeting and outlined my plan.

'We will build a fort that we can defend from the only direction a landing can be made. It will be large enough to house us all and some of the livestock and provide space for gardens. As we reach better terms with the natives here we will expand and establish ourselves more fully on the island.'

There were murmurs of agreement and I continued, 'I propose we name the fort after our king, whom we loyally served until driven to desperate action by one unworthy to bear the good king's commission.'

I was sincere in this statement and it was roundly cheered. I ordered all hands to remain on the ship for the present until we discovered the disposition of the natives. Those in canoes kept their distance and we saw saw none on the beach or in the trees beyond. Despite this order, Quintal and Sumner beckoned to a canoe lingering a little off from the ship and had themselves taken ashore for what purpose I know not. When I heard of this I sent a boat after them and they were brought back. Matt Quintal, a useful fellow in a tight corner, was a handful to a commander and so I dealt with him in the only way I could. I was waiting for the boat when it brought them back soon after dawn broke in a cloudless sky. I stood so that the miscreants would be facing directly into the sun rising dazzlingly above the horizon. I clapped a pistol hard to Quintal's head.

'I'll let you know who is master here.'

He stared balefully at me for an instant, then dropped his head. I ordered them both to be put in irons to contemplate their disobedience, but I made sure they received their rations of rum and food so that they might feel that I was severe but fair.

With my authority clearly established I went ashore with an armed party and marked out the site for our fort. It was to be a hundred yards long on each side with earth walls twelve feet thick at their narrowest measure, the whole to be surrounded by a water-filled ditch eighteen feet wide. A drawbridge would give entry to the fort which would have a four pound gun mounted at each corner with the swivel guns placed as needed on top of the walls. Almost the first structure put up was a flagpole flying the Union Jack. The cheers that rang out when the flag was run up startled the birds for a quarter mile around.

I drew up lists and rosters and set the people to work on the building of the fort and clearing of the ground for gardens. I released the pigs, intending for them to breed in the woods and provide food and sport. The goats were kept tethered. Tom Ellison milked and cared for them and saw that they were deployed to clean up food scraps and rubbish around the tents.

'Congratulations, Fletcher,' Peter Heywood said when the work was well underway and proceeding smoothly. 'You just might succeed.'

I looked around at the scene of order and industry, with even Quintal and McCoy wielding axes. 'I'd say I have succeeded, Peter. Or rather we have.'

Peter gave one of the smiles I had come to know as sceptical. 'Have you talked to any of the Toobouians?'

I confessed I had not.

'I have. Their language is much the same as that of Otaheite and you know I have a proficiency in it.'

'Yes. I'm busy, Peter. Your point?'

Peter pointed to where Churchill, Millward, Burkett and two of the Otaheitean women were digging the moat, about fifty metres of which had already been dug. 'The Toobouians fear that you mean to exterminate them and that is their mass grave.'

'Ridiculous.'

'Nevertheless, they think it. What's more our pigs are ruining their gardens. They fear starvation.'

I laughed. 'They can't fear extermination and starvation both.'

Peter made a gesture I found hard to interpret and walked away to his task of carrying rocks to reinforce the fort wall. The last few months with its good food, adequate rest and lately hard work had built him up so that at seventeen or so he assumed the character of a man. I knew he was still disaffected, despite his occasional friendliness, and I dreaded him becoming an enemy.

George Stewart remained my stoutest supporter and he informed me of the behaviour of Churchill, Sumner and Millward who had not secured women of their own. 'They pester the women of the other men,' George said, 'and speak of raiding the native village.'

'I'll flog the man who does that,' I said, 'and you may tell them so.'

A few days later I beheld the sorry sight of these three, naked, attempting to enter the fort unseen at dusk. I had been alerted to their approach by one of our lookouts and I confronted them.

'What have you wretches been about? Where are your clothes and weapons?'

Since Heywood's information about the Toobouian's complaints, no man had gone about unarmed. These three must certainly have had either muskets or pistols with ammunition, and clothes and other possessions besides. I drew closer and saw that each was bruised on the arms, legs and back. Sumner had a pronounced limp.

'The natives took them, Mr Christian. We were set on by a large party and had no chance.'

'I ask again, what were you about?'

Churchill, who had the most spirit, spoke up. 'Women, Mr Christian. We went abroad to get some to join us.'

'Force them, more like. You have put us all in danger by providing these natives with guns after causing them great offence.'

'God damn it!' Churchill cried. 'They were willing enough to whore their women at first when they planned to kill us.'

'Just so, and then a fool like you would have been prick deep in one when the attack came.'

Churchill raised a fist and all the pent up doubts and anxieties that had been building inside me came to a head. I put aside the musket I'd been carrying and rolled up the sleeves of my shirt.

'Would you try me, Charley?'

'Hit a captain and I hang.'

'I'm no captain and at this moment nothing but a man like you who calls you a bloody fool and will speak stronger if need be.'

Churchill took a stance that showed he had some acquaintance with the ways of the prize ring. 'I may hit you?'

'You may, if you can.'

By this time a goodly crowd had gathered, as in a schoolyard when a fight takes place. Churchill and I were of an age and a size, with him rather heavier. Within seconds, the on-lookers had formed a square and were urging us to fight. There was no question of a second's knee being offered or a referee being appointed. The rules, I suspected, would be those followed by Jack Slack and others who had brought the prize ring into such disrepute, which is to say, none.

Churchill, although bruised, appeared to be free in his movements as he circled, testing the ground with his feet and spitting on his fists. His nakedness did not worry him, indeed he seemed to glory in it and his prick seemed to be stimulated by the prospect of a fight. From the way he comported himself I suspected him to be a rusher, a cross-buttock man who liked to dump his weight on a fallen opponent in an effort to drive out his wind and break a rib or two. My own preference was for the technique of Mendoza who elected to hit sharply and often, while staying out of reach until his opponent was worn down by loss of blood or exasperated into making a mistake.

To test this theory, I advanced, slanting my body sideways and gave Churchill a sharp rap on the cheekbone which drew blood. He gave a roar of fury and rushed at me. I dodged and clipped him in the ribs as he floundered past. I judged him not to have good balance, rare for a seaman, and it was an easy matter to deceive him with feints and swaying my body sideways as he lunged straight ahead. He then changed tactics and tried to corner me against the on-lookers, hoping for support from one of them. None came, but with a quick thrust of stiff fingers at my eyes, he almost brought the matter to a close in his rascally favour.

Annoyed, I peppered him with light blows. After a few minutes he was breathing hard and I became careless. He rightly judged my flicked left to be a feint, stepped inside it and got his arms around my chest. I felt the strength still in him and knew that unless I broke his grip he could cut my breath and throw me. Luckily, his naked body was slick was sweat and I pushed hard against him within his grasp and slid down and out.

My style of fighting did not appeal to the audience and I had a sense that I had fewer supporters than opponents. Although I had escaped the hug and throw, I had lost wind and slightly wrenched my left shoulder in getting free. Churchill was struggling to re-gain his balance and I would never have a better chance. Although I knew it would pain my shoulder, I hit him twice with my left fist on the ear where he wore a ring. The ring cut him and more blood flowed. He threw back his head in pain and fury and I smashed him in the throat with a straight right hand blow that had all my weight behind it. He went down in a heap, gasping for air and helpless. I stood over him and drew back my foot. He put up a begging hand and I moved away.

I wish I could say that my victory over Churchill confirmed my authority and brought dissension to an end, but this was not the case. Liquor was one cause of trouble. Try as I might I could not keep our supplies safely locked and drunken fights and days where men were unable to work because of their over-indulgence were common. I allotted tasks to those most suited – McCoy and Coleman to man the forge to keep the tools in working order; Hilbrandt to cook; Byrn and Ellison to watch over and maintain the boats, the rest to work on the fort and act as guards in shifts.

For some weeks the work proceeded reasonably well, with the walls reaching six feet and the ditch well advanced, but the lust for women eventually caused many to lay down their tools. The natives became hostile, refusing to trade for food and threatening any who ventured far from the fort. To my great regret a war broke out between us and the Toobouians. There was wrong on both sides with the likes of Quintal and Sumner attacking natives in an attempt to steal women and only succeeding in wounding men and burning houses. The natives attempted to lure our people with women and then attack them and some suffered minor injuries.

'We must meet with the chiefs and arrive at a solution,' I said to Stewart after one such affray.

'They are playing a waiting game, Fletcher. They think to starve us out and may succeed, unless some of us kill others over the women and our number is reduced so that they feel able to launch an attack.'

He was right. 'I'll force their hand.'

'How?'

'I'll take control of a *marae*, seize the statues and sacred objects.'

'Jesus, that's a bold step.'

And so it was but it achieved its object. The party I led did some damage to the sacred grove and carried away many of the objects of worship as well as an arsenal of spears and clubs of special value. Tinarou, one of the chiefs, sent word that he wished to meet Titreano, their name for me, to discuss the return of their relics. This I agreed to do. Accompanied by a heavily armed party, including Stewart, Coleman, Martin and Morrison to balance the hot heads like Quintal and McCoy, I met the chief and his advisers in a clearing on the outskirts of his village.

'We will drink kava,' the chief said.

This muddy concoction prepared from the root of a tree was by no means welcome, for after several bowls one loses the use of one's legs. I sat with the chief, while the supporters on both sides stood at a distance. We had brought gifts and some of the objects they so fiercely cherished. We discussed the exchange. I declined more kava which I knew to be an insult, but the time had come to make our wants known.

'We demand wives for our men. Young women.'

Tinarou, old and fat as the aristocrats among the natives always become, shook his head and pulled a face as if I were a child. I flew into a rage and ordered my men to withdraw with weapons at the ready. The natives watched us go and followed at a distance. On our retreat we threw some of the sacred objects into the deep bush and left broken spears and clubs along the path. It was a declaration of war and I knew then that with the desire for women not to be satisfied and the natives implacably hostile, our Toobouai commonwealth was doomed.

In the days that followed my authority was challenged by Churchill, McCoy, Quintal and others. They broke the lock on the storeroom where the grog was stored, helped themselves and became roaring drunk, threatening everybody and especially the Otaheit-eans among us. Churchill led raiding parties for women and strayed livestock. They were opposed by a strong force of Toobouians and repelled. Angered beyond measure, they increased their armaments and on the next couple of encounters, in which I had to take part or lose all influence over our lives, we killed more than fifty natives, including women and children.

Let no one think this cruelty sat easily with me. Loving Isabella as I did and looking forward to the birth of my child with its mixed blood, I regarded the natives as people with the same feelings and sentiments as ourselves, however differently expressed. I felt each death I had witnessed as I would the stroke of the cat, and thoughts of B— and his floggings came to my mind and I cursed myself for a monster.

I contrived several covenants between myself, Churchill and his adherents and others, attempting to restore harmony, but to no avail. By early September we were a rabble with several factions contending and all trust absent. Those without women refused to work on the fort and proposed to cast lots for the Otaheiteans to become their slaves. This could not be permitted and I rallied sufficient level heads against it and also against a mad scheme to murder every Toobouian male on the island and take the women by force.

Work came to a halt, lookouts abandoned their posts and there followed three days of disputation about our future. I slept scarcely at all and became weary and low in spirits. At least none was for making for Botany Bay or some other British settlement, all knowing full well that, innocent of mutiny or not, justice was blind. In the end exhaustion calmed everyone down and it became possible to take a more or less orderly vote, although some voted at the behest of others out of fear or in expectation of favour. It came down to whether to return to Otaheite or not, and before a vote was taken on this I made a stipulation.

'I will carry you and land you wherever you please. I desire no one to stay with me. But I have one thing to request, nay, demand. That you will grant me the ship, allow me a few gallons of water and leave me to run before the wind, and I will land on the first island the ship drives. After all I have done I cannot remain at Otaheite. I will live nowhere I may be apprehended and brought home to cause grief to my family.'

I meant every word and was astonished at the effect. Ned Young was the first to speak. 'We will never leave you, Fletcher.'

Others took up the cry, 'We won't leave you, Mr Christian.'

In the end, I had eight men with me; the remaining sixteen voting to return to Otaheite. I had tears in my eyes as related business was conducted – agreement that I might have the ship, and that there should be an equal division of everything of use and value that remained with us. And so my grand plan for a harmonious common-wealth, safe and prosperous, came to nothing, and almost every man amongst us had blood on his hands.

Nine men

WITH GREAT EFFORT, EVERYTHING THAT had been taken ashore from the ship was now restored to it. I had Will Brown collect saplings and seedlings of breadfruit, bananas, yams, plantains and other things and store them in the great cabin. I gave an ironic smile to see the area resembling once again its character when B— was in command of the ship, although we took many fewer plants.

On 18 September we weighed anchor and bid a sombre farewell to Toobouai. I could not help but reflect on Ned Young's words earlier – 'God help the next vessel along.' We had done these people a great damage and I resolved not to allow any such calamity to happen again if I could prevent it.

My spirits were low as we made the passage back to Otaheite yet again, but at least I had now the firm knowledge of the men who had cast in their lot with mine, to experience together whatever awaited us. My list this time was short:

Ned Young
Will Brown
Isaac Martin
Alexander Smith
Matt Quintal
Will McCoy
John Mills
Jack Williams

On this list there were no surprises except perhaps for Brown who had taken no part in the mutiny. He evidently held to his resolve to be quit of England, and, as a steady man, I was glad of him. Ned Young, too, was a valuable supporter. Jack Williams had been helpful on the fateful day I seemed to recall, but scarcely an actor. It was he, however, who had branded B— a thief over the matter of the lost cheese and he rightly feared B—'s revenge should he survive. He was a quiet type but I fancy he had a yen for adventure, which was certainly before him now.

I was more surprised at the decision of some to remain at Matavai Bay. Churchill, Sumner, Thompson and Burkett would hang for certain if taken which they must have known. Churchill's hatred for me may have infected the others, but their states of mind I did not know. Most of the others had taken an active part; Millward and Muspratt prominently and others less so, and why they chose to remain I never ascertained as they seemed to fear to converse with me. Certainly, we nine were embarked on a risky enterprise and some may have felt the odds against us to be too long. My main concern among those who had not supported me was for Peter Heywood, George Stewart and Jem Morrison, and I sought out each of them on our four-day passage.

'I beg you to reconsider, Peter,' I said to him as we shared a meal on the first night out. 'You may not have meant it, but you were armed during the mutiny and the captain will never forgive you.'

'You're assuming he survived.'

'I have a sense that he has.'

'You wish it?'

'I do. After the bloodshed on Toobouai I don't like to think of more deaths at my hands.'

'It wasn't your fault.'

I shrugged. 'Nevertheless, you know a ship will come to Otaheite to search for us and, even if the captain did not survive to damn you, there will be those who will not tell the same tale as you.'

209

'I can't help it, Fletcher. I was no mutineer and I believe in British justice.'

At that I smiled. 'So do I, which is why I don't care to wear anything around my neck – to do so reminds me of the noose. You are old enough to hang, Peter.'

'I know, but the truth, Fletcher, is that I cannot bear the thought of never seeing England and my family again.'

There was nothing more to say. I put my hand on his shoulder and moved away. George Stewart I encountered later smoking his pipe on the afterdeck. 'George, I thought you were with me.'

'I was.'

'Until?'

He gestured over his shoulder. 'Until I saw what happened back there. It will happen again with that set of villains you have for company.'

'Ned Young and Will Brown, villains?'

'Three against six.'

'You have villains enough among you – Churchill and his crew.'

'A minority, and with much to keep them in check.'

'The captain will blame you for not saving him. He'll find a way to damn you along with all the officers who did not enter his boat.'

George puffed smoke and shook his head. I recall this because his relaxed and confident manner impressed me. He then made the reason for it clear. 'I firmly believe the captain to be dead and all who went with him. I think those of us who remain on Otaheite can construct a convincing narrative to shield us from blame. The ship wrecked, many lost, some saved – something of the sort.'

I had to admire his coolness, mistaken though I believed him to be. 'Your plan depends on our disappearance for ever.'

'Yes,' George said. 'It does. Take care you don't let me down, Mr Christian.'

Our friendship's end was sealed with those words. We had been close and cooperative and I wonder still if things worked out as he hoped. I doubt it.

Morrison was a strange character. Much better educated than the run of seamen and with a smattering of Latin and Greek to his repertoire. He had a garter tattooed on his thigh with the motto *Honi Soit Qui Mal Y Pense*. For all that, he was a tough sailor who knew his job and did it well. From things that had been reported to me, I suspected that he had been touched in some way by Methodism, for he had been heard praying in an enthusiastic manner and I had myself heard him complain about B—'s bad language. He had taken an interest in the natives on both Otaheite and Toobouai, and I hazard a guess it was born of an impulse to convert them. I had not had much contact with him and, now that it was to be severed, I wished it had been more, for he interested me considerably.

'You are resolved, Jem?' I asked him.

'I am, Mr Christian, but I thank you for allowing the vote and for arranging matters in such a civilised fashion.'

'Thank you. I never meant for there to be bloodshed or suffering. I consider that I did what was necessary.'

To this he made no reply and I continued. 'You know, Jem, Isabella, my woman, is with child and so will others be before long. Wherever we end up we will need people of education to teach the young. You could be of great service and be worthy of reward and respect on that account.'

He shook his head and said nothing. That was the carrot, next I offered him the stick. 'I know you took no part in the mutiny, but I have heard that you discouraged Mr Fryer from attempting to retake the ship.'

'I did that, to avoid needless bloodshed.'

'Do you think a court martial would see it that way?'

He knew exactly the tack I was taking but he was not moved. 'I've thought the matter through, Mr Christian, and I believe I can hold my own in any court where I am accused of mutiny.'

'With Latin quotations?'

'If need be.'

'I wish you well.'

'And I you, Mr Christian.'

We reached Otaheite without mishap, but we had worn out our welcome at Matavai Bay as I suspected, and the deception that we had practised on our last call had been called strongly into question by a Captain Henry Cox of the *Mercury*, who had called at the island and deposited one John Brown, a troublesome fellow, at his own request. Not surprisingly, Cox had been puzzled at our story of what had happened to B— and part of the *Bounty* crew, and had passed his doubts on to the natives.

I met this John Brown but once and then briefly when he came in a canoe to the ship. He bore the marks of a drunkard and prosed like a Methodist, a most dangerous combination. I have no doubt he gave us a very bad character to the natives after we departed.

Isabella, who spoke to some of the few people who came out in canoes to greet us, told me to be careful for the Otaheiteans now were disinclined to believe anything we told them. She warned me against attempting to trade for food or even filling our water casks.

'They are angry, Fletcher, at your lies and those of . . . others about the great captain Cook.' I had told her not to mention B—'s name in my presence. I conferred with Ned Young and we laid our plans. A number of men and women had come on board and we made them welcome, feeding them and allowing them the run of the ship. They eagerly accepted some watered rum.

Having made the division in lots of all that we agreed, the sixteen who were to remain on Otaheite boarded the large cutter which was loaded to the gunwales with their possessions. Each had a musket, a pistol, a cutlass, a bayonet, a cartridge box, seventeen pounds of lead and three gallons of wine. Not Byrn who, through his blindness and disagreeability, could not be trusted with weapons or wine. It had been agreed that they should also be allotted an anvil and a grind-stone.

With Quintal and McCoy, I took them the half mile to shore where they disembarked. Some of their *taios* came to greet them and to assist in the unloading of their goods which was done with despatch. Thus the time came to farewell a mixed band of men – some I despised, some I had no feelings for, and two I loved.

It was a moment not without tension. We had taken some people from here without their consent and I had no way of knowing how this would be received. These men were with us in the cutter and they sprang overboard as soon as they felt able to swim to shore. They were met on the beach and departed quickly. But the fear in me remained.

If Peter Heywood and George Stewart had got wind of the state of affairs on the island – and both could have communicated with the natives as Isabella had – they might well have been inspired to make a last effort to retake the ship, rather than let their last link with civil-isation pass over the horizon. I watched them closely for any sign of such an action, but they merely looked eagerly towards the people gathering on the beach and shouted greetings.

I helped unload the cutter and watched as the men waded through the shallows to the dark beach. George Stewart left without a word, but Peter Heywood looked back as he reached the sand and I sprang into the water and splashed towards him. We shook hands.

'I have something to tell you,' I said.

'What, Fletcher? You'd best be quick. Quintal is impatient to be off.'

'Bugger Quintal. The captain was an arsenic eater. He was mad from it at times and could not be trusted. He would have brought us all to grief one way or another.'

'What?'

'I saw him. He prepared small amounts on a set of scales.'

'My God! Have you evidence?'

'None, I threw it overboard after the mutiny.'

'In God's name why?'

'I scarcely remember. I thought none would believe me. It would be thought I had invented it to justify my action.'

'Why tell me now?'

'It might help you if you are ever charged with this crime.'

I saw the doubt in his eyes and could read his thoughts: the word of a mutineer against the holder of the king's commission. I released his hand and waded back through the lapping waves to the cutter.

Back on the ship with night drawing in, Ned Young and I did a head count of the natives. We had eighteen women aboard and six men. Two were Toobouians who had thrown in their lot with us back on the island and so earned the enmity of their fellows. The other four Otaheiteans thought they were aboard merely to enjoy themselves. Similarly with the women; only four were with us voluntarily.

'We must have enough women,' I said to Ned, 'otherwise the trouble we have had will be repeated.'

Ned agreed and late that night when all others aboard were asleep, we cut the cable, hoisted sail and stood out past the reef awaiting a favourable wind. When dawn broke, the natives coming on deck were alarmed and asked to be returned home. I told them we were merely visiting another part of the island, but they soon divined the truth and became angry and distressed. One young woman, bolder than the rest, dived overboard and struck out for the distant reef. Brown had had his eye on her and urged us to go after her but I refused.

'She's a brave lass,' I said, 'and deserves her freedom if she can win it.'

We then took stock of our captives, whom we fed and gave gifts to in the hope of soothing them. The Toobouian men persuaded the Otaheitean men that they would be well treated and have adventures and would eventually be returned to their home. The women remained distressed and their sorrow was increased when we separated out eight who were old and plain. *Bounty*, being a small ship and now but lightly laden, was easy to handle even with her severely reduced crew, and we took her close to the island of Moorea where we could expect inquisitive canoes.

'Keep her out of swimming distance from the shore,' I ordered Quintal at the helm. 'And the rest of you wave and beckon and draw any canoe near.'

Several canoes put out and our stratagem worked. We gave the natives nails, axes and knives and persuaded them to take our eight old women with them. This was accomplished with much wailing and tear-shedding by those who were leaving and those who remained, but we hardened our hearts and completed the transaction. Strange to say, within a few hours of this the women ceased to protest and before the day was out they were in earnest conversation with Isabella and the other wives.

That night we learned the names of the women, and allotted them to ourselves and the native men. As had become my habit, I drew up a list:

Self	Isabella
Ned Young	Susan
Jack Williams	Pashotu

Matt Quintal	Sarah
Alex Smith	Paurai
Will McCoy	Mary
Isaac Martin	Jenny
Jack Mills	Vahineatua
Will Brown	Teatuahitea

There were but three women left over for the native men and I left it to them to come to an arrangement. Only the Otaheitean Talaloo, through status and force of character, secured a woman of his own, Nancy. The others, Timoa, Nehow and Menalee were to share Mareva and the Toobouians, Oho and Tetaheite, were to share Tinafanea.

And so our party of twenty-seven sailed off into the vast Pacific in search of a safe refuge, a home, and a place where we might begin new lives such as no people before us had ever known.

Search for a home

FEW OF THOSE ON BOARD *Bounty* knew how large the Pacific Ocean really was and how its islands were situated. Apart from myself, only Ned Young and Will Brown had any knowledge of navigation; the natives had no concept of distances at sea whatever, being accustomed to only short voyages to nearby islands, although, as I was to learn, they had legends of voyages made over vast distances by ancestors. But these legends were thought almost to have taken place in another world, so distant were they in time. The result of this was that our search for a home took us so long and covered such trackless seas that it defied the understanding of most of our company.

On our passage from Toobouai to Otaheite, I naturally gave no one any true hint of where I intended to look for our home, but it occurred to me to lay a false trail. In conversation with some of those who were to remain on Otaheite I mentioned Duke of York Island, which lay to the north-west. But this was never my intention. Having slipped the cable at Matavai Bay, I directed our course in search of the Solomon Islands where Quiros had tried to establish his New Jerusalem. The advantage of this course was that it took us below the latitudes most used by previous British explorers.

'Spanish navigation was not worth a pinch of snuff,' I had heard B— proclaim, and I hoped that this would be the common opinion among our nation's sailors. Quiros had declared some of the islands he had moved among to be but sparsely inhabited or not inhabited at all, and this was our first requirement. After the experience at Toobouai, we sought to be merely settlers, not conquerors. Nevertheless, we needed provisions and water and on our voyage put in at several islands unsuited to our final purpose, but able to provide what we needed.

At these places we traded but did not linger as the familiarity of the natives with our needs and desires and the structure of our vessels suggested they were on the routes our ships customarily travelled and we had no way of knowing whether pursuit of us was already in train. We traded, were thieved from, and left. On one island, called Mangai by its inhabitants, canoes came out with pigs and coconuts and a vigorous trade got underway. These natives were bold fellows and several came on board. One expressed admiration for the pearl buttons on my coat and in a spirit of friendship I gave him the coat.

'Show your friends,' I said.

An athletic youth, he leapt onto the ship's rail and displayed himself to those in the canoes below. I had turned away when I heard a shot ring out. The native was struck full force, threw up his arms and fell into the water.

'He stole your coat, Mr Christian,' McCoy said with the smoke still coming from his musket.

I advanced on him, forcing him back against the mast so that he dropped the weapon. 'You villain. I gave him the coat.'

McCoy shook his head but showed no other emotion. The life of a native meant nothing to him. The friendly trade ceased at that instant. The natives on board left the ship, pulled their dead comrade from the water and paddled away, making loud lamentations. I swore at McCoy and assigned him a series of unpleasant duties but there was no other punishment I could invoke. Every hand was needed for the sailing of the ship and in any case, with our search tediously prolonged, I felt the diminishing of my authority day by day.

Quintal, in particular, came close to challenging me when I directed him into the rigging to check on a sail.

'Send young Tom,' he said. 'He climbs like a monkey.'

'You forget, we left him at Otaheite.'

This checked him and he obeyed the order but unwillingly and did a poor job so that I had to send another up after him.

The ship itself was in poor condition. With all the plants that had been taken on at Toobouai, the livestock and the provisions traded for in the islands, her decks were disorderly and dirty with no prospect of cleaning them. She was taking on water through sprung planks in her hull and worm-eaten timbers. At each island we put into the story was the same – hostile natives, difficulty in getting water and increasing anxiety among our people, especially the Otaheiteans and Toobouians. At last we reached Tongatabu in the Friendly Islands, which was within a hundred miles of Tofua where the mutiny had taken place. I felt as if I had come full circle in a quest so far fruitless and that a hard decision had to be made.

I had spent hours poring over the charts and books B— had left behind. I may say that many of these carried notes written in the margins by B—. Any account of Cook's voyages was heavily annotated with angry expressions at the neglect shown to B—'s own contributions. Whether this anger was justified I cannot tell, but the language was immoderate, many people being described as damn fools and bloody liars. To do B— credit, it must be said that his hand was a model of neatness and clarity compared to my own wild scrawl.

One book of particular interest was Captain Hawkesworth's, published in 1775, containing accounts of numerous Pacific expeditions, such as by Cartaret, in 1767. A passage in Hawkesworth quoted Cararet's discovery of an island. I have the book in front of me, and the passage marked:

Upon approaching it the next day it appeared like a great rock rising out of the sea: it was not more than five miles in circumference, and seemed to be uninhabited; it was, however, covered with trees.

Cartaret had named the great rock Pitcairn's Island after the young officer who had first sighted it. Trees, I reasoned, suggested water and tillable soil. As marked on the charts, Pitcairn's Island was far from the common sea routes, being in an area not favoured by winds or nearby island groups which could provide provisions. I struck the chart with my fist and resolved that Pitcairn's Island should be our home.

The island's location was given as latitude 20° 2' S, longitude 133° 30' W and it was estimated to be about a thousand degrees westward of the Americas. Apart from the appeal of its physical characteristics, I was encouraged, strange to say, by another piece of information — Captain Cook, the supreme navigator, searched for it twice but could not find it. I concluded that there must be some mistake in the bearings given, but that the island existed could not be denied and therefore it must be possible to find it. It was marked on no chart and I had only the probably incorrect bearings to work with, but what could be better for a refuge?

When I told Ned Young of my decision he echoed the question that had been put to me earlier.

'Can you find it, Fletcher?'

'I can,' I said while thinking: or die trying. That was not a thought to make known. I told Ned to let everybody know that the ideal place was determined and that, happily, it was in those warm latitudes we had come to love; south of Otaheite but the milder for that. Ned spread the word and soon a deputation comprising Quintal, Smith and McCoy paid me a visit.

'We have but one question, Mr Christian,' Quintal said. 'How far?'

'I'll not lie to you – the better part of a thousand miles.'

'You can take us across a thousand miles of ocean and find a speck five miles around?'

I showed them the charts and the navigational instruments. 'I could take you to England if you wished. To the fleet at Portsmouth, let us say.'

That had its effect. They knew full well what that would mean. To a man they agreed to make the voyage.

'Stay a minute,' I said. 'To make this voyage we will have to beat against unfavourable winds and go south to latitudes colder than those we have been used to these many months. It will mean hard work upon a hard working ship. Far easier to go north to Otaheite.'

Quintal shook his head. 'Likely the women would leave; likely the Indians there have killed those that stayed.'

'Or a searching vessel has called and hanged them on the spot,' Smith said.

'I trust not,' I said, putting my hand on the chart. 'But those are the risks set against this plan.'

Will Brown had evidently been listening outside the cabin. Now he entered and displayed a pot in which a seed had sprouted. 'Tobacco,' he said.

The three gave a cheer and Brown, Mills and Quintal departed. Smith hung back, apparently wishing to talk and I bade him be seated.

'I'll warrant those cold latitudes are nothing compared to the Horn, Mr Christian.'

'Nothing,' I said.

'I have something to get off my chest, now that we are all free men and set to begin new lives in an untouched land.'

I was surprised to hear him speaking in this way as he had never had much to say before and seemed more a man of action than of words. Smith was powerfully built, quite a few inches shorter than me, though with the breadth and muscle of a man much taller. He was much marked by the smallpox. We had one thing in common though – he was tattooed, perhaps more than anyone of the company, on the body, arms and legs. I knew little about him, save that he had been useful in the mutiny and thereafter, and I had been told that Samuel, the clerk, had been teaching him to read. That marked him out as interesting. He carried the nickname of Reckless Jack. For what reason I knew not.

At this time, with the decision made and doubts set aside, and the love of my Isabella secure, I was yet hungry for talk and association with my own kind. I pulled out my pipe and shared my tobacco with Smith.

When our pipes were going he said, 'My name is not Smith, but Adams, Jack Adams.'

I puffed and said nothing.

'It's a common enough tale, mine, Mr Christian.'

'Mr Young has set our new course. Our pipes are alight. I would hear it.'

What follows catches his words as nearly as I can recall.

'You probably wonder why I joined in the mutiny and stayed with you, Mr Christian. I'll try to tell you. I come from a seafaring family, Irish, but of the Protestant faith in so far as there was any religion at all. My father was a Thames waterman and it was while he was working for a coke merchant of Wapping that he got drunk and was drowned in the river. I had a brother and two sisters, one married, and our mother died soon after leaving us orphans. I was born in sixty-six, making me twenty-four years of age today or tomorrow or sometime soon, for I am not sure of the exact date.'

At this I saluted him with my pipe.

'I was twelve years when we was made orphans, more or less.

Thrown on the parish we were, all but the married one, and you can guess at my way of escaping the bloody workhouse.'

'The Navy.'

'Yes, sir, the Navy. I joined as a nipper and spent ten years at faithful service.'

I was scribbling figures on a scrap of paper as he spoke. 'That brings you pretty close to joining *Bounty*.'

'Pretty close, sir. All but a month or so after I deserted from the *Hyperion*.'

'Ah,' I said. Every man in the King's Navy knew the story of the *Hyperion* and her commander, Abraham Bucholtz. If ever a man deserved the appellation of a flogging captain it was Bucholtz. On a Mediterranean voyage of no particular consequence, he had half of his crew savagely flogged. Three men, when threatened with a repeat dose, had struck the captain. He suffered no serious injury but had the three put in irons and on a meagre ration of bread and water for the remainder of the voyage. Court-martialled at Portsmouth, the offenders were sentenced to be flogged through the fleet, which would have meant the administration of many hundreds of lashes. Such was their weakened condition that two of the men died and the third was rendered unfit for service or work of any kind. Bucholtz earned no reproach.

'Two of those men were my mates, Mr Christian,' Smith said, 'and as good sailors as you'd hope to see.'

'Until driven too far,' I said.

Smith nodded and put down his pipe, obviously much affected by his memories. 'I deserted the *Hyperion* and changed my name, but the sea's the only trade I know and I was told that Mr Bligh was not a harsh man.'

'Nor was he, once.'

'And a skipper had a care for his crew.'

I nodded.

'So I signed on, but I had made a pledge that I'd not suffer further injustice of the kind I'd known on the *Hyperion*. I was flogged, and hard, you may be sure of it.'

'So when you were flogged at Matavai for the theft from the cutter . . .'

Smith shook his head. 'Aye, there was no justice in that and it heated my blood, but there was more to my pledge. I vowed to kill the man who flogged me unjustly. You'll never know, Mr Christian, how close I came to running him through with a bayonet when he was bare arsed on the quarterdeck.'

'I'm glad you did not, for I might then have done the same to you. But what stayed your hand?'

Smith took up his pipe and puffed it back to life. 'You might have heard that I've been learned to read.'

'By John Samuel.'

'Aye, a good man. I've continued reading since we sent them off, but in one book only.'

I closed my eyes briefly. 'The Bible.'

'Yes, sir. I began with Samuel and continued with Jem Morrison.'

'I still can't see why you were merciful. An eye for an eye and what have you.'

'No, sir. I follow other texts and above all the true commandment.'

'Thou shalt not kill. I followed it myself, though I'm not much of a man for the Bible.'

'So I've noticed, Mr Christian. There being no services aboard.'

'Nor will there be until we are safe and settled. Religious disputation is a curse. Well, an interesting tale to be sure . . . Adams. Is there more to tell?'

'Just this, sir. I would rather I kept the name Smith for now. My grandmother's name it was, and I had an uncle by the name of

Alexander. But, Mr Christian, should I die I would like you to put my true name on the marker.'

The religious talk had sapped my patience. 'You're younger than I am. Why talk of dying?'

'I fear the Indians, sir. I fear they will turn against us.'

That concluded our talk and I marked Smith as one, like Morrison and many others, made soft-headed by religion.

I had put a brave face on our long voyage in quest of Pitcairn's Island, but in fact the search tried the resolve of every last person aboard. The high latitudes we entered as we beat westward brought a cold never before encountered by the natives and they suffered greatly from it. As well, the skies continued grey for weeks at a time, with the sea the colour of iron in what must be the emptiest stretch of water on the globe. We sighted no land, no birds, no flotsam or jetsam, no life other than fish. At the appropriate time, we bore north into welcome warmer climes, and I kept *Bounty* on a course designed to bring us to Cartaret's bearings and told no one of my alarm at finding nothing at that point. Like Captain Cook, I could not find the great rock where it was supposed to be.

I sat in the cabin with Isabella, now large with child, sleep not far away and pondered the matter deeply over several pipes and draughts of brandy. The ship was quiet, moving smoothly under light sail. Either Cartaret was mistaken in his location or Hawkesworth had misrepresented his bearings. Which? Or could both be wrong? I was drunk and resolved to spin a coin on the matter. The coin settled on its end and I laughed. There was nothing for it but to explore these waters. I went to bed oddly happy. If the island was so hard to discover, I thought, how safe it must be should we find it.

On the evening of the next day, with the sky dark and the wind gusting, a shape arose rose on the horizon, dead ahead. There was no mistaking it from Cartaret's description. This was Pitcairn's Island

and the date was 15 January, 1790. I stood on the deck as Ned Young, Will Brown and others congratulated me on my navigational skills. I accepted their praise as I knew I would need every ounce of authority to make a success of our endeavour if this was indeed its sticking point.

I looked about and thought I saw Smith on his knees, but he may have been simply about some ship's task. I ordered rum all round.

The year 1790

THE WEATHER CONTINUED STORMY, and all we could do for the next two days was stand off and sail around the island at a distance, examining it and searching for an anchorage. It was like no other place I had ever seen, rising from the sea to perhaps a thousand feet at its highest point and thickly wooded. I could distinguish palm trees only, but Brown reported that a variety of trees grew, many of them fruit bearing. Our chief concern, apart from finding a landing place, was that the place might be inhabited, because it would be easy to defend. We coasted about in full view of anyone who should be ashore but saw no signs of life other than the sea birds that wheeled about uttering their mournful cries.

From the deck, Ned Young and I swept the island with our spy glasses.

'No smoke, no movement,' Ned said. 'This place is uninhabited, unless by pygmies who live in holes, wear fur coats and eat their food raw.'

'Have a care. Some might think you serious.'

'This is a good place, Fletcher. You have done well by us.'

'I hope so, provided we can find a place to land.'

I took sightings and went below to consult the Hawkesworth book again now that I had located the island precisely. Whether the error was Cartaret's or in the printing of Hawkesworth's book I know not, but Pitcairn's island was misplaced by five degrees of latitude and over two of longitude. Anyone sailing by the only directions available would need persistence to find it, or luck, or both. For our purposes an entirely happy circumstance.

By the middle of the day the weather had cleared, the sea had become calm and we were able to venture close to the cliffs.

'I can taste them now,' I heard McCoy say to Smith.

'What, mate?'

'See them birds? Where there's birds there's eggs. What I'd give for a platter of fried eggs.'

'Soon enough,' Smith said.

In the clearer air, not heavy with rain or spray, we espied breaks in the cliffs along the north-eastern coast line. I ordered the large cutter lowered and Will Brown, Jack Williams, Will McCoy and myself, along with three of the Otaheitan men, entered the little cove we were to name Bounty Bay. It was scarcely more than a dimple in the coast-line, but we could see a narrow beach at its head and the cliff beyond was less steep than in other places.

The men put aside their muskets and rowed in while I guided them clear of half-submerged rocks that would have tested our vessel's wormy planks. As it happened, the water itself took control. We were picked up by a breaking wave and carried furiously forward over any further hazards to be thrust onto a beach, less wide than a cricket pitch is long, at the base of a cliff.

'This island permits people to land,' Will Brown said, 'but does not exactly welcome them,'

I looked at the rowers with their lifted oars, trained seamen still, and saluted them by waving my musket, which, I then realised, I had clenched in my hands throughout the landing. 'And isn't that just what we want?'

We hauled the cutter the last yards through the shallows and pulled her onto the sand. As I stood on the beach I had a sense of reaching the end of a long journey, but not of finality. So much lay ahead, more, I trusted, in terms of years and work and responsibility, than those that lay behind me. I directed the Otaheiteans to investigate the cliff to find a path while the rest of us looked to our muskets lest we had been deceived by natives with powers of concealment beyond our comprehension.

Our natives discovered a way ahead of a kind, although it was steep and rough. I ordered them to watch the boat with McCoy as their guard, while we made the climb.

'Fetch me some eggs,' McCoy said.

We climbed the steep cliff with difficulty, going down on hands and knees at times, but not being forced to stop. At the top we found the land never level but with a large section reasonably flat, enough so certainly to permit houses to be built and fields and gardens. The surrounding slopes and valleys were covered with vegetation and I could hear, if not see, a stream running freely. In this, I was mistaken as it proved, and my error was no doubt due to my wishing to see the place in the best possible light.

The day was bright and clear and the whole scene presented itself as green and pleasant. A soft, mild wind blew in the tree-tops and I could hear the sea crashing against the cliffs far below but at no great distance directly. As I looked across the stretch of ground that would require the chopping down of a good number of trees and a fair degree of levelling and clearing, a thought entered my mind to make me smile. I wished I had a horse to ride around the island, but I knew I would never see a horse again.

Will Brown strode off to examine the trees and scratch at the soil while Williams and I wandered about, still with our muskets at the ready, although there could be no doubt that not a single soul lived on Pitcairn's Island.

'You like the place, then, Mr Christian?' Williams said, mistaking the reason for my smile.

'I do, Jack. And you?'

'Well enough. A bit small.' He was a Guernsey man I knew, and had been heard singing snatches of songs in French, not unpleasantly.

''Twill suffice. Our needs are not great. Safety is the thing.'

'Aye. Might I look for some eggs for Will?'

'You don't have to ask. We are to be free here, with no man, no master.'

Williams seemed astounded at this notion. He pulled off his cap, scratched at his head and rested the butt of his musket in the thick grass. 'What about the Indians?'

I had been giving much thought to how we would live together with the natives in this new world to be of our own making, and had not come to any firm ideas. 'That's different,' I said, knowing that it was no answer at all.

Williams left his musket with me and went off. Will Brown returned from his investigations with his face aglow. 'Fine soil this, Fletcher. Grow anything it will. I would I had more seeds than tobacco.'

'You'll have enough to keep you busy, Will, with Teatuahitea to help.'

'She's a fine lass and a great improvement on my shrew at home, and ...'

I cut him off. 'This is home, Will.'

'So it is. I was about to say I am about to father a half-Indian, a thing I never dreamed of.'

'You'll not be alone in that, and we have to give thought to the raising of them. I believe we should teach them to be ...'

Brown had used a bayonet to scratch at the soil. Now he cleaned it with handfuls of grass and gave me a searching look. 'Yes?'

I laughed. 'I'm more Manx than anything else. Let us say I would see them grow up as British.'

Brown nodded. 'And yet their mothers' skills will be needed here – for gardening, fishing, medicines and more.'

'What more?'

'I've made a study of these people, Fletcher. Their religion relates to the land and the sea and the sky. I don't understand it more than a little, but I think the women will need to hold to their gods here.'

I spat and swore and felt like firing my musket in anger. 'A pox on religion. I thought we'd have enough to worry about with Smith and his Bible prosing.'

Brown shrugged and said nothing more. I did not let this detract from my enthusiasm about the island, raised still further when Williams came back with his cap full of good-sized eggs. 'The birds nest on the cliffs,' he said, 'and getting the eggs is easy for a man not afraid of heights.'

'And a good rigging man like yourself is not, eh, Jack?'

We made our way back down to the beach with the going easier downhill than up. Brown had some leaves and bark which he said he'd attempt to identify from some of the books Nelson had left behind. Mills was delighted at the sight of the eggs and placed them carefully in the boat as we rowed back to the ship.

'Titreano,' Talaloo said in the Otaheitean tongue, 'there were no people to be seen?'

'None.'

'I wonder why. The island has water and trees and birds. All such islands have people as we have seen.'

Will Brown understood a good deal of the language and he spoke up. 'I may be wrong, but I thought I saw signs of gardens, very over-grown.'

Talaloo looked at me inquiringly.

'There might have been people here in the past.'

'Perhaps the island is cursed.'

I would have hit him had he been in reach. '*Mamoo*! And I'll flog you if I hear you speaking such trash.'

There was no word for flogging in the island language and the expression I used may have been wrong. Talaloo glared at me and bent to his oar, saying nothing.

On the ship I assembled the company and told them of the advantages of the island, particularly its absence of people, isolation and defensibility. Brown waxed enthusiastic about the fertility of the soil and McCoy displayed the eggs. To the natives I spoke of the things Brown had stressed and made no mention of the possibility of it being inhabited in the past. Isabella spoke on my behalf of the water and the flowers and the birds which seemed to make an impression on the native women, although the men showed signs of resenting her contribution and her role in the scheme of things as my wife.

I observed Talaloo closely through these proceedings. As the only native with a wife of his own, due to his rank in the native society, I expected him to be more amenable to our plans than the others, but he remained implacable, if not hostile. He would repay watching, I concluded, and immediately reproached myself for falling into an attitude of suspicion such as Smith had expressed.

The day had drawn on and the sea was rising with busy currents and swells that made it too hazardous to take *Bounty* any closer to our new home. After some dissension with the likes of Quintal and Smith, who were eager to see the island, it was agreed to take her in on the morrow and find a safe anchorage off the beach to permit us to strip her and land everything useful from her stores and construction.

One thing Ned Young and I agreed upon in private consultation was that the ship was in poor condition after her long, hard voyages, and that there was little chance of making significant repairs.

'She will have to be beached, Fletcher,' Ned said.

'Or scuttled,' I said.

'A final act.'

'As in any drama.'

Ned laughed. 'This is certainly that. And it would fill the theatres of London.'

At that we both laughed but, with the waves lapping at *Bounty*'s scarred and barnacled timbers and a great rock presenting as our final resting place, we both felt the need of brandy to ensure our night's rest.

The next day we did a thorough inventory of the vessel, marking down everything useful that could be carried away, whether it was presently fixed or not. Thanks to Quintal we still had some of the carpenter's tools, a fact Quintal did not hesitate to remind us of. With the meat and bread from the stores and the livestock and the fruit and vegetables we had taken from Otaheite and Toobouai, we would be able to feed ourselves until we could grow our own food. The sea teemed with fish and the island was alive with birds.

Ned Young rapped a stout bulwark. 'There's enough timber in her to build a dozen houses.'

'Yes,' I said, 'or another ship.'

'I thought this was to be our home.'

'An idle thought,' I said.

'A dangerous one, Fletcher. The sooner we strip and scuttle her the better.'

Ned had a knack of dismissing doubt. 'We'll start today,' I said. 'There's a week's work in it at least and we'd best take advantage of the fine weather. We'll bring her in as close as we can and use the cutter to carry the goods ashore. Some of the timber we can float. Sails first, we'll be living under canvas.'

We were in my cabin and Ned looked around at the books. 'Will you share the books, Fletcher? I've a mind to read some.'

'We'll share everything,' I said, winking at him. 'I admit I've put my own name under that of the original owner in some of them.'

He took a book and examined its spine.

'William Dampier's *A new Voyage Around the World*,' I said. 'My favourite, I think.'

'The pirate?'

'Buccaneer. And in a way responsible for all that has befallen us.'

'How so?'

I took the book and showed him the passage where Dampier extolled the virtues of the breadfruit. B— had written in the margin that it was this that had given Sir Joseph Banks the notion to take the breadfruit from Otaheite to feed the slaves in the West Indies.

He replaced the book. 'No novels?'

I laughed. 'Can you see our late captain reading novels?'

I have mentioned that we worked a week at stripping the ship. I can now record further details. Happily, Isabella discovered a better path up the cliff. Though still steep and heading first one way and then another, it was firmer and wider for the most part and she was certain that it had been prepared by native people some time in the past.

'How can you be sure?' I asked. 'Perhaps white men have landed here before?'

She shook her head. 'No, Fletcher, look.' She unwrapped a bundle and showed me pieces of pottery very like those we had seen on Otaheite and Toobouai. 'There were houses here, and cooking fires and a *marae*. The people made stone images and carved in the rocks.'

'How long ago?'

She shrugged. 'Many seasons.'

'Did the people leave, or did they die?'

She smiled and fingered the pieces of pottery. It was as if the question had no meaning for her and I realised that I had little idea of the natives' view of history. I was ignorant of the way they marked out time and how they accounted for the behaviour of people long dead. They had no written records but long memories and much tradition preserved in stories and myths. Peter Heywood had translated one such legend as best he could, but it seemed to assign human form to fish and plants and I had merely been amused by it as one would be by tales of magic and dragons.

News of the previous occupants spread quickly among the natives and I was relieved to find that none put Talaloo's pessimistic interpretation on the fact. Isabella reported that all were pleased by the signs that people of their own kind had lived and worked here before. I suppose it would be the same among us if we came upon a deserted village, of which there are many in England, in what had been thought a wasteland. In any event the natives, the dour Talaloo included, worked with a will at the dismantling of the ship.

Living half on shore and half on the ship, we made trips without number in the laden cutter, transporting provisions, tools, fittings, weapons and ammunition, rope, nails and all our personal possessions. We ripped up the lining of cabins and storerooms and floated the timber ashore together with unbolted yards and booms. I ordered the hatches to be lashed together to construct rafts to help with the work. The women bent their backs to hauling these rafts ashore. With difficulty, the galley stoves were lowered into the cutter and taken ashore, where, with other heavy items, we used ropes and pulleys to raise them to the top of the cliff, a distance of three hundred feet or more. The weather continued fine and warm and we sweated freely under the sun, all stripped to the waist and becoming as brown as the natives.

Eventually the moment came to fell the masts and Quintal, Mills and McCoy went happily to work. Watching them, I realised that they hated the ship itself and any thought I might have had of preserving her in any guise would be opposed. As the masts came down, splintering anything in their paths and falling so as to be sawn to manageable lengths, lashed together and floated ashore, I felt a pang at the death of the gallant little vessel that had carried us so far. I realised, reproaching myself for the thought, that I had shared a desire with B—: to bring the ship home without losing a single man and that, unlike him, I had done it.

I cannot bear to write again of her burning and there is no need. One thing I must add; her guns, every one, went to the bottom with her and I was glad, taking this to be a sign that our lives were here-after to be peaceful.

Quintal's action had deprived us of much timber and some metal, all of which could have been useful, but reproaching him would have been to no avail and I gave no thought to punishment. There was to be no flogging or putting in irons on our island. We got less work than we might have from Quintal and McCoy while the grog they had salvaged lasted, although all were grateful for a tot at times. By the end of February we had everything hauled up to the plateau where we intended to make our village.

Still living in tents made from the sails, we began the arduous task of clearing the trees and scrub to provide sites for our houses and gardens. The flat section provided a view out to sea but we were careful to leave a screen of trees so that our presence would not easily be detected. At first, we penned the livestock together, apart from some pigs and goats we let run wild. Later we would divide the animals equally. It was with some reluctance that I agreed to McCoy's urging that we kill the dogs lest their barking be heard out at sea should a vessel happen by. Indeed I had no authority to prevent it as, once our lives were conducted ashore my position among us was one of equality, save only that all but Ned Young and Will Brown continued to address me as Mr Christian. About this I was not sorry. I had no wish to govern as I had learned on Toobouai that it was a thankless task. I wanted only to live in peace with Isabella and our child and cultivate my garden.

Lest there should be doubt in the future about our family arrangements, I now set them down as they stand. I am mated with Isabella, Ned Young with Susannah, Will Brown with Teatuahitea, McCoy with Mary who had a babe in arms not McCoy's, Quintal with Sarah, Zac Martin with Jenny who had been Smith's woman previously and carried his initials in tattoo on her arm, Mills with Vahineatua, Williams with Pashotu and Smith now with Paurai.

The Toobouians, Oho and his young nephew, Tetaheite, were to share Tinafanaea. Only Talaloo had a woman, Nancy, of his own as I have said. The other Otaheiteans, Timoa, Menalee and the youngster Nehow, were to share Mareva. The natives were accustomed to sharing women, as we had seen on Otaheite, this arrangement seemed as fair as we could contrive. The natives offered no objection.

I questioned Isabella as to the women. As one from the chiefly caste of Otaheite, she held some sway among them and knew their minds.

'They would prefer to be the wives of some of the white men,' she said.

'Some?'

'Not Quintal or McCoy.'

'Ah.'

'Bad men.'

'Yes. Perhaps they will get better.'

Isabella said nothing to that.

When it came to the division of the cultivatable land the matter was simple. Will Brown did a rough survey and concluded there were about ninety acres that could be so described. This we divided into nine lots which we drew for, so that each might have an equal share. The rock pools we allotted similarly.

I had been mistaken about the stream. There was a fine spring that provided abundant sweet water but it was some distance from the settlement and carting water was sometimes burdensome. That aside, there was no fault to be found with the place. The climate was mild and without the wet season that made Otaheite unpleasant for months on end. When our first winter came we scarce noticed the difference. It would be a good climate to grow old in without the cold season to stiffen aged joints and bones. We learned that the rain fell steadily through the months but seldom too heavy, and there were a great many clear, cloudless days when the air was like nectar and the horizon was distant and sharp in every direction.

The clearing of the square around which our houses were to be set was done by all hands and proceeded quickly. Then each man marked out the setting of his house and we drew lots to decide in which order they should be built although this arrangement broke down and the houses went up piecemeal as we found the time and could persuade others to help. Here the natives were of much use, knowing how to weave palm leaves to provide a strong thatch and how to construct walls that could be moved aside in the warmer weather. We built the houses solidly to stand against the winds, which were occasionally strong, from the ship's timbers. Each was to much the same design with two levels, the upper for sleeping and the lower for cooking and eating. Having no glass, the windows had shutters only. We built the roofs with a pitch for the rain to run off.

I can speak only of the houses of Ned Young, Will Brown, Jack Williams and my own, for I have not been inside the others long enough to take note, but the houses I speak of have proper bedsteads with mattresses stuffed with leaves or feathers, and with low tables and chests beside them such as you would find in any respectable dwelling. There is yet something of *Bounty* about all our houses for we wanted nothing to do with dirt floors and built proper flooring from the ship's decking. In my own house the ladder leading to the upper level is one from the ship, slightly cut down to fit. I have my sea chest by my bed and my uniform hanging on a wall. We all have tables and chairs, some taken from the ship and some built by our own hands with our precious supply of nails. With our supply of oil and candles ended, we burn oil wrung from the flesh of the coconut in our lanterns. It gives but a dim and smoky light, but as we live the greater part of the time out of doors it matters little. I almost wrote less than it would at home, but I must try to avoid such expressions.

The native men and their women built their own huts in their own style in a clearing some way apart from our square. They assist us in all things – the work in the gardens, the carting of water, fishing, the collection of the eggs from the noddies and terns on the cliffs and the hunting of the now wild pigs and goats. All food produced by labour and won from the land and sea is shared and it can be our proud boast that nobody goes hungry on our island.

The first upset to our industrious and tranquil way of life came when Jack Williams' wife, Pashotu, died of an affliction of the throat which stopped her breath. Williams had established a forge and his skills were greatly in demand for the mending and sharpening of tools, for none of us were agriculturalists and we damaged the tools regularly. Williams, who had not yet completed his house, could not endure being without a woman while the rest of us, mostly comfortably housed although McCoy and Quintal had lagged behind in their building, had one. He demanded to be given one of the natives' women. This most of us opposed, knowing it would cause resentment among the natives.

'He might come after our women,' McCoy said.

Quintal laughed. 'Come after mine and I'll roast him in his own fire.'

'We need his skills,' Will Brown said. 'Perhaps we can persuade him to wait a while.'

'For what?' Ned Young said. 'For a canoe-load of women to be washed ashore?'

I write this some time after the meeting. By this, after we had been on the island some months, Young and I had grown apart. The reason for this I know not. He spent more time with the natives than with his former shipmates and Isabella told me that Quintal had taken to calling him a nigger on account of his West Indian blood. He had become cantankerous and I increasingly found the company of Will Brown more pleasing, so I came to his defence on this occasion.

'Jack's no Goliath,' I said. 'If we flatter him for his forging and say things may change in the future as Will suggests, he may calm down and accept his lot.'

'I wouldn't,' Smith said.

'Jack has not your force, Alex. He's no bull, more a fish to be played on a line.'

'You have a way with words, Mr Christian,' McCoy said, 'else that bastard of a captain would be in a watery grave.'

That sobered the meeting. I undertook to represent our views to Williams but I was wrong in my assessment of his character. He demanded a further meeting and had evidently rehearsed his statement.

'If you will not give me a woman I will leave the island in the cutter. I claim it as my due. I am a wronged man.'

Young laughed. 'You would go to your death.'

'I claim it as Mr Christian claimed the ship after Toobouai.'

Young laughed again. 'It smacks of your plan to leave the ship on a raft, Fletcher.'

'It was never a serious plan, nor should this be for you, Jack. Mr Young is right. You could not survive.'

The meeting, conducted in one of the remaining tents, broke down into passionate discussion, with some for allowing Williams to leave and others insisting that he stay. I was tired after a hard day's work clearing land for a garden and failed to see Quintal and Young slip away. McCoy produced a half bottle of rum, which, he said, was all that was left of the ship's store. We all had a drink and McCoy pressed a good measure on Williams in particular. The meeting broke up without result.

In the morning we found that Quintal and Young had holed and sunk the cutter, the jolly boat being useless from the start. From that moment on, Jack Williams neither delved nor dug, he took payment for his work with the tools in food and did the work slowly in a slovenly manner.

At about this time, on one of my wanderings about the island, I discovered a cave situated in a high rocky outcrop to the west of our village that afforded a view of the sea and the approach to it which I only stumbled upon by accident, it being rough, very steep and much overgrown. The trouble with Williams and the disaffection displayed by Young had troubled me and caused me to be low in spirits often and to seek my own company. On finding the cave I felt a conflict of emotions. On the one hand I welcomed it as a refuge, a place for quiet contemplation out of sight and sound of other people. On the other I saw it as a possible fortress, a place to make a last stand should we ever be discovered and attacked. Over time I stocked it with food and weapons and ammunition, unbeknownst to all others. I spent much time there and in my blacker moments saw it as a place where I might die by my own hand rather than be taken. I saw myself climbing to the highest point over a sheer drop to the sea boiling against the cliff below and shooting myself. My body would be swept away. A fitting end to a villainous mutineer, some might say, but this scene, though it came often enough to my mind, never infected my brain so as to cause it to happen without reason. I was resolved to live as long as I could, and fruitfully with Isabella, on Pitcairn's Island.

I have neglected this journal for some time, busying myself with my house and garden and taking myself off to my private place. But I have need to record an event that has transformed me in ways I struggle to understand and yet welcome with a full heart. Isabella miscarried of the child conceived earlier to our sorrow, but she conceived again almost immediately and on Thursday, the tenth day of October in the year 1790 our son was born. I looked down at the tiny creature with his brown skin and dark eyes and saw clearly in his features the faces of my brothers and myself. His head was longer than with the natives, the nose thinner and more pronounced and the chin longer and firm. The sight gave me a pang that caused me to catch my breath.

Isabella was alarmed. 'Fletcher, what ails you?'

'Nothing. Nothing. A fine child, perfect in every way.'

'Pick him up, Titreano. Carry him.' She seldom used my island name and her doing so brought it home to me how different our feelings were. She saw me now as an island chieftain, the father of her child, a chieftain in the making, and his birth confirming her status as belonging to the highest order in island society. My reaction was otherwise – I saw a Christian, a member of a family with a long and honourable heritage dating back to the Norse warriors who raided the British coast, taking what they wanted, settling where they chose. I never felt more Manx, more connected by blood to my forebears, than at that moment.

I picked the child up. He was wrapped in a shawl made from the lining of a jacket Peter Heywood had left behind. Since the mutiny we had realised the foolishness of the heavy formal clothing we had been obliged to wear, and went about dressed appropriate to the climate. The dark-skinned mite lay in the soft white cloth defence-less, yet looking up at me with bright, alert eyes, slanted like his mother's. The set of his thin lips reminded me of my brother Humphrey, who was known for his stubbornness whether right or wrong. A Christian family trait, perhaps.

'You will put the water over him, Fletcher,' Isabella said.

'What?'

A perfect mimic of our actions as many of the islanders were, she made a gesture that was unmistakably that of christening a child.

'Who told you of that?'

'Paurai. Do not be angry.'

Smith's woman, of course. He had been preaching and teaching as I suspected he would. At another time, in another mood, I could have been angry, but not with my child in my arms and my wife looking at me as though I were the king of the world. I muttered something and Isabella looked at me in surprise, not understanding. I realised that I had spoken in Manx, the language I have been writing this journal in. Why it had come to me to speak it then I know not, but I was disposed to agree to her request. The Norse men had abandoned their dark gods for the Hebrew one and I had no wish for the child to grow up heeding the island gods with their sacrifices and other cruelties. Christening and Christianity, by contrast, were harmless rituals and beliefs.

'We will sprinkle the water over him,' I said, 'and name him Thursday October Christian.'

It was a whim that amused me, but Isabella took it completely seriously. 'And who to perform the ceremony? Must it be a special person?'

243

Smith was the origin of this piety but I had no wish to have his bull-like presence in the office. I thought of the drunken parson who had played chess with my father. 'No,' I said, 'just a friend.'

Will Brown duly christened the child with Teatuahitea, Smith and Paurai, Martin and Jenny in attendance.

When I began this journal I wrote that I hoped it would serve as a record for my children of the events that led to their lives being what they are. Now that a child is actually in existence I think it a poor thing, true enough in substance but lacking spirit. I find myself to be virtually cured of my black moods and hopeful about the future. This feeling may derive in part from the peace that flows from the sight of my son at his mother's breast. It seems a blessing, almost as if the fates have given our union, and the strange circumstances that brought it about, their approval. I fear I am falling into a religious frame of mind against all my previous instincts. God help me, I have taken B—'s Bible, having never possessed one of my own, up to the cave and spend time thumbing through it, enjoying the stories and admiring the language, though I have never embraced the book as the truth. Dead is dead and God merely an idea to comfort the oppressed and afflicted.

Thursday October is barely a month old and Isabella has told me she is with child again. Nor are we alone in this fertility. As the year draws to a close, the cries of babies can be heard around our square – Young's, Quintal's, Mills's and the Otaheitean child brought by Mary, McCoy's wife, was joined by a child of their union.

I suppose it could not be expected that nine men of different temperaments, upbringing and education, thrown together by extraordinary events, would live in perfect harmony. So, at the end of our first year I set down my account of our community's divisions. Williams, I fear, is a solitary figure in his widowhood and has none but the most necessary communication with the rest of us and little with the natives. He works his forge after a fashion as I have said, hunts a little, gardens not at all, and still has not finished his house. He trades goods with the natives for food and his unfinished house is said to be threadbare, while he goes about in rags, ever complaining. I have attempted to draw him out and used the few French words I know in an effort to amuse him but to no avail.

Ned Young and Alex Smith are much together bonded, I think, more in their interest in the ways of the natives and, I suspect, in sharing the favours of the women of the native men, and making available their own wives. Young seems to have taken a vow not to speak English, for I have not heard him do so for these many weeks. He and Smith have let their hair grow and wear the native bark skirts most of the time, although Smith arrays himself in shirt and breeches on Sundays to conduct a service of his own contrivance from the *Book of Common Prayer*. I have attended once or twice but cannot abide it. In his ignorance, Smith takes the Bible as true with a dangerous enthusiasm.

Jack Mills, Will Brown and Zac Martin work industriously in their gardens and, with Will's advice and help, are the most successful in the raising of crops. They have aided each other in the house building and have strong structures in place. Will, a Leicestershire man of about my own age, had worked in the Kew Gardens in London and seen something of polite society. He is thin and fair of skin although he darkened as did we all under the sun. I have mentioned his rent cheek and dropped eye, which made some wary of him, but I find him a steadfast friend.

It remains to write of Quintal and McCoy, who spend much time together and have less communication with the rest even than Williams. They are fractious fellows, quarrelsome even among themselves, and lazy. Both fathers now, they pay little attention to their families or their houses and prefer to shoot birds and pigs for meat and bargain with the natives for other foodstuffs. The most alarming portent of their behaviour is their treatment of the islanders they attempt to compel to work on their houses and in their gardens. Our houses are at a distance but cries can be heard at night.

'They beat the men,' Isabella told me, her eyes fierce. 'The men fear them. They beat their women.'

It is doubtless true and such is our lack of governance that none has the authority to interfere. Smith has resolved to take the Bible to them, but I reckon it will have little effect. The situation will resolve itself in time, but not, I fear, happily.

And what am I to say of myself, Fletcher Christian, gentleman, late Acting Lieutenant of HMS *Bounty*, as I sit scribbling in my cave with a warm wind blowing such as never blew in Cumberland in December? What is there to say but that I am a man divided. I yearn to see my mother and brothers and grieve for the distress they may now be feeling if word of the mutiny has reached England. I miss the sea and can scarce bear to make fishing expeditions in the cutter, re-floated and partly but poorly repaired, as the others do. The natives have built canoes for this purpose, but all of us know that our world is bounded by the distance we may safely venture from our rocky shore,

But I have a wife, a fine child and another on the way and I cannot starve or be cold; I can incur no debt, break no law nor be subject to any injustice. I am a free man. How many in the great wide world can claim as much?

And yet the divisions of which I have written present almost every day, principally Smith's ever-increasing Biblical babble. It sustains him no doubt, and Isabella reports that some of the women are drawn to it, especially to its fire and brimstone aspects. I recall that Smith originally showed interest in the softer texts. It seems that he has changed his tune.

The year 1791

WE ARE BUT A MONTH into the new year and have already had cause for great alarm and fear. Towards the end of January a huge storm got up. It raged mostly out to sea but high winds and lashing rain tested our houses and gardens. The best built structures survived but those of Williams, Quintal and McCoy were severely damaged and will require much labour to repair. The natives' huts, cunningly placed as if they could predict such forces, suffered no serious damage.

My yam patch, on the cooler side of the island where I had built a temporary shelter, like a summer house, of which I am especially proud, was almost washed away and I plan to establish it more firmly in the future with better protection. Though I find the vegetable bland, Isabella is fond of it and when prepared as a mush it is much enjoyed by Thursday October and will be, no doubt, by his brother or sister due to arrive in the middle of the year.

But more alarming than the storm itself was its aftermath. Three bodies were washed ashore. They were caught in the rocks, the storm having scoured away almost every speck of sand from our narrow beach. One of the native women, searching for shellfish, found them and raised the alarm. Strange to say, although I am accorded no rank above any other of the white men here, it was to me that the duty fell to examine the bodies and organise their burial. They were obviously sailors, reminding all present, even Quintal and McCoy, that we had all been seamen with our lives at risk. Something of my old shipboard authority was temporarily restored to me. I wondered how many of the others missed, as I did, the sound of the bells aboard ship tolling the hour.

Almost every person on the island had gathered around the corpses. They had not been in the water long enough for the fish and other sea creatures to disfigure the bodies but they were much battered and torn by the rocks. One, the largest of the three, was black, a powerfully built African with thick lips and woolly hair. The others were white men, smaller, and one a good deal older. They wore canvas trousers and flannel shirts. The African wore one heavy sea boot, the others were bare-footed.

I lifted my eyes to scan the water.

'What?' Will Brown said.

'I'm wondering whether they came from their ship itself or from a boat, and whether there will be others.'

Quintal waded into the shallows and retrieved part of a broken oar. 'A boat, Mr Christian.'

'Aye, likely the ship went down.'

The natives withdrew to discuss the matter among themselves. We stood silent for a while, each with his own thoughts. My mind jumped to the launch into which we had put the captain and his fellows. If they had encountered storms such as the recent one, their fates could well be the same as the dead men at my feet.

Mills put the question on all of our minds. 'What manner of ship? There are blackamoors in the Navy. I've seen them.'

'Not many,' McCoy said.

Martin bent down from his considerable height and lifted the shirt-sleeve of one of the men. Keen-eyed, he had apparently seen part of a tattoo on the man's arm and when the cloth was lifted an intricate image of a bird was revealed. The tattoo was old, the colours faded, and the skin had been affected by the salt water, but the bird was still discernible. It was nothing like the tattoos we had seen in the Pacific and which almost all of us bore.

'That's a redskin tattoo, or like to one,' Martin said. 'I'll wager this man is an American. The Indians make marks such as this and many sea-going men carry them.'

'You're sure, Zac?' I said.

'I've seen them often, Mr Christian, on boats sailing from Nantucket and New Bedford. I disliked the marks and was told the method was painful.' He moved his shirt aside to show the small Otaheitean star, similar to my own, on his breast. 'I found this painful enough.'

'What kind of ships? Navy?'

Martin straightened and shook his head. He was a few years older than me, and his brown hair was showing streaks of grey. 'Whalers.'

At that I fancy we all breathed sighs of relief. Our chief fear was of British naval vessels. American whalers were unlikely to pay the great rock we inhabited much attention, and even less likely to land as they went about their trade. Whales we had seen aplenty, and the natives had lamented that the water was too rough and the canoes they had built too fragile for them to attempt to hunt the young. Isabella had told me that it was an occasion for great ceremony when a young whale was killed or one was washed ashore in a condition to be skinned and eaten. The bones made useful tools, she said, and the teeth were decorative.

'We have little to fear from whalers,' I said.

Quintal, McCoy and Williams, indifferent to the fate of these unfortunates, absented themselves after insisting that their clothes and anything that might be in their pockets be divided and drawn for by lot. Ned Young watched them go and shrugged. 'Anything to avoid digging,' he said.

I bent and drew the shirt sleeve down over the tattoo. 'We can't bury them without a great deal of work carting stones. The pigs would soon root them up. We'll have to weight them and give them their sailors' burial.'

Ned Young nodded and, looking back, it seems as though this was the last moment at which we in close accord.

We stripped the bodies, wrapped them in native cloth and lashed heavy stones to their chests. Smith, in his stumbling fashion, read a passage from the Bible, something to do with 'all flesh being grass'. With the help of some of the natives, Will, Mills and I got them into the canoes and took them out past the breakers where we consigned them to the deep.

The discovery of the bodies cast a certain amount of gloom over the community for a time, reminding us as it did that, although we were hidden away, chance could at any day lead to our discovery. For some time I was not the only one to mount a high point almost daily and scan the sea to the limits of vision aided by a spyglass. After a while, however, we have resumed our normal habits, to whit gardening, hunting, collecting eggs, keeping our houses in repair and tending to our families.

It concerns me that we have few recreations. The natives play ball games, tossing a ball constructed of leaves and grass, which appear entirely uninteresting. McCoy, Quintal and occasionally Williams and Martin gamble over cards and dice. From my youth I was fond of competitive sports: running, jumping, throwing, shooting and particularly cricket, which we played at school and on the green at Cockermouth. I excelled as both batsman and bowler and the impulse came upon me to construct a bat and devise a ball. Only Will Brown and Mills among the men showed any interest. Brown had played the game when young and Mills had seen it played but had never handled bat or ball. I carved a bat from a length of wood from one of *Bounty*'s hatches, and spent much time winding coconut shell threads around a tightly knotted piece of rag to construct a ball. The result was not entirely satisfactory as the ball had a tendency to come apart after being struck several times. Nor would it bounce well on the uneven surface of our pitch. Nevertheless, Mills proved a canny bowler with an ability to flick his wrist and cause the ball to spin, and Brown was adept at throwing down a wicket from a distance. Isabella and several of the women joined in when their duties permitted and some merry times were had.

I write of things now past in the hope that matters have been put to rest, although I fear more conflict and pain lie ahead. Two events occurred within weeks of each other; the one happy, the other sad and the cause of much trouble. My second son was born in the middle of the year. I named him Charles after my brother and he was christened once more by Will Brown. He promises to be a sturdy, bonny lad like his brother.

A few weeks later Smith's wife, Paurai, fell to her death while collecting eggs on a high rock above the sea. Smith was at first greatly cast down but quickly recovered and demanded that we support him in taking women from the islanders. Quintal, McCoy, Williams and Young readily agreed, giving them a majority. I raged at Young, telling him that such a move would produce nothing but dangerous enmity.

'They are cowardly fellows,' he said, 'and two of them but boys. They cannot stand against us.'

He must have known this not to be true and I can only conclude that he wished to frustrate me or perhaps had grown bored at our quiet life and sought some excitement. With a majority against me and Mills wavering for fear that Smith's choice might fall on his woman, I had no choice but to arm myself along with the others and present our demand to the natives. Quintal and McCoy surprised the Toobouians Oho and Timoa and took Tinafanea. Smith and I presented our muskets to the Otaheiteans and told them that they must surrender one of their two women. Smith, in his bull-like manner, said that the choice was his and that Talaloo must give up Nancy, who was also known as Toofaiti. Talaloo protested, his face a mask of fury, but Smith pointed a pistol at his crotch.

'You must go to Jack Williams,' Smith said, and the woman appeared to go willingly enough.

'I'm taking the other,' Smith said as we left the hut. 'She's younger and better looking.'

'You've made two enemies.'

Smith shrugged. 'I have four friends.'

'God help you with such friends.'

'I believe He will,' Smith said.

And so it was done, leaving the six natives with but one woman between them. Isabella seemed unconcerned.

'The women will still go with our men as before.'

'Christ!' I said. 'Smith will kill Tinafanea if she does and Oho and Tetaheite as well.'

'Why?'

It was impossible to make her understand the value we put on one woman cleaving to one man. When I tried she laughed and said the idea was stupid. I told her to caution the women against being unfaithful to their new husbands but whether she did I know not. Truth to tell, I know little of what passes between the women, who spend much of the day together and only repair to the houses at night. Although I speak occasionally to Menalee and Oho, I know nothing of what is in their hearts or those of the other native men. We are two groups apart and what the children will make of it when they are grown I cannot guess.

For a time an uneasy peace held, with the natives apparently accepting their lot. But in fact Talaloo and the two wronged Toobouians were plotting to kill us all. This was revealed when Isabella heard Taifiti singing a song as she went about her tasks. Her song contained the words 'Why are the dark men sharpening their axes? To kill the white men.' On hearing this Isabella rushed to me.

'They mean to kill you! They mean to kill you!'

I was minding the children at the time and feeling nothing but goodwill towards the world so that her panic was a shock. When she made clear to me her suspicion I did not stop to think. I seized a musket and ran to the hut Oho and his nephew had shared with Talaloo since the women were taken. Oho was outside and he shouted a warning to the others and fled into the bush. Talaloo and Tetaheite broke through the back wall of their hut and followed Oho into the bush.

'Damn you, Fletcher, you should have shot at least one,' Young said later when I recounted what had happened. I did not tell him that I was by no means sure the musket was loaded and that I could not, in any case, shoot an unarmed man in cold blood. News of the plot had spread like wildfire around the settlement and Quintal and McCoy had swiftly rounded up the three Otaheiteans, tied them hand and foot and deposited them in the broken hut. We held a meeting, with all the natives, including the women, out of earshot.

From the first, I knew that this was the end of our society. Quintal, McCoy and Smith were for killing the three Otaheiteans in captivity and hunting down and killing the three who were at large. McCoy, who seemed to be drunk, although as far as I knew there was no liquor on the island, was their spokesman. 'We can't sleep peaceably in our beds with any Indians alive,' he said. 'We must kill them all.'

This I could not countenance, nor could Mills or Will Brown. Young seemed divided, as he had drawn closer to the natives since our arrival on the island. It crossed my mind that he might have known of the plot, indeed been a part of it, but I dismissed the thought as too troublesome. All was lost if we turned against each other.

'Would you include the women, then?' I asked McCoy, hoping to mock his proposal.

'I might,' he said. 'Why did Nancy not tell us of the plot outright?'

At this Williams protested. 'She did so in her own way.'

'Slyly, mayhap,' McCoy said. 'They are all sly. It is their way.'

'Even your Mary?' I said.

'I keep her in line with a rope's end, and will do the same with her Indian brat.'

The talk went on far into the night with tempers fraying and our ears alert lest the three natives launch some kind of attack. Every man at the meeting was armed with a musket and pistol.

'What weapons had they when they fled, Fletcher?' Will Brown asked.

'None. But they may have crept back and secured some. We cannot be sure. At least we know they have no firearms.'

We had allowed the natives the use of muskets to hunt pigs but had insisted the weapons be returned after any such expedition. Many suggestions as to how to deal with the situation were raised and hotly debated, including that the three plotters be captured and put in canoes and sent away from the island.

At this Young laughed in his mocking fashion. 'Then they would die as surely as Bligh and his lickspittles. More merciful to shoot them on the spot.'

'As we should have done then,' Quintal said.

Argument then broke out about the conduct of the mutiny such as had not been heard among us before. Pistols were raised, and I learned that Quintal and others had spoken of taking the ship at various times during our long passage to the island. I was enraged and my anger brought this matter to a close but did not resolve the question at hand. It is strange to relate but my authority, partly restored when we found the bodies of the sailors, was further confirmed. I ordered Quintal and McCoy to bring the Otaheiteans from their prison so that we might question them. This they did. All three were desperately afraid of Quintal and McCoy who had handled them roughly in the past. Still tied at the wrists they stood trembling before us, no doubt expecting to be shot.

I attempted to calm their fears and, as the one who spoke the native language best, I questioned them closely about the plot. All three swore they knew nothing of it and would have betrayed it to us instantly had they known. I believed them but most did not and several were for shooting them. It was Young who proposed a compromise.

'We may test their loyalty by sending them to hunt and kill the others,' he said. 'With a limited supply of powder and ball and one musket between them. If they succeed they will have proved worthy of our trust.'

I was doubtful. 'Talaloo is of the chiefly caste. They will be reluctant to raise a hand against him.'

Young shrugged. 'Their lives depend upon it.'

The plan found favour with a majority and the natives agreed when it was put to them. They were kept secure for the rest of the night and set about their mission the next morning. In the morning Toofaiti was found to be missing. Quintal laughed and said that she found Williams too ugly and not man enough to hold her. Williams on this occasion showed a rare flash of spirit. He struck Quintal a severe blow which felled him. Then he stood over him.

'Damn you, Quintal! Talaloo beat her as you beat your woman. She hates him. The bastard must have come down and taken her. I'll kill him myself if I get the chance.'

What followed no white man witnessed and I can only write of it as Isabella has told me from her questioning the other natives and the women in particular. Whether this account is true in all respects I know not. Certain it is that the others deputed Menalee to attempt to kill Talaloo as the most dangerous of the fugitives. Menalee took to the bush unarmed and scouted for some days, returning with the news that Oho was in the southern part of the island while Talaloo, Tetaheite and Toofaiti were in the west. His opinion was that all were hungry so he took some food hoping to win Talaloo's trust by agreeing to enlist with him against us. On this occasion Menalee was issued with a musket.

'He tried to kill Talaloo,' Isabella said, 'but the gun made no sound and Talaloo began to fight with him. They fought hard and Talaloo called on Tetaheite to help him but he was afraid and took no part.'

'He is a coward?'

'He is young. Toofaiti then came up and Talaloo called for her help. She took up a big stone and as Menalee held him down, she beat Talaloo's head with the stone and killed him.'

'Her husband.'

'He had mistreated her. She was not of a rank with him. She would rather the white man, though he is lacking in his manhood, and Talaloo had forced her to go with him.'

As we saw, Menalee returned with Toofaiti and Tetaheite whom we confined. I examined the musket and found its lock to be rusted. I wondered who had issued it but could not discover. The women, with Brown and myself as guards, ventured into the bush to the site where the fight had taken place and they made for Talaloo a shallow grave covered by a heavy canopy of rocks, proof against the pigs.

Toofaiti returned to Williams and Tetaheite was kept under close guard, and so this bloody time ended, as it was agreed to leave the fugitives to starve and weaken themselves before another attack on them was made. It was agreed that Menalee should hunt down Oho, now the only danger. He had been seen sneaking close to the settlement and doubtless was hungry and lonely, for in the normal state no native spends much time alone. Oho was a powerful man and it was decided that Timoa should be allowed to accompany Menalee in their hunt for him, but our trust was not such as to issue a firearm.

Again, I can only testify as to the result of this action and place faith in the version of events given to me by Isabella because Menalee and Timoa refused to speak of it to me or the other white men. They pursued Oho until he was close to exhaustion and then, drawing near, spoke to him soothingly. They said that we had decided to forgive him and to let all the natives live in peace, sharing the one woman left to them. Whether Oho believed these blandishments or not is impossible to say, but he ventured out and friendly conversation took place with Menalee and Timoa sharing food with Oho. As was their custom, Menalee and Timoa undertook to comb Oho's hair as a seal on their friendship. As Timoa was performing this service Menalee cut Oho's throat from ear to ear.

The natives returned to the settlement and told the women what had been done. With Mills and Quintal, who wanted to be sure the man was dead, we accompanied the women into the bush and found the body. The slash across the throat had been forceful, almost severing the head, and Quintal nodded his approval.

'Menalee made sure of him. He knows where the power lies on this island.'

I was not so sure. It was a savage act, stamping Menalee as a man of violence after Quintal's own heart. The flies and ants, having feasted on the spilt blood, had already begun the process of reducing the body to dust. We left the women to dig a grave and put up a cairn of stones as before, and returned to the settlement.

'What of Tetaheite?' Will Brown said.

Quintal laughed and spat. 'McCoy and me can work him till he's too tired to do any mischief.'

I am recalling these events, now some time in the past, and am by no means sure I have all the details correct. I am writing on the last day of this year, which I feel inclined to call the year of blood. Had it not been for the death of the two women, things might not have come to this pass, but I cannot be sure. The thought of the natives sharpening their axes still haunts me, together with Toofaiti's slaying of her husband and Menalee's savage slash. On Otaheite, although we knew of the natives' savage ways, we little thought they could come to affect us, being people apart. But now we are not people apart. With still more children born, we are united in blood as well as in our occupation of this small space. I trust Isabella; I wonder if the others trust their women as much. I wonder if they sleep easy in their beds. I do, but I would I had a dog to alert me to danger by day and by night.

Another great concern is the hypocrisy of Smith. His faith is of a savage kind and he delights in expounding on bloody tales from the Bible. He was ardently in favour of the killing of the natives and cites the passages about the sons of Ham in support of our subjugation of them. But, hypocrite that he is, he is forever prosing at them to accept Jesus as their saviour to my disgust and their great bewilderment.

The year 1792

I HAVE TAKEN TO SPENDING less time in my cave and therefore write less in this my journal. Considerable work is required in the gardens to feed my family for I fear their appetites are large. I am also somewhat afflicted by pain in my hip which, I believe, derives from a fall from a horse when I was a boy. It has troubled me little in the intervening years but now, especially when the weather turns damp, the hip does not move freely and pain courses down my right leg. Isabella, ever attentive, rubs the hip with warm oil which gives some relief but, as I approach my thirtieth year I feel some of the weight of time.

Nevertheless, I delight in my children, both growing strongly and never ill. I remember my own childhood illnesses and especially those of my brother Humphrey who was often abed for weeks. Children not robust died frequently in Cockermouth and every family had stones and markers in the churchyard bearing the names of those who died young. Not so here. All children born, and I am now uncertain of the count because the families live so much apart, have thrived on the ample food and in the sunshine. I write now on the birthday of my mother, the eighth of May, and my heart is heavy that I will never know if she still lives and whether she has overcome her difficulties. I hope she has.

My son, Thursday October, grows apace. He walks and talks. His speech derives partly from his mother and partly from me. I doubt he will understand either English or Otaheitean fully, but what matter?

He is a Pitcairner as we are all growing to be. My only shoes have worn out and I go barefoot. English cloth rots in this climate and I have but one good shirt and one pair of breeches surviving. I wear them occasionally because Isabella likes to see me so dressed, otherwise, like the others, I cover my loins with native bark cloth alone. We hack off our hair to shoulder length and use scissors but rarely to trim our beards and moustaches. Although some of us have razors, nobody shaves.

On looking at the children the other day at play, seeing those able to crawl and walk and hearing the mothers singing to those at the breast, the thought came that we must one day have a school. Our materials for this are of the scantiest – no books suitable to young minds, no chalk, no slates and very little paper. As to teachers, few of us can read and write and none, I fancy, has the temperament of a teacher. Smith would welcome the role to infect the children with his new-found piety, but I do not suppose the children would flock to him. I must talk to Isabella about it. It may be possible for us to instruct one of the younger women and so prepare her for the task, or the matter may have to be delayed until one of the children who shows promise can be so guided. My mind is much on thoughts of the future of our colony.

Resuming at a later date. I feel isolated and apart from my fellows. Much has changed in the associations between us, partly under the influence of grog. McCoy, from Aberdeen, who had worked in a distillery before going to sea, knew the secrets of producing alcoholic drink from plants. I have mentioned his conduct at one of the meetings at the time of the natives' plot. Later he came to me, respectfully but obviously drunk, and boasted of his prowess. He offered me a tin mug full of a clear spirit.

''Tis from the ti palm, Mr Christian. It makes a fine mash and a bonny tot. Have a taste, sir.'

I sipped at the brew and found it fiery to the point of causing my throat to seize. 'God save us, Will, that's a devil's brew. Do you not water it to drink?'

'Not I, sir, nor Matt or others. We have a taste for it, since we have not enough tobacco and the other usual comforts of a seaman's life.'

Will Brown's tobacco plants have failed to thrive, and we had to ration the supply we had taken from the ship. Unused to being sparing with tobacco, most of us, myself included, lamented the want of the soothing smoke whenever we felt like it. Something of a tippler in earlier days, I had grown used to being without grog and, if the truth be known, missed coffee more than any other stimulant. I handed back the cup.

'You have a woman of a night, Will, and children around you. Something no British sailor has.'

McCoy downed the contents of the mug in one swallow. 'A lazy black bitch,' he said. 'Growing fatter on yam and taro by the minute. Good day to you, Mr Christian.'

Sad to relate, Mills, Martin and Brown have taken eagerly to McCoy's brew, so that Mills and McCoy have began to work together between drunken bouts. Likewise, Martin and Will Brown, who is somehow cast down by not producing a child and jealous of me, have begun to associate with Quintal, always a drunkard from Portsmouth onward. I retreat more and more into the warm circle of my family, not wanting to associate closely with those strange men who are truly apart in their several worlds – Williams, Young and Smith. Young and Smith's houses and gardens are adjacent but they have little contact and I wonder what effect this solitariness will have on us all. Only McCoy and Quintal can be called friends and it is a friendship mainly of the cup.

I discuss all with Isabella who tells me that the native men and some of the women have tried McCoy's drink but do not like it. They wish the kava plant grew here but it does not. I have no yen myself for that muddy brew, but its effect of causing paralysis of the legs and sleepiness is less dangerous than that of the grog. I give two instances. Not long ago Mareva came running up to me as I was working in my garden.

'Titreano, they are killing Timoa,' she shouted.

'Who?'

She babbled hysterically in Otaheitean so that I could not understand her. I grabbed a bayonet and ran to the plantation jointly worked by Quintal and McCoy, or rather by the natives they forced to work for them. Coming upon a small clearing where McCoy had his still, I found Timoa tied to a tree with his arms raised and tied to branches above his head. McCoy's arm was drawn back to deliver a blow with a knotted rope. Timoa's back was already bleeding.

I put the blade to McCoy's neck. 'Belay that, McCoy, or I'll cut your bloody throat.'

Quintal, drunk, was seated on a log watching the beating. He stood but, either from seeing my expression or from drunkenness, quickly sat down.

McCoy dropped his arm and I used the bayonet to cut Timoa free. He dashed away, howling.

'You fools,' I said. 'To make enemies of these men.'

McCoy spat close to my feet. 'Men? Niggers. Thieves. That black bastard stole my yams, a full bushel, I swear.'

Not for the first time I cursed myself for not allotting the natives larger plots. As it was all but Menalee, to whom I had assigned a section of my own garden for his personal use, were obliged to work for the others and take what food they were given to be supplemented only by what their woman gathered. True, all the natives had put on flesh, none was starving, but their resentment and thieving were understandable.

McCoy and Quintal were both drunk but I attempted to reason with them. 'How can you be sure Timoa stole the roots?'

Quintal waved his mug. 'Mareva told on him.'

There was nothing to say. From Isabella I had learned that all the native women despised the men for their weakness. Likely Mareva had been pleased to see Timoa punished and was only alarmed at the severity. Perhaps it reminded her of events aboard the ship, as it did me. I left, cast down and full of foreboding.

Some time later I came down to the settlement after spending most of the day in my cave. I had intended only to go up and search the horizon for signs of shipping or any floating wreckage that might be coming our way. It happened rarely, but a few useful pieces of timber had been washed ashore and once a wounded infant whale had been trapped in the shallows and was quickly despatched and cut up by the natives. But rain fell heavily soon after I arrived and persisted for most of the day. I had some food with me and was disinclined to negotiate the steep track in the wet so I remained warm and dry in the cave, reading over some of B—'s books – John Byron's highly interesting *Narrative of a Shipwreck* and Dampier's *Voyage to New Holland*. I was interested to see that Dampier's departure in the *Roebuck* had been delayed by the Admiralty's inefficiency. His plan to enter the Pacific by the Horn had thus been frustrated. Unlike B—, however, he had the good sense not to attempt it, knowing that the season was unfavourable.

On returning home near to evening I found Menalee lying near our house in a shelter that we used to store tools and other items. Isabella had provided him with water and a grass mat and he was groaning in his sleep, obviously feverish. I approached and saw that his back was badly bruised and cut and that his wounds had dirt and a white substance in them. Isabella was at first reluctant to tell me what had happened, fearing my anger, but at last she spoke.

Menalee, she said, took a pig McCoy had been fattening to feast on with Quintal, Brown and Mills.

'They found Menalee roasting the pig and were very angry. The red face beat him with a stick and then with a rope and put dirt and salt into his back. They left him to lie for a long time until he found the strength to crawl to our house. He is hot but he shivers. I think he will die.'

By the red face she meant Quintal, who had a scraggly ginger beard. His complexion was fair and unlike most of us, he did not darken in the sun but merely looked ruddy and weatherbeaten. I told Isabella to cover Menalee with a blanket and to get him to drink water if she could. I knew she made potions against sickness and I knew she would do all she could for the poor fellow.

I went to Quintal's house unarmed, not trusting myself with a weapon. Quintal and McCoy were cleaning their muskets when I arrived. They were chatting and tried to ignore me but I stood so close they could not but look up.

'You're a brute, Quintal.'

'What's this?'

'You beat that man's back to meat, then you tortured him.'

'Not so, I thought the salt would help heal the thieving black bugger.'

'What of the dirt?'

He shrugged and made no reply. I leaned against a house post that was none too firm. 'Well may you clean your weapons, for you've near killed the only one of the natives we can trust.'

'He stole my pig,' McCoy said.

'There are other pigs, but if Menalee turns against us with the others you have mistreated God help us all.'

'Are you afraid, Mr Christian?' Quintal said and from the glow in his eyes I could see that he had been drinking McCoy's Aberdeen poison and was beyond fear for the moment. I reached down and took the musket from his hands. 'I'll tell you this, little Mattie, red face.' I used the Otaheitean word insultingly. 'If Menalee dies I'll gather a majority to have you executed for his murder. I might give you the choice of being hung or shot.'

Quintal sneered, knowing this to be an empty threat. 'And if the bugger lives?'

I flung the musket down on the sand, undoing his work. 'Then I'll deal with you myself.'

At this Quintal stood and faced me. He was the shorter by some inches and had grown fat through over-eating, drinking and doing little work, but he was thick in the neck, broad-shouldered and deep-chested, and his bulk and drunken anger almost made me take a back step. 'And how would you go about that, Mr Christian, sir? Would we duel like gentlemen with pistols or sabres?'

McCoy laughed.

'I'd thrash you as I thrashed Charley Churchill on Toobouai.'

'Charley had been beaten with sticks by the Indians and was bruised. I'm fit as a bull and fought many a time in the booths. I reckon you'll find me a harder nut to crack, sir.'

His contempt made me want to attack him there and then but I controlled myself. 'We'll see.' I turned and left them.

Menalee's fever lasted for several days but did not prove fatal. I am writing now shortly before going to fight with Quintal. I have insisted that the natives should know nothing of this, for if they were to see two white men fighting it would do nothing but lower our prestige still further. The fight will take place at the yam patch a distance from the settlement. Brown, who has no taste for pugilism, has agreed to keep the natives busy at a distance. At his instruction and with a promise of a reward if they are successful, Timoa and Nehow are to go fishing in their canoes while Tetaheite is to help Brown repair a fence. One of the women is close to her time and the others are in attendance and indifferent to the doings of men.

I confess to uncertainty. On consideration, Quintal bears the scars of many fights. Although carrying flesh nowadays, he is powerfully built and light on his feet. He was a considerable rigging man, work requiring strength and balance. I have no doubt I can excel him in science, but I am plagued by the pain in my hip and am not near as nimble as I once was. The bout is unlikely to be conducted according to Broughton's rules, probably unknown to Quintal. As I have written, I attended a few mills as a youth and admired science more than brawn. But, as in the brawl with Churchill, there will be no second's knee or referee, no ropes or calling time. Quintal and I are old enemies now, he blaming me for allowing B— to live, me never forgiving him for burning the ship as and when he did. I suppose this moment was bound to come.

I write now with considerable difficulty on the day after the fight. I have swollen and bruised hands and a wrenched back from when Quintal caught me in a perfect cross-buttock throw. I hobbled to the cave where I am now writing. Quintal was a formidable fighter who knew more about milling than I expected. His bulk made him slow but I discovered to my cost that he had extraordinarily long arms, giving him a reach greater than his height suggested. There is little to report about the fight. Quintal threw me several times and I knocked him down about as many. He landed many heavy blows on my body and I hit him about the head until I discovered it was as hard as a rock and switched my attack to his belly. To my surprise, Quintal fought fair and seemed to enjoy the battle. McCoy, Williams and Smith urged him on while Mills and Zac Martin offered me support. Young and Brown were absent.

Truth to tell, neither of us was in proper condition for a bout and it ended after about twenty minutes indecisively with both too exhausted to raise our hands. Quintal was somewhat marked around the eyes and nose and had lost a tooth, causing his mouth to bleed. I was battered around the ribs and, with my other aches and strains, was glad to call a halt. We parted without shaking hands.

And so our third year on Pitcairn's Island finds us divided and opposed, one against another, with the natives beaten down and unhappy. Isabella has told me that it was vain for me to think that word of the fight would not get out. Williams told Nancy of it and she spread the news among the others, women and men. She says some believe Quintal was victorious and others think I won the fight. All are puzzled by it. None more so than Menalee, who, since his recovery, has avoided me as much as possible. Useless to tell him I fought on his behalf, as he would not understand such a departure from what he would think to be normal behaviour that is, that one remains true to one's tribe no matter what.

Smith has conceived a mad plan to baptise all the children. He would do it by total immersion in the sea. I understand that some of the women are intrigued and willing to allow it and would submit to it themselves. Our men are mostly indifferent; neither Will Brown nor myself would allow Smith to touch a hair on our children's heads. He grows more passionate in his delusions day by day.

'Your children will go to hell, Mr Christian,' Smith told me. 'And you with them.'

I shook my head. 'You are making a hell here of what could be an Eden.'

He went off, muttering about blasphemy.

2 January, 1793, early

MY HIP AND BACK TROUBLE HAS caused me to leave off going to the cave. I have brought this journal down to the house and now plan to write in the early hours of morning when no one is astir. I do not sleep well. Troubled by my body and in my mind. At least writing is easier now that I have devised a way to improve the quality of the oil, by straining it through a fine mesh, and have improved the wick after experimentation with the coconut shell threads. I have the shutters closed and if anyone is curious about the light showing, let them be. B—plainly intended to write a great deal because his supply of ink, most of which, although not all to judge by the arrangement of the pots when I took possession of the writing materials, was left behind will serve me for some time to come.

I wonder what the year will bring. Our gardens are all well advanced and food is in abundance. The fish in the sea seem inexhaustible, but I fancy the bird numbers have declined somewhat as a result of our egg collection. We have ducks but they are a poor lot, reluctant to lay. Our spring continues to flow and to give no anxiety. I do not know if others have considered it apart from Brown and myself, but if the spring were to dry up we would be forced to collect rain water from the rock pools which would be arduous. It occurs to me that this may have happened in the past and caused the previous occupants to leave the island. A doleful thought.

The pigs are troublesome, the goats less so. Both provide good meat when they can be shot but they have grown cunning and require skilful hunting and shooting. We have half-tamed and tethered one to provide milk. I find tracking through the bush difficult and my family eats less meat than others. Isabella is skilled at fishing and shell collecting so we never go hungry or lack variety. Fools that they be, Quintal and McCoy have taught the natives to shoot. They issue them with muskets and a limited supply of ammunition and send them hunting on the understanding that they can share in the results, the worst cuts no doubt. Tetaheite is said to have become a good shot, the others less so, not liking the sound of the report. Why Quintal and McCoy trust the men they have so abused puzzles me and I can only ascribe it to laziness and drunkenness. McCoy in particular appears to be drunk a good deal of the time and his woman suffers accordingly.

Because *Bounty* was intended to go on a very long voyage, much of it in uncertain waters, there was a great supply of powder and ball aboard. We brought it all ashore – enough to last beyond our lifetimes if used wisely. With drunken louts and hostile natives the firearms represent a significant danger and I have thought of wetting or otherwise corrupting the powder. But the anger such an act would cause could bring about more trouble than that I seek to avoid. And there is always the possibility that we have to defend ourselves. So I take no action. Perhaps the muskets and pistols will fall into disrepair in the hands of such fellows.

Thursday October and Charles thrive and the children all play together and are amiable, totally unaware of the divisions and hostilities that exist among their elders. In my darker moments I admit to myself that they are the hope for the future of Pitcairn's Island, so far away from any other human on earth, and I can only hope that they display the best characteristics of the two races, not the worst.

It is some months since my last entry. Life continues along its usual lines and I have no need to write anything down, there being nothing of moment to record. Nor are my own thoughts and feelings worthy of notice. Suffice to say I waver between contentment and a feeling of futility. The cause is obvious. I was a young man of promise with a marked out career path that could have taken me to great heights. Who knows what deeds I might have done, what honours and riches accrued, what love affairs undertaken, what friendships made? And now I am a peasant farmer, scarce even a yeoman, having no kinsmen, no servants and no reputation among my neighbours. Still, there are the blessings of Isabella, who will never know I named her after one I sought and lost, and my children. Isabella has but lately told me she is with child again. When I think of the women we admired in England – the pale, thin creatures, many of whom were killed by their first child, I am glad Isabella bears and brings them forth so easily. We both hope for a daughter.

We speak, Isabella and I, mostly of domestic matters – the house, the children, food, my ailments. She has seen me writing but shows no curiosity about it. I have offered to teach her to read and write, but she merely smiles and shakes her head.

'A white man's thing,' she said once when I pressed her.

'And our children?'

'First they must learn to fish, dig and hunt.'

Others have their crosses to bear. Young suffers from some affliction of the lungs which, at times, makes it almost impossible to draw breath. This seems to be happening more often and he is drawn and thin from the pain and effort. His coughing is distressing to hear, but he does not spit blood so that at least it is not consumption that has hold of him. Added to that, his remaining teeth pain him greatly and this has given rise to an event which has sealed our hostility forever.

'I am suffering the torments of the damned,' he said to me, 'from a tooth as black as coal. Your Isabella is skilled at knocking out teeth in the heathenish way they do.'

'Who told you this?'

'Susannah.'

'She is young, would she know?'

'Damn you, she says so. I pray you ask your wife to rid me of this tooth.'

I talked to Isabella and she admitted that she had knocked out many a tooth in a ceremonial fashion. I clacked my own sound teeth at her. 'I trust you never have to knock out any of mine. Young has a sick tooth and asks you to remove it.'

'He is no friend of ours, Fletcher.'

'True, but he is in great pain and to have him in our debt might be useful.'

'The ways of white men are strange. He is an enemy. Perhaps the tooth will kill him.'

I kissed her. I am married to a savage who lives by a savage code. 'Our ways are strange. I ask this of you.'

We went to Young's house and found him lying on his bed groaning with the pain. The side of his face was blown out as though his mouth was full of air. His breath came thinly but regularly.

'Quick,' Susannah said, 'while he breathes well.'

I supported him. Isabella placed a stick to hold his mouth open and had him point to the tooth. His breath was foul and I could not bear to look. Isabella had a long thin stone which she put to the tooth. She held a rounded stone in her hand and brought it sharply down.

'Jesus Christ!' Young's closing jaws snapped the stick and a part of the shattered tooth sprayed from his mouth in a welter of blood.

'You black bitch!' He tore free, sprang from the bed, seized a club and struck Isabella a glancing blow on the head. She yelled and fell back. I stood and slammed my fist against his temple with all my force so that he fell back stunned.

'You've killed him,' Susannah cried.

'I'll be damned if I have,' I said. 'Fetch me a knife and send to McCoy for some of his poison.'

I was speaking in Otaheitean as I did most of the time and the two women understood me. Susannah left the house and returned with a gourd of the spirit just as Young was coming to his senses. McCoy staggered in after her. Young was lying on his bed with his chest covered in blood.

'Dead, Mr Christian?'

'No. If he drinks all of this will he feel any pain?'

McCoy laughed. 'Not if he drinks the half of it.'

I propped Young up and had McCoy hold him while I poured the spirit into his bloodied mouth. He gagged on it but swallowed several times and then appeared to welcome it flowing down his throat. He opened his eyes and looked at me as though I was his executioner. Then his eyes closed and his breathing became thin and ragged. I cared not whether he lived or died. I prised his mouth open, took up the knife Susannah had provided and cut the stump of the diseased tooth out of his jaw as though I was digging up yams. Young moaned but remained still through the operation. When the dark, bloody root came free I threw down the knife and slopped more of the spirit into his gob.

'If you have such a thing as a clean rag, soak it in water and put it in his mouth. Clean him. He might live. I care not one way or the other.'

McCoy, suddenly sober, looked at me, seized the gourd and drained it. 'He was your friend, Mr Christian.'

'I have no friends now in this accursed place.'

I left the house, noticing that Isabella was whispering to Susannah. Later, she told me that she had advised the younger woman as to what potions to prepare and what chants to sing. Young survived, but we have not spoken from that day to this.

Isabella defies nature, at least in so far as English women are concerned, by becoming more beautiful as her pregnancy advances. She performs all her tasks both inside the house and out with a cheerfulness that shames me when I descend to the depths. As I have written, I sleep little and am plagued by headaches and dimming eyesight. I fear that our English eyes are not well adapted to the constant bright sunlight and the reflection from rocks and the sea. I have taken to wearing a hat woven of leaves, giving some relief, but no doubt looks comical. I am not alone in these disabilities. McCoy, in particular, shows signs of madness from his constant intake of strong drink and any scratch or insect bite he suffers immediately turns ulcerous. His woman has told Isabella that he eats little and then mostly meat.

'His blood is bad,' Isabella says, and I suppose that is as accurate a statement on his condition as any.

But I am writing now in the early hours of the morning in May as the weather turns cooler and more restful sleep is possible. This night I have slept for six hours and feel refreshed and would write of happier things. What comes to mind is my better associations with Jack Mills and Will Brown. They have detached themselves somewhat from McCoy and Quintal, whose rages have become intolerable. Smith and Williams remain apart, although Smith preaches constantly to those who will listen and consigns to damnation those who will not. Although not the youngest of us, he is perhaps the most healthy which, of course, he attributes to his faith. If it came to a trial of strength between us I fear he would win. If he should try to assert some kind of authority born of the

Bible, I know not what the outcome would be. I give him a wide berth.

'I confess to you, Fletcher,' Brown said to me recently. 'I am reluctant to die here.'

Although we were young men yet, thus our thoughts ran on death, so sadly had things developed. I said, 'I thought you found it a gardening delight.'

He glanced at me to make sure I was joshing him. 'Just so, but there's more to life than plants.'

'As our captain found.'

'Aye, to his cost. Do you look ahead, Fletcher?'

I was in one of my eyesight-dimmed periods and I held out my hand. 'At times I can scarce see beyond my arm's length.'

'I've remarked the hat. You are not alone in that. Quintal squints like a loony. But you know my meaning, surely?'

'Aye. You think to leave the island.'

'I do.' Will looked about him. We were seated on logs in the yam patch I was trying to develop at the edge of my garden, not wanting to walk daily to the more favoured place. 'You've thought the same?'

I had. The notion had been growing in me, springing from a number of seeds. Strange to say, one was a wish to hear music again; not the scratching of Byrn, but a proper band in full flight. I have no skill in music myself and admire those with the talent all the more on that account. Another seed was my reproach to myself that we had not established a meeting place in our settlement. Our village lacked a centre and we should have known better than to omit it. Surely any group of people, and especially one so strangely composed as ours, needed a place to discuss problems as they arose. We had nothing such and had paid a price for its lack.

'I have thought of leaving,' I said. 'Ever since the first deaths by violence.'

'How?' Brown's voice was but a whisper.

'By building a boat, how else?'

'Where, Fletcher? Where could we go?'

I had thought about it long and deep, having by now decided, against everything in my head before, that our settlement on Pitcairn's Island was doomed to failure. I would need allies, secrecy, violent action almost certainly. I had more of a dream than a plan. Could I trust Brown? I wavered, then spoke. 'America,' I said. 'Where Englishmen have broken free of tyranny.'

It was a statement I never thought to make – unpatriotic, treasonable and hateful to a loyal Englishman. But where else in the world did we have a prospect of freedom if we left the island? Brown, a practical fellow, seemed not taken aback by the idea but by the chances.

'It's thousands of miles away.'

'Aye. It's a dream.'

'I'm shrivelling here. Could it be done?'

'I've studied the charts, Will. A sturdy craft, well provisioned and manned, has a chance of reaching Mexico.'

'Jesus, what manner of people dwell there?'

'Indians, and Spaniards.'

Brown shook his head. 'Spaniards, enemies of England.'

'Not at the time we left and who knows, now?'

Brown smiled. 'I grew up on stories of Drake and the Armada.'

'As I did, as a Manxman. There were tales of Spaniards cast ashore and breeding brown-skinned babies with Manx women. I was ever swarthy myself.'

'I doubt a Spaniard would have a chance to plough a Manx woman in that hue and cry. He'd more likely be ploughed himself.'

Just for that moment it was pleasant to think about battles and victories of long ago, but it did nothing for our present purpose.

'D'you recall the sailors washed up here dead some time back? Americans, Zac Martin deemed them, and I believe he was right. American ships may be in these waters hunting whales. If we are out there we might fall in with such a vessel and find favour with them.'

'Oh, Fletcher, that's a happy thought. Martin might be with us in this plan.'

'He might.'

And so I, who had acted on the spur of the moment in the mutiny, albeit with a hideous fear to prompt me, fell to plotting on Pitcairn's Island with Will Brown, Jack Mills and Zac Martin. How might we escape from the trap we had fallen into, threatened as we were by ill-treated and wronged natives and former shipmates who had lost control of their lives and desires?

It is nigh impossible to do anything in secret on the island. One's business is everybody's business, so we four had to invent a story to cover our being occasionally together and the work we engaged upon. My plan was as follows – we elected to help the natives construct better fishing canoes, those they had being very inferior and apt to take on water in rough weather. Quintal and McCoy continue to compel the native men to work for them and Williams and Young remain apart, indifferent to what we others do. We have told the women nothing of the plan but our intention, when we leave the island, is to take them and the children with us if they desire to go. We will build three substantial canoes, using some of the timber from the ship which has not found its way into our houses and some which has. Mills and Brown have the skills and we have the tools. My plan is to build the canoes in such a way that they can be fastened together at the last moment to make a large craft, capable of carrying a dozen people with provisions for a long voyage.

Quintal and McCoy are drunk every night and the native men too exhausted to do anything but sleep as soon as they lay their burdens down. It might be necessary for us to constrain Young and Williams when we make our escape. So be it. We will do them no harm. Once again, I have insisted that no blood be shed in this action which could be seen as a second mutiny, as we take our leave of the agreements which have hitherto bound us together.

I will leave Pitcairn's Island with some reluctance. It had seemed the perfect place to begin our lives anew but it was perhaps a narrow vision. I suppose we could have sailed *Bounty* to America at the outset, but I doubt the idea was in anyone's mind or would have found favour. At that time we were tied to the islands by history and our experience to date. We thought not of the wider world. England and Otaheite were our boundary points. From necessity, we have come to take a broader view.

Apart from the hazards of the projected voyage, our problems are many. Secrecy, above all. We are sworn together to say nothing of our plans to our women or anyone else, whatever the temptation or provocation might be. So far, the bond has held. Another problem is our health and strength.

'Zac has strained his back,' Will Brown reported to me a day or two ago when we were working on a keel board for a canoe.

Martin was the tallest man in the company, standing close enough to six foot, and his figure was gangly but strong. He would be a vital member of our party for his strength and especially for his American origin. We were still a long way from ready, with the work progressing slowly, but it was a bothersome detail. Happily, Jenny, Martin's woman, was skilled in the native arts, and she restored him to full strength by rubbing his back with vegetable and fish oils.

'God, you stink, Zac,' I said when we next met.

Martin laughed. 'She bids me keep the place oiled. It feels so much better I cannot refuse.'

For myself, I have taken to swimming to relieve the hip pain and it seems to be efficacious. The salt water and the hat have helped my eyesight. I was ever a strong swimmer and in this climate the water is mild all the year about. It pleasures me greatly to be able to go down the path to the beach without pain, swim and plunge under the surface, and make the climb again. The remains of our ship lie on the sea bed, not so far out, and, as my strength increases, I think to swim there, dive down and see her one last time. I may, but on my last swim I saw a shark circling and so I may not.

I spoke of the shark to Menalee who laughed and said that the sharks could do him no harm. He is sullen, like his fellows.

I am writing now on a day worthy of mark – 20 September, 1793. 'Tis almost dawn and I've slept well since Isabella has told me that she expects our child to be born this day. Our daughter, as we trust. Work on the boat, as I now think of it, progresses well, and it excites me to think of taking ship again for a new world with my wife and three children. Surely this time we can start afresh, leaving all the old divisions and hatreds behind us. As light peeps through the shutters I extinguish the lamp, stretch and rise from my table. I hear the birds greet the dawn and I am full of hope.

I know how the morning will progress, having been through the process twice before. Isabella will send for the women she wants and they will assemble to do what is necessary to draw the child safely forth. It is no place for a man. I will breakfast on goat's milk, fruit and taro and go forth to work my yam patch. A goodly supply of yams will be needed for our next voyage to freedom.

Postscript

On 20 September 1793, the day his daughter was born, Fletcher Christian was shot and killed by the Polynesian Menalee.

Acting in concert, the four Polynesian men on Pitcairn also killed John ("Jack") Williams. John Mills and Isaac Martin were shot and beaten to death; William Brown was battered by a stone and then shot and killed. Alexander Smith (aka John Adams) was wounded but not killed and given amnesty.

At some time in 1796, William McCoy, in a drink-induced delirium, threw himself from a high rock and was killed. Late in 1799, John Adams and Edward Young, again in a dispute over access to women, killed Mathew Quintal. Young died of a respiratory disease in 1800, leaving Adams as the only surviving mutineer when he met Henry Corkill of the whaler Emerald *in 1807.*

A search of Massachusetts records has revealed that a Henry Corkill, born in Boston in 1775, was killed in 1812 in a skirmish between the militia, in which he was serving as a Captain, and a British troop. Corkill's nearest of kin was given as a sister, Isabelle, so he evidently did not realise his dream of creating a family.

In a remarkable feat of navigation, endurance and leadership, William Bligh took the open launch through the Endeavour Strait to the then Dutch-held island of Timor, losing only one man in the process. On his return to England

Bligh, as naval law required, was court-martialled for the loss of his ship. He was exonerated. After serving with distinction in the French wars he was appointed Governor of New South Wales, only to endure another mutiny at the hands of the 'Rum Corps' in 1808. He rose to the rank of Vice-Admiral and died in 1817.

The crew of the Bounty *who remained on Tahiti, including some who were mutineers and some who were not, were taken into custody by Captain Edwards of the* Pandora *who had been despatched by the Navy for that purpose. The prisoners were held in a locked cage on the ship and, when she struck a reef and foundered, a number of them drowned. The six named by Bligh as active mutineers (including Peter Heywood) were tried for mutiny in England, found guilty, and sentenced to death. Heywood had influential connections and was pardoned; James Morrison was also pardoned on the recommendation of the court; William Muspratt escaped the rope on a legal technicality. 'Young Tom' Ellison, Thomas Burkitt and John Millward were hanged. Heywood went on to achieve a high rank in the Navy and neither at his trial nor subsequently spoke of what Fletcher Christian had told him of Bligh's arsenic taking.*

On Pitcairn on the day of the killing of Christian, the wives of the mutineers killed all of the Polynesian men. As the last white survivor of the saga of the Bounty, *John Adams was found by Captain Folger, chancing upon the island in the whaler* Topaz, *in 1808. His report was slow to reach England, by then too enmeshed in the Napoleonic Wars to pay much attention to an event almost twenty years past. Adams died of natural causes on Pitcairn in 1829.*

The descendants of the mutineers and their Polynesian partners continued to live on Pitcairn, joined by other settlers. Owing to population pressure causing food shortages, the Pitcairners were moved to Norfolk Island in 1856. Subsequently a number of families moved back and today people who can trace their ancestry to Christian and his comrades live on Pitcairn and Norfolk Island, in

Postscript

Australia and New Zealand and elsewhere. At the time of writing some of the Pitcairners are embroiled in legal proceedings regarding the sexual abuse of under-age females. One of their defensive strategies is to assert that they are not subject to British law as a long-term consequence of the mutiny on HMS Bounty.

Peter Corris

Appendix: The crew of HMS *Bounty*, and list of Polynesians taken to Pitcairn Island.

The crew of HMS *Bounty:*

Lieutenant William Bligh	Commander
John Fryer	Master
Willam Cole	Boatswain
William Peckover	Gunner
William Purcell	Carpenter
John Huggan	Surgeon
Thomas Ledward	Surgeon's mate
Fletcher Christian	Master's mate
William Elphinstone	Master's mate
Thomas Hayward	Midshipman
John Hallet	Midshipman
Edward Young	Acting midshipman
Peter Heywood	Acting midshipman
Peter Linkletter	Quartermaster
John Norton	Quartermaster
George Simpson	Quartermaster's mate
James Morrison	Boatswain's mate
John Mills	Gunner's mate
Thomas McIntosh	Carpenter's mate
Lawrence Lebogue	Sailmaker
Joseph Coleman	Armourer

Charles Churchill	Master-At-Arms
John Samuel	Clerk and steward
David Nelson	Botanist
William Brown	Assistant botanist

Able seamen:

Thomas Burkett, Michael Byrn (fiddler), Thomas Ellison, Thomas Hill, Henry Hillbrandt, Robert Lamb, Isaac Martin, William McCoy, John Millward, William Muspratt, Mathew Quintal, Richard Skinner, Alexander Smith (aka John Adams), John Smith, John Sumner, Robert Tinkler, Mathew Thompson, James Valentine, John Williams.

(Source: Hough, 1994.)

List of Polynesians taken to Pitcairn Island:

Men	**Women**
Oha	Mauatua (Isabella)
Titahiti	Mary
Menalee	Sarah
Timoa	Susannah
Nehow	Jenny
Tararo	Vahineatua
	Mareva
	Pashotu
	Paurai
	Prudence
	Teatuahitea
	Toofaiti
	Sarah (infant)

(Source: Lummis, 1999.)

Acknowledgements

My wife, Jean Bedford, gave me the idea and the researches of my daughter, Ruth Corris, greatly helped the execution. At Random House Meredith Curnow and Roberta Ivers showed their faith in the book and greatly improved it by their suggestions.

Anyone who has read Caroline Alexander's superb *The Bounty* (HarperCollins, 2003) will recognise the debt I owe to this book. Likewise, I acknowledge the great usefulness of Trevor Lummis's *Life and Death in Eden* (Phoenix, 1999) and Richard Hough's *Captain Bligh and Mr Christian* (Arrow, 1994).

I have endeavoured to remain true to the historical facts as far as they can be determined, but as Gregory Dening has demonstrated in his *Mr Bligh's Bad Language* (Cambridge University Press, 1992), the story of the *Bounty* has played upon and stimulated the imaginations of poets, playwrights, musicians and filmmakers for over 200 years, and I am merely one of that number.